SHOW A LITTLE LOVE 1

CHARLOTTE AFRICAN AMERICAN WRITERS

Written by:

Clayton F. Brown,
Tony L. Bellamy,
Ulyssess McDowell Jr.
Sheila E. Bell

authorHOUSE®

AuthorHouse™
1663 Liberty Drive
Bloomington, IN 47403
www.authorhouse.com
Phone: 1 (800) 839-8640

Published by AuthorHouse 03/24/2020

ISBN: 978-1-7283-5141-4 (sc)
ISBN: 978-1-7283-5140-7 (e)

Print information available on the last page.

Dedication: *I'd like to dedicate this book and the second one to the members of the writers group.*

Charlotte, North Carolina the year 2000, on a breezy fall rainy night, at the Independence Library conference room approximately 75 people filled every space. Fire codes were being broken as the umbrellas' dripped water on the floor of the recently remodeled library. A writer's group was being formed. It was the same night another local writer's group also had a scheduled meeting, however, all of its members and interested people found their way to the Independence Library looking for something different and new. Standing at the front of the room leaning on the podium was a middle age man, who recently moved from California (the Bay area) proclaiming he would like to start a writer's group. He had no name for the group; he only knew what his proposed short, mid and long term goals were to be.

There were a variety of people within the audience listening to what he had to say. From the expression on his face, it was easy to assume he realized the type of audience he had assembled through his advertising. Educators, lawyers, doctors and ex-convicts shared the same space. For an ice breaker, he began to talk about his time spent in the Bay Area and how he wrote a poem and presented it to the professors of a writers group on Berkley campus. After giving the copies of the poem to the professors that sat at the round table, he was asked to step outside while his poetry was reviewed and they would let him know if he could join the writers group. He stepped outside in the dark as the rain saturated his hat and the cigarette he was smoking broke in half. At this point he became a little perturbed, within a few minutes someone came to the door asking him to come back inside, they've made their decision. The leader of the group stated he liked the poem and welcomed him into the group.

Clayton decided not to join the group. He said they were too stuffy. Now, he stands before a group of people proclaiming to produce a different writers group. A place whereas the experience writer can come and share information. Sell their books and give pertinent feedback of their travels. He began to go over the short term goal.

"Our **short term** goal is to establish boundaries and structure at the meetings and bring in authors to share their experiences."

"For our **midterm goal**, we shall gain community awareness of our group. We will present a showcase of artistic work and donate the money to charity."

Both of the above goals were accomplished within two years. During the course of accomplishing those goals Clayton knew in order to be the leader of a writer's group he had to become a writer. Therefore, he started to write his first novel. His thinking was if you are going to *talk the talk,* you need to *walk the walk.* His novel "Under the Green Tree," spread like a wild fire. The ladies from one end of North Carolina to the other were coping exerts from the book and faxing some of the stories to their friends while they were at work. Clayton began conducting book signings state to state, but he did not forget the goals of the writers group. Stories from his book reached the North Carolina Art Society in Raleigh, and he was asked to come to the black tie affair to receive the first time author award for the works of "Under the Green Tree."

The writers group accomplished its short and midterm goals. For the midterm goals a community performance was produced by Clayton at the Afro-American Culture Center, uptown Charlotte. Two standing room only shows were produced, which consisted of a one act play with the plot being the contracting of the HIV/AIDS virus. The actors were from Queens College theatrical department. There were singing and dance performances, poetry, authors and vendors. To top it off, for the ten dollar ticket the group catered food to feed the entire audience for both shows. All of the proceeds were donated to the local AIDS foundation. Two years later the group did the same thing at the Mint Museum also uptown Charlotte, this year the money was donated to the Battered Women Shelter.

At that meeting on the dreadful cold rainy night, Clayton also told the group they would write a book (some of the members).

"This book will be different; we will write a novel in which the reader will not know we've changed authors. The transition will be so smooth it will be difficult for them to know we switched authors."

"Awe, we can't do *nothing* like that," blurted someone from the audience.

"Oh yes we can," Clayton quickly retorted.

Within the decade of the group's existence they managed to write two novels together with members from the group. The titles of the books are "Show A Little Love 1 & 2." So, his **long term** goal was also achieved with the group. The group lasted for 10 years and it's been 10 years since they've united. Some keep in contact via social media, others have drifted away. But the memories of the group and what they've placed into people lives will never be forgotten. The expression on the children faces when the group would travel to the surrounding middle schools and read to the students and perform writing skits, the joy can never be reproduce.

To everyone that has ever been affiliated with the Charlotte African American Writers Group (CAAW) I wish you well, and thanks for all the beautiful memories and the times we shared together, remember the term we used to always say to each other, *"keep laying down the ink."*

Clayton F. Brown

Contents

Acknowledgements

Clayton F. Brown

Thanks to Almighty God for giving us the breath of life to be able to relay the story of Belinda Norris. I'd like to thank the rest of the authors for sharing a dream with me. Most co-authored novels are a compilation of individual short stories. What we've accomplished with *Show A Little Love 1* is a sharing of the same story while expressing our individuality as writers. We carried the story of Belinda while inputting our own unique style and flavor. We've made it where the reader can feel the different authenticity of each novelist. I thank them all for their hard work. Thanks to those that rendered their thoughts pertaining to the novel while it was in its making. We cherished your views and comments, and your critiques were embraced with gentle consideration.

Tony L. Bellamy

Special thanks are in order to God, the original creative entity. To my loving family, you guys are the real stars in my crown. To the wonderful writers of CAAW, I will forever be indebted to you for your support. Finally, to all of my readers, please realize that I am blessed by you on a daily basis. Your commitment and support will forever be etched in my heart.

Ulysses McDowell Jr.

I'd like to thank my immediate family, and all of my extended family, relatives, and friends. Here are the names of my parents and siblings: my father, Ulysses "Crocodile" McDowell, my mother, Dorothy "Rucker" McDowell, known affectionately as "Dot," my sister, Ellen Anderson "Nita," my brothers, Larry "Mac" and Kevin "K-Mac." You guys are the greatest, and so are your families. Thanks to Clayton F. Brown and the entire CAAW group. You have motivated me to finally put the pen to paper. It was a joy working on *Show A Little Love 1*. I hope this is only the beginning of something special and big. Thanks again. Thank you, God, who has never let me down, and who deserves all credit, if any credit is due. See you in the next novel. *Semper Fi!*

Sheila E. Bell

Being a part of writing *Show A Little Love 1* has been a remarkable experience for me. It's made me realize the power of the pen and the uniting of the mind, even though we are hundreds of miles apart. Writing a novel without having met any of you in person has truly been a unique experience. I want to thank Clayton F. Brown for allowing me to be part of this talented group of people. I feel like I've known you all my life. I certainly want to thank my family and my three sons, who support me in all of my writing endeavors. Finally I must always give thanks, praise, and honor to God my Savior for blessing me with the gift of writing.

Introduction

Show A Little Love 1 is a combination of stories written by four multitalented individuals with diverse backgrounds. Synergistic powers were at their best in the creative process. Clayton F. Brown, Sheila E. Bell, Ulysses McDowell Jr., and I consider ourselves fortunate to have been a part of this project. In life we all are subjected to unfortunate situations. How we handle adversities determines the outcome. Belinda Norris' life wasn't any different. Although endowed with beauty and financial security, her inability to overcome the demons from her past led her to indulge in sexual promiscuity and reckless behavior.

Belinda Norris' perfectly sculptured body became a liability she randomly used to destroy other people's lives. Unwilling to accept the consequences of her decisions and mistakes caused her misery and pain. Guilt-ridden, she believed a good man would never take up residence in her life.

Show A Little Love 1 provides food for the soul. The power or unconditional love and forgiveness are two essential elements depicted throughout this novel. Belinda must learn the bonds of true friendship cannot always be measured and tested. Filled with suspense, mystery, and betrayal, *Show A Little Love 1* captures the essence of what life affords to those who constantly live on the edge.

Tony L. Bellamy

Chapter One
The Game

Shivering, despite the blaze in the fireplace, I pulled my wool throw blanket up to cover my chilled shoulders. Small bits of marshmallows floated at the top of my hot chocolate while it rest on my reading table. The telephone and my writing pad also sat next to my rocking chair. This was my comfort zone, a quiet place for me to think—about being lonely. Beautiful, I knew I was, perhaps too pretty. I was baffled. I couldn't understand why I looked the way I did, and was still lonely. I thought it was because of the family curse. My mother often told us about some old lady who she thought put a curse on all of her children; because the old lady didn't like her.

Without a doubt, my mother was gorgeous and her beauty was passed onto my siblings and me. I thought it was the curse that would leave me bewildered after numerous relationships that seem to last forever—but didn't! *And,* I wished my mother had found a way to remove the curse from the Norris family a long time ago.

My long straight hair complimented my unblemished skin, both, should have been more than enough to embrace an active social life. God knows I had a body that would turn heads every minute of the day. I was five foot five, one hundred and twenty pounds with a tight stomach and firm uplifted breasts. My small waistline accentuated my full hips. *What in the world I'm doing in this house all-alone? I hadn't had a man up in here, in a while!* I thought while lifting myself out of the rocking chair to turn the wood over in the fireplace.

I ought to call somebody, maybe Sharon is at home. I contemplated with dismay while taking aim towards the telephone.

Sharon Bait was a little on the heavy side, but she was sweet and stayed down the street from me. Sharon was a school teacher with two other jobs. She stayed busy. Too busy, I would think, and her husband Bill was in school fulltime; he also had two jobs. With so many jobs between the two of them, I would tease her sometimes about being Jamaican. Like the

1

Jamaicans, Sharon and Bill had the reputation of having two or more jobs. Whenever I called her to go somewhere with me, she would be so tired it was pathetic.

A few months ago when I received my income tax refund check, I gave her a call to see if we could go shopping. I remember it so well...

"Sharon, hello... this is Belinda."

"Hey Belinda, girl what've you been up to?"

"*Just chilling,* I have my Income Tax refund in my hands and I'm ready to go shopping." I was too excited, walking around the kitchen with the telephone receiver up to my ear, pacing the floor as I spoke. "You want to go with me?"

"Belinda, I don't have any money," she paused. "That man of mine, Lord, I just don't know!"

"What do you mean, Sharon?"

"We've been struggling for so long, and it just doesn't make sense."

"I hear you Sharon, "I replied in a calmed voice to ease her tension.

"You know I have three jobs Belinda?"

"Yeah, I know Sharon."

"I'm paying for my husband's tuition and my student loan. He has two jobs and he's going to school full time."

"*How y'all living?* When do you spend time together?"

"We don't, sometimes it's just hello and goodbye!"

I could imagine her shaking her head on the other side of the telephone.

"Belinda, our sex life is just a quickie here and there."

"At least you are doing better than I am. Self-satisfaction isn't all that pleasing, I'm still lonely!"

"I don't know why Belinda? You're too pretty not to be having a handsome guy knocking your door down."

"Yeah, maybe that's the problem; too pretty girl!"

"Don't worry it'll change. I had a dry spell like that in college."

"*Oh really?*" I made it seem as though she shouldn't have had a dry spell. Although, I knew she'd better be glad Bill came along, or she would've been out to dry for a long time.

Sharon's strong demeanor would sometimes run men away. She was always trying to prove to the world how educated and smart she was. I always thought people who were smart didn't have to prove it. To top it off, she could stand a visit or two to Jenny Craig or some sort of weight watchers clinic. But, that was my girl, whatever!

"Yeah Belinda, before Bill came along I didn't understand why I was so lonely." Sharon started laughing to herself over the phone.

"What's so funny?" I asked her, while she was just *busting up.*

"I was just thinking about how Bill didn't have a car when I was in College. That fool would get on his moped and travel for three hours on back roads in the snow, just to come see me."

"Sounds like you two were made for each other," I said sarcastically.

"All right Belinda lets not go there!"

"I'm just playing Sharon." We started laughing, although I meant what I said. They were the perfect couple whenever they were together.

"Sharon, don't worry about the money I'll get you something, just don't be greedy, okay."

"All right Belinda let me put something on," Sharon replied, then we hung up the telephone.

Sharon and I had a great time that day. We shopped for hours until we were exhausted and had spent most of my money. I didn't mind sharing my funds with Sharon, her heart was genuine and Bill was also my friend. We were close but not inseparable. I kept away from sharing my inner most secrets with her. Her efforts to open up to me were admirable; however, I refused to carry on conversations relating to my past. My past was my secret; it was a dark, painful secret that haunted me. Knowing she would look at me differently, I couldn't share with her what I did to my best friend, Candace. Whenever she would strike up a deep conversation I would evasively change the subject. When she would talk about her marriage, I'd start another conversation.

I didn't want her to share anything with me about Bill that was personal. Their job situation was enough, but she would still make the attempt to talk about their sexual life intimately. Heavens knows if she'd known about my past she wouldn't have brought up that conversation. She must have suspected I wanted to keep our relationship on a different level. I found it hard to share the event that left my heart in the state it was in with her. How could I've been so stupid?

People make mistakes; I assured myself—but Candace was my best friend, and for me to loose trust with my best friend, it was devastating. I was from Dorchester, Boston and she was from the south. Our life styles were different, mine was wicked and wild. I used to hang with the wrong crowd; drinking and carrying on, always having a good time.

While growing up in Dorchester most of my girls would put their best

3

friend's old man to a test, just to see if he was the faithful type. Then we would report back to our girlfriend and let her know the real deal about her man. It was a juvenile thing to do, especially when some of my girlfriends would find themselves caught up in the moment; when finding out if their girlfriend's man was faithful. Of course, we were young when we would tempt the young men whose head on their shoulders weren't in control of their action in the heat of the moment.

Peer pressure was a dangerous weapon when I was young and living in a middle class life style. In my neighborhood we'd all hang together, cute girls of course. Flocking like a pack of birds, seven to nine of us, sort of like a gang. We were all attractive; therefore putting young men to a test wasn't as damaging to a girlfriend as it would be when she became an adult.

During my younger years our attitudes were carefree. Although, a lot of my girlfriends were caught up in *The Game*, and when a friend was the victim they would take the news of a friend sleeping with their boyfriend, as though it was nothing. I wouldn't go all the way! It didn't take much for me to know and let my girlfriend know if her boyfriend was unfaithful. To some, they could've easily considered this group of girls, were no more than a bunch of *sluts*. We didn't think that way! The guys that wouldn't cooperate with our childish test of being propositioned would make threats of telling their girlfriend of our actions. Little did they know, she already knew—she just didn't know who from the group would be doing the enticing or when it would occur.

On summer days we'd gather at the park, someone would have music playing while we walked around in our cutoff jean shorts with the frizzles dangling around the edges of them. Young we were, with not an inch of fat displaying, while nearly eighty percent of our body parts showing. Janice, one of our girls strolled to the group with Richard one-day. He was cute, but in retrospect that would be an understatement; he was fine as *hell*! Flawless, he was and with an irresistible smile. Richard's smile was a major turn on to me. He was tall and handsome; his deep soft eyes were the kind that seemed as though they could look right through a person. His broad shoulders and quietness just intensified his appearance. Richard was smart and athletic; he just had it going on. Janice was falling head over heels for this guy, and it was time for our approval.

When they strolled up to the group, it was all in my mind that I would take him on a temptation ride. The way he looked, I had second thoughts about going all the way with him if things did get out of hand. Janice knew when she introduced him to the crew he would be *open game* for the crew's game of temptation.

After that day in the park, I wore so many tight cut off shorts and halter-tops to display myself to Richard everywhere I knew he was going to be. He finally caught on to what I was doing. One day Janice told me that Richard's parents were away and she was going to be with him on Friday. I thought this would be my opportunity to intervene, so I walked to his house and knocked on his door. When he opened the door he was surprised to see me. My game was laid back, and every time he saw me in the neighborhood, I'd delivered small amounts of temptation towards him. *Sort of like reeling him in.*

"Hi Belinda, what are you doing here?"

"I was in the neighborhood, so I thought I'd knock on your door and ask for something to drink." I said, while batting my eyes, then turning my head looking around. "This sure is a quiet neighborhood."

"Oh, okay Belinda; come on in." He waved his hand directing me to come inside. Hastily, I stepped into the house before he would want to change his mind.

Richard's mother really had the place laid. The pictures on the walls resembled centuries of a family tree. There were so many grandparents; the photographs clearly indicated they only had black and white cameras during that period of time. Some of his grandparents were on horses in the photos.

"Hey Belinda, have a seat." Richard waved his hand indicating for me to sit on the sofa.

"Can I get you something to drink?"

"Yeah, some juice will be fine." I looked around in a pleasing way. "Oh, you have a lovely home."

"Oh thanks, my mother is always doing something to it. I'll be right back."

Before Richard returned I had positioned myself for an enticing mood. My skirt I knew was too short and tight; was well above my knees. My nails and hair was ready for a fashion show. How could he resist? I poured on the charm and unlike a lady; I was all over him when he returned. To my amazement he constantly pushed me away, telling me how much he was going to try and make things work with Janice. That didn't stop me though, I must have tried two more times, and then I stopped.

"I'm going to tell Janice that you came on to me Belinda!"

"No Richard, can we just keep it between ourselves? I don't want to hurt her!" I said, in a sweet innocent voice.

Although, I was far from being innocent with him, I just faked it. I really didn't care; she knew the rules of the group and it was inevitable when it was going to happen. I just didn't understand why he didn't go for it. Definitely, I looked better than she did. She was cute and everything, but could never compare to what he had in front of him. Was there something wrong with him? I thought for a second. If he didn't tell her; that was another way we would know if he were faithful to a girl in the crew.

I told Janice what had happened and she was pleased, but she waited a few days for him to tell her; he did. After that incident, two more attacks were placed on him from different girls in the group. They also failed to turn him out. Richard started walking around like he was the man. He really had the big head and thought he was God's gift to women.

A girl named Sheila Johnson placed the fourth proposition on Richard. Although I thought I had it going on—I must admit, Sheila was too impressive. She was tall, with a nice short hair cut style that complimented her graceful stride. She was too close to perfection, and a little on the quiet side. Sheila's pose would have any man drooling at the mouth. When she decided to tempt Richard I was with her. We sat on the bleachers at the football field, watching the players hit each other with their sturdy shoulder pads.

"*Dang girl!* He knocked him to the ground." Sheila said, as her quietness seemed to be aroused from the violent playing of the guys from the football team.

"Girl, he'll be all right. Watch, he'll get up in a moment." Just as I said that, the young man was back on his feet shaking the stunning blow off of him.

"I hope they don't hit Richard like that, Belinda. Have you been watching how he's been looking over here at me?" Sheila looked at me, knowing it was time for her to come on to him.

"Yeah girl, 'cause I know he's not checking me out. That fool turned me down!"

"Don't worry I'll take care of him." Sheila retorted. "I'm going to catch him right after practice is over, *bet* he won't turn me down!"

"*Oh really, Sheila?*"

"Yeah girl, I left that storage room door opened, the one by the stairs to the gym." Sheila nodded her head in the direction of the gym.

"Oh really, I guess I better leave so he won't think I have something to do with it."

"Yeah, you probably should leave. But not yet! When he looked over here again I'm going to through him a kiss with my lips."

Sheila smiled, thinking she could reel Richard in. Then, I noticed Richard looking towards Sheila's *way* and Sheila puckering up her lips; sending him a smack from her lips across the football field. I was sure he caught on I could see his cheekbones lifted through the face of the helmet as if he was smiling.

"Belinda, I'm *gonna* get him in that storage room and turn him on so bad, he'll be begging for me."

"Go ahead, more power to you, 'cause we done tried. It seems like he's not budging. Janice must have him whipped good." I started laughing for a second while watching Sheila sending signals to Richard from the bleachers.

"She may have whipped it on him, but just the fragrance from my body is going to drive him crazy. Girl it's going to be like him at the entrance of a tunnel and me saying, no! He'll be so hot and bothered, *ya know*, if he gets that close."

"Girl, you gonna go that far?"

"Yeah girl, if I get him to go into the storage room that's enough to tell our girl Janice. But just for turning y'all down, I'm going to take him to another level."

"I hear you. I'd better get out of here and let you work it!" I snapped my finger twice and we laughed together, pushing each other gingerly.

Practice was over and the guys rushed into the locker room to shower and change their clothes. I knew Richard caught every signal Sheila was throwing at him. Just as I thought he was the last one coming out of the locker room. Probably so none of the other fellows would know he was trying to talk to Sheila. I thought to myself, while watching Sheila sat in total anticipation.

"Bye Sheila," I said while noticing Richard coming towards the bleaches. His head was swollen from thinking every woman wanted him. Perhaps he was playing a game on us; turning us down? Nevertheless, I knew he wouldn't be able to resist Sheila.

"Okay bye Belinda, I'll let you know how things went."

I walked away from the football field that day thinking about Sheila. At one of our parties Sheila taught us the game of *choo choo*. Most of our parties were invitation only; we kept a list of the guys that were at our previous parties. We always tried to keep new faces. In four or five rooms stood a guy blindfolded with only his under garments on. Five or six girls would get in a line formation. Our crewmembers would be the first three girls in the line and the rest would be *wanna bee's*. They would do anything to be a part of our social realm; just like the guys that were inside the rooms. With the *wanna bee's* at the end of the line, we'd grab a hold of each other's waist.

With all of the drinking and smoking going on in the living room, we would hold on to each other and *choo choo*, circling the living room; imitating the sound of a train. Sheila would be at the front of the line; we would march at a half step (sort of like a line of Sorority girls in College) up to the first room. In the dimmed lights of the room, stood a young man unaware of what was going on. Everyone kept the game a secret, and we always recruited new guys to be in the rooms.

The guy stood in near darkness, blindfolded, waiting for the unknown. Some would take the spare time while waiting for us to come into their room and excite their manhood; preparing their minds for the ultimate surprise. The shy guys would have fear of not knowing what to expect, arousing themselves would be far from their minds.

Sheila stopped the train in front of him, and at a soft tone she began to teach us the train's objective.

"Hi, how are you doing?" She said in a sweet voice, while staring at his manly physique.

"Find and yourself?" He responded, but wondering what was going to happen as he waited in eager anticipation.

"I'm all right, but I always can be better."

"Oh really, and what can I do about that?"

"First of all, let me do the questioning!" Sheila retorted. "And always keep the blindfold on. We are not going to hurt you, okay?" Sheila spoke softly to ease his discomfort.

"Okay baby, whatever you say. You sound so good."

"Thank you baby." Sheila said, and then she turned and winked at us as if she wanted to say, 'I've *got* him now.' Sheila grabbed his hand and placed his index finger into her mouth. Unaware of where she was going with this game of *choo choo* we stood and watched her moves with amazement while she seductively sucked his finger. With her other hand, she unveiled the tight mini skirt that covered what all mothers stressed to never be displayed to the opposite gender.

Bare from the waist down she stood; we watched in total admiration and anticipated her next move. I'm far from being attracted to the same gender, but I have to admit, we were all in a state of shock while looking at Sheila's bareness. Flawless Sheila was, and from the waist down her nudeness was as close to perfection as anyone can get. Her creamy skin with long delectable legs was as smooth as a baby's butt. Her female center of gravity was shaped as if an artist had designed it; she was beautiful without a doubt, and she handled herself in such an elegant manner.

I watched as she took his finger out of her mouth and placed it on her soft spongy hairs. Warmth and wetness must have trickled through the guy's fingers then throughout his entire body. We watched as he began to shake with the blindfold on. With his hand still in place, he massaged her wetness. Sheila continued to talk to him at a soft tone.

"How are you feeling baby?" Enticingly, Sheila whispered.

"I feel good baby!" the guy said as if he was in Heaven.

"Yeah, me too," she responded, and then Sheila lowered his hand down to his side. Instantly she pulled her mini skirt back to its' rightful position.

"Hey baby, I'm standing here totally nude. Tell me the first thing you would do to me when I'm in your arms?"

We all stood quietly wondering where this game of simple assault was leading up to, waiting to hear what he was going to say.

"I'd kiss you all over, and treat you like I know you need to be treated."

Whack! Sheila had slapped the daylights out of him. Then she quickly ran to the back of the line and began the sound of *choo choo*, we all caught on and joined in with her. The guy stood with the blindfold on; as instructed he didn't remove it, nor did he move from his position. Sheila taught us how to use our beauty just to dog men out.

We went into the next room and played the game again. I performed it just as Sheila, perhaps a little more as I can recall the sensation of the physical touching also trickling through my body. It was like a rush being in total control of those guys. It seemed as though they were so desperate to be in the company of beautiful women; we learned that they were willing to take any punishment we'd apply to them.

My hand somewhat hurt after slapping that guy silly, and the thought of giving into his will did sped fast through my mind. At around the fourth room Celeste was at the front of the line. She was fairly new to the crew, and she lived on my block. When Celeste was doing her thing with the young man and they were at the touching stage; Sheila had to come to her aid.

Quickly, Sheila ran from the end of the line and gently tapped Celeste on the shoulder, reminding her to stay on her course. Celeste was getting caught up in *The Game*. She was going with the flow of the guy's hand and she was getting aroused from his touch. It's a good thing Sheila came to her rescue; they were about to act like dogs in heat.

Celeste asked the guy the magic question, while his hands were at his side. His response happened to be the correct answer.

"I'm standing here with nothing on, tell me, what's the first thing you would do when I'm in your arms?" she asked.

"I'd take this blind fold off, so I can see what I'm about to get!" the guy responded.

Sheila snatched Celeste from the front of the line and indicated for one of the *wanna bee's* to come forward, her name was Rosalyn. She was a quiet girl that lived on the same block as Sheila. We dropped her off in the room when the guy answered the question correctly.

What went on in the room after we left, we didn't know. The serene expression from their faces when they came out of the room would be the only indication of what had happened.

It was amazing how the girls would think the gentle serenity expression of their faces would disguise what really went on in the room; it was a dead giveaway. We knew when something happened. The *wanna bees* thought we would let them into the pack if they had sex with these guys; some of them we wouldn't, despite the fact they had compromised their morals. They had to be cute, in order to stand next to us!

The game of *choo choo* taught me how easy it was to manipulate young guys' minds. They would do anything to be next to a girl in our pack; that they thought was so fine. The young women that eagerly wanted to be a part of the crew were weak! To actually think peer pressure can make someone do things or bring out the worst in a person was kind of silly. I never did get caught up in the game, I knew it was just that; a game! While sitting in the living room of the party I would just drink some alcohol to unwind.

I was surrounded by three or more guys that had the intentions of getting me drunk to have their way—I knew that game too. I would just let the liquor touch my lips and pretend I was getting as drunk as they were. Soon they would leave me alone, and I'd watch their stumbling bodies walk away. Females' minds are much more matured than boy's I would think. Unfortunately, I guess at that point of my life I really couldn't find Mr. Right if he'd came along and pinched me.

Those were some fun times at the parties, never in my wildest dreams I'd think I could be in as much control of the young men's mind in my neighborhood as I did. It was indeed intriguing. Guys are something else, we'd lie to them just for GP—general purpose.

It was the older women at the beauty parlor that would lay down the lessons. When I'd get my hair done they would be laying the womanhood laws down as if their philosophies were always right. They would be talking about the different ways of dogging men. How could we not think on this type of level? It was being handed down to us from the older ladies that knew what had worked for them for years.

Mrs. Tyler would sit in the chair with her rollers and I would listen to her talk to the other women. It was like listening to a motivational speaker in progress.

"Child, I remember one time I was dating Leroy. Now he was a trip. Girl, one time he came to my house and banged at the door late at night like a mad man!" she said to the other women.

Curiously, I'd try to listen; couldn't turn my head though, she would've thought I was being nosy and not finish her story.

"Yeah girl," she said. "I would have someone else up in the house *just 'a* whipping it right!"

She looked around to see who was paying her any attention, but then continued.

"Leroy would be knocking at the door in the middle of the groove, like a natural born fool! I'd sneak the other guy out the back door and get myself together. Then I went walking to the door and the first thing my Leroy said was, '*Who's* that you *got* up in here! I heard you at the back window, you were *just 'a* moaning and a screaming, what's going on up in here!'" Mrs. Tyler laughed.

"I told him that I was just having a bad dream, then I heard him knocking at the door. I'd put on this innocent look too child," she said. "Leroy was furious, but I'd managed to calm him down, I said, 'Baby now you know *ain't* no man been up in here. I was having a nightmare that's all you must have heard. Now baby come on here, and give it to me,' I had him then."

"That fool said, 'yeah, I know you wouldn't give it to me, if someone else been up in it.' I almost died." Mrs. Tyler laughed at what Leroy had said. Then she turned her head to see if anyone was listening before she continued.

"Girl men are so stupid it is pathetic, he just felled up in it and didn't even realize he was getting sloppy seconds. We got the power; we just need to know how to use it," she said, laughing enthusiastically with her counterpart.

With all of the knowledge we were receiving it would be obstinate not to use the lessons on the silly young men we were dealing with.

After all, sometimes it seemed as if they were just asking for it. So we gave them what they needed, the pleasure of being dog. Now, that I think about it, this is what they really wanted, to be dogged and miss-used. Just a perfect body can make them drool and be worked or molded in anyway we needed them to be. This is the type of teaching the older ladies of the neighborhood were instilling into the minds of the younger generation. We had no choice but to try it on them.

Mrs. Tyler was a trip; her lessons in the beauty parlor were indeed one to be reckoned with. Her pose, style and the way she dressed set the tone of a woman that had the experience of womanhood; she could control any man. The way she dressed, her hair and nails made me think even in the Garden of Eden she would've been in control. High maintenance she was, any man could easily see. Sometimes I wondered if loneliness accompanied that strong demeanor of hers.

It would take years for me to experience that deep dark side that existed in her persona. Truly, I'd wonder how a woman of such caliber dealt with the absence of companionship. Perhaps it didn't mean that much to her.

While she sat in the chair at the beauty shop, I could somehow see there was a good possibility this woman was concerned about being lonely, as I too am able to share with her today.

Later that night after leaving Sheila at the bleachers waiting on Richard, I was upstairs at my house when the police knocked on the door. My father with his strong wisdom that he's so eager to share with anyone strolled to the door.

"Who is it?" He said with a curious snarl.

"Police, we need to talk to Belinda Norris!" roared an authoritative voice. My father opened the door and invited them in. Two policemen stood in the living room talking to my father. Although, I couldn't hear what they were saying, I knew it had to be serious.

From in-between the rails of the banister I watched their lips moved. Then my father turned away from them and yelled my name. Quickly, I stepped back behind the wall leading to the banister. His voice bellowed in such a manner I thought the walls were shaking. The terror that existed inside of me prior to a whipping, had overcome me.

"Belinda, get down here now!" he shouted.

I was nervous as I walked down the stairs that for some reason were carpeted from the top to the bottom. I always wondered what Daddy was thinking when he put carpet on the steps. Maybe he didn't want to hear us walking up and down the stairs. At the bottom of the steps my father met me. Instantly, I clung to him for his comfort and support. I knew from the expression that was on his face, he had not a clue as to what the police wanted with me. Fear had escalated inside of me; to the point my stomach was bubbling like it had ginger ale inside of it. My father escorted me into the living room where the two oversized policemen stood. The one that seemed to be the senior officer spoke first.

"Hello Belinda, I'm Sergeant Howard and this is Officer Davidson." He pointed at the other policeman as if they were going to put the cuffs on me.

"We'd like to ask you a few questions." Sergeant Howard said, as he stood back examining my demeanor, then turning his head glancing at my father for a moment.

"Sure, what is it you want to ask me?"

"Belinda, we were told you know a young lady name Sheila Johnson."

"Yes I do. She's a friend of mine." I said curiously, while noticing Sergeant Howard waiting for me to finish my sentence.

"Tell me Belinda, when was the last time you saw her?"

"Just a few hours ago," I was curious at this point, not knowing where this interrogation was going, but I knew I had to define my position on the matter. "I left her at the football field."

"There's a good possibility you were the last person with her." Sergeant Howard kindly accused, but waited to see how I would respond to his comment. Now, I knew something was wrong.

"What do you mean the last?" The first thought came to my mind was that Sheila was dead.

"What's going on?"

"She was found brutally beaten, and her clothes were ripped off of her." Sergeant Howard stated firmly. "Sheila was assaulted and raped!"

"Oh no, that can't be true! I was just with her."

"What were y'all doing?" he continued to ask me one question after the other. "Why did you leave her?"

"We were sitting on the bleaches, watching the football team practice. I left because she was waiting on Richard."

"Richard! What's Richard's last name and where does he live?"

The sergeant became more demanding, thinking he may have a lead on the situation.

"I left as he was coming out of the locker room." I began to mentally remember him walking over to where Sheila was sitting.

"How is Sheila doing?"

"She's still in the hospital, in a state of shock. Somehow she's lost her speech, could be from the trauma."

"Oh Daddy!" I grabbed my father's waist and hugged him for comfort. *"Oh my God!"* I screamed.

"Now Pumpkin," my nickname Daddy always called me when he's trying to ease me through discomfort. "Everything is going to be just fine."

Daddy put his arms around me, but I knew he had not a clue if things were going to be okay.

"Isn't it Officer?" Daddy asked for reassurance.

Tears cruised down the side of my face while I held onto my security blanket, my father. Just the thought of knowing Sheila was hurt, made me cry and *boo-hoo* furiously. *I shouldn't have left her there. What could have happened to her?* I thought to myself.

"We need you to show us where this Richard lives." Sternly, Sergeant Howard said, then he glanced at the other officer as if he needed his okay.

"Don't worry baby, Daddy will be right behind you." My father said, but with his wholesome wisdom he thought for a second.

"As a matter of fact, why don't y'all just follow us officer. If this boy did have something to do with this girl Sheila, I don't want my daughter in harms way. If she *rides* with you in the patrol car, he might start shooting or something." Daddy stopped for a minute to see their response.

"Be best if I take her. We'll point out the house and you guys can do what you have to do. I'll safe guard my daughter."

"Okay, that sounds like a plan Mr. Norris." The sergeant looked at his partner insuring he understood what was to take place.

"We'll call for back up once we get there."

"All right!" the other officer said. "Let's go folks!" Officer Howard anxiously hurried us out of the door.

14

Richard's street was quiet and quite dull looking. I told my father where to stop. The police were directly behind us when we stopped in front of his house. The entire time in the back of my mind, I knew Richard was aware that I knew he was going to be with Sheila. I was frightened. If it was in him to do something like this to her, what would he do to me for knowing. She must have pushed him over the edge. I could only assume he lusted for Sheila so badly he must have lost his *dag gone* mind, when she told him no.

I didn't get out of the car when we stopped; I merely stuck my hand out of the window, pointing my finger indicating to the officers that we were in front of Richard's house. The moment Daddy drove away, two other patrol cars arrived. All of the cruisers had their blue lights flashing, alarming the entire neighborhood of their presence. As Daddy drove off I turned around in my seat watching the excitement. When the officers exited the cruisers, I could see them running. They were holding their pistols with one hand as though they were trying to remove the safety guard. Richard ran out of the back door of his house and the officers caught a glimpsed of him.

"*Police!* Halt or we'll release the K-9." Sergeant Howard yelled. Richard ignored them and continued to run. Daddy slowed the car down, and while Richard ran from the police in-between the houses, I could swear we made eye contact. He ran through his neighbor's backyard and soon the entire block was filled with spectators. Behind the house in the backyard the officers released their K-9 on Richard. His athletic abilities were too much for the donut eating police officers. Richard was jumping fences and running extremely fast. The K-9 caught sight of him and that was all he had needed.

When Richard jumped around one of the neighbor's tall fence, quickly the K-9 ran around the house at top speed staying on Richard's path. The dog caught up with Richard and thrust his heavy body onto Richard, knocking him to the ground. The K-9 pinned Richard down, his jaws locked around Richards's forearm, as his immense fangs pierced the skin of Richard's arm and blood splattered all over the yard. It seemed as if the dog was trying to rip Richard's arm off.

Finally the police arrived to Richard's rescue. They arrested him and left a couple of patrol cars to guard his house until they received the search warrant. Later, in Richard's room they found traces of bloodstains on his clothing in his dirty clothes hamper. My dad told me about it the next day. In the hospital the doctor extracted semen from Sheila and skin tissue from her fingernails. Through DNA testing they were a perfect match to Richard.

The bloodstains on his clothing found in his house matched Sheila's blood. Sheila must have pushed him to a breaking point. From that day on I no longer wanted to participate in the crews game of playing with the young men's mind. The situation with Sheila and Richard had taught me a valuable lesson; after all it could have happened to me. Sheila was hospitalized for I don't know how long, and she was only able to make sounds. She was sounding like a deaf person when they spoke and couldn't hear the sound of their words. No one could understand her but her younger sister.

Her family found out about the crew's little game and they were angry with all of us. They thought our little game was cruel and soon something of this nature would happen. Her family felt we were responsible for what had happened to Sheila; and our crew dispersed after that. I managed to forget about Sheila and the crew, although I never could forget the look in Richard's eyes when he stared at me.

A few months after Sheila's incident, I started receiving threatening letters in the mail, at first I thought they were a joke, but I soon learned to take them serious. They scared Daddy to the point he notified the police. I knew Richard was locked down in prison. Whoever was sending those letters obviously meant business. The letters were coming at a frequency of about once a week; they were horrible!

"I'm going to cut, slice and dice you up. You cannot get away, each day I watch you. Waiting, waiting for the right time to kill you Belinda! I'm going to do it slow, so you can feel the pain. I'm going to peel your skin off of you while you are still alive and replace it with a layer of hot tar, before I slice your throat."

The words were cutouts from the newspaper, making it difficult to match or trace anyone's handwriting. Whoever it was that wanted to end my life, I had not a clue.

The police advised Daddy to keep me close to the house whenever I wasn't in school. Things really became hectic. I was ready to leave Boston.

That next fall I went off to College, Columbia University in New York, it was totally different having my freedom and independence. My mother and father wouldn't be waiting up for me and there was no curfew, I loved it! Although I always made sure someone walked me to my dorm, college was so much of a carefree life. It was up to me how well I progressed in my classes. It took some time to deal with all of the freedom; I had a few friends, but none to compare with Sheila and the crew. While being in college it seemed as if our friendship back home began to diminish, everyone was going their separate ways. I guess we were all growing up, and all of the bad things we had done came to a halt after what had happened to Sheila.

Occasionally I'd drop a card, hoping someone would read it to her, I heard she was still disabled and probably would never regain her mental stability.

My senior year I fell in love with Carlton Hamilton. We were business majors, Daddy didn't like the idea. He wanted me to be with someone with a more prominent profession, a doctor or lawyer perhaps? It didn't matter to me though; Carlton was fine. In so many ways he reminded me of Richard. Although I couldn't imagine him in those orange coveralls they wore in lock down.

After telling him about Richard, I have to admit I did get aroused during one of our sexual episodes when he put on a pair of those coveralls with chains wrapped around his ankles and his hands were cuffed behind his back. It was a complete turn on to me when I peeled it off as much as possible to get to what I wanted. I never did figure out how he had put the handcuffs on behind his back. But, the joy of seeing absolutely nothing under those coveralls was a complete turn on. I actually thought I had Richard from prison during our episode.

After graduation we had a huge wedding in Many, Louisiana. Many, is a small town about an hour drive from Shreveport. It was Carlton's hometown; my parents flew in and met their new in-laws. Carlton's parents adored me and my parents were happy for me after seeing that Carlton did come from a respectable family.

They had a ranch with horses and all kinds of animals on acres of land, it was huge. The wedding was set up outside on a beautiful day. Janice, Veronica and Celeste from the crew flew in for the wedding; they were my bride's maids. Lustful eyes protruded out of the sockets of the gentlemen's head at the wedding over my three friends. If only they knew how treacherous these women could be they probably would've had second thoughts. Janice and Celeste still lived in Boston and Veronica had made her home in Brooklyn, New York.

Celeste was still wild, she had a carefree attitude, and the girl had excitement written all over her. For a moment I thought Carlton had to get some more liquor the way she was sucking it down, but the girl stayed in control.

Since Carlton and I were business majors both of us were recruited right out of college for jobs at First Interstate Commerce Bank, located in Rochester, N.Y. There we bought our first home and were the happiest couple anyone could imagine, everything was going so right. We had the large three thousand, seven hundred square foot home and the expensive cars. The walk in closets was large enough to sit my parent's living room in it, they were proud of us. We even had a person to come and clean for us twice a week.

Things started to change for us after I became ill one year. I had a tumor the size of an orange resting on my ovaries. After the operation I could no longer have kids, it put a heavy burden on our marriage. Somehow I felt Carlton understood and would embrace the idea of adopting.

Carlton was upset; but pretended to be supportive. Nevertheless, things took a turn for the worst. He started hanging with his friends all times of the night; at least this is what he said to me. The telephone would ring and when I answered it the person on the other end would hang up. Whenever Carlton answered the phone he would speak as if he was talking to one of his male friends. Paranoia began to set in on me while sobering in my miseries about my marriage. To top it off, I started receiving those letters again that I was getting in Boston.

My life and marriage was going downhill, I could feel it. Finally after years of putting up with him coming home at 3'oclock in the morning, the doorbell rang at around 2:30 in the morning. I was frightened but I knew I had to answer it. I draped myself with the soft silk housecoat he had given me for an anniversary gift; although I wanted a *dag gone* Jaguar.

I walked down the stairs to see who was at the door. It was the police and they delivered startling news. My previous experience with the police coming to my parent's home was an indication to me it was some bad news I was going to receive. Carlton, my husband, the man that I loved but doubted his faithfulness was dead and they wanted me to come and identify the body.

Once I had a grip of the situation, my first question was, "How?"

The officer merely replied, "Heart attack." Carlton always told me he had a heart murmur, but I had no idea the severity of his health issues. The things that ignited his heart attack would later be told to me. At the morgue they slid open the long cold drawer where Carlton's cold purple looking body was. His body was nude, and he displayed a settle look as if he was at peace with himself. I cried and turned my head away from my husband's body.

Quickly the strong arms of the officer wrapped me and disallowed my weak body to penetrate through the floor. I delivered a nod indicating that it was him. Tears flowed down the side of my face as I rested my head on the officer's shoulders.

Then it dawned on me that my husband was lying there on the slab covered with a sheet, with not a stitched of clothing on.

"Where are his clothes?" I asked the officer.

"Mrs. Hamilton," he turned and looked at the other officer. Right then I knew I didn't want my name to be Hamilton any longer the way they looked at each other. I wished he had addressed me by my maiden name, which I was soon to regain after receiving the startling news he was about to tell me.

"We wanted you to read the police report. But since you asked, and you do have a right to know."

"I would think so, he is my husband! Now what happened to his clothes?" I demanded.

"This is the way your husband was found. He was engaged in sexual activity when he died."

Reluctantly, the officer said then he waited for my response. The room started getting smaller, and it seemed as though I was turning in circles. My head was tight and feeling extremely heavy, like one of those heavy balls in the gym.

Get a grip girl! You are not about to pass out here. You knew he wasn't faithful! How could he die under another woman? How could he go out like that? Dang! I thought to myself before responding to the officer, while they just waited to see how I was going to handle the news.

"*Oh, really?* I guess he went happy. Now it's my turn to be happy. I'm *gonna* sell that big house and spend his insurance money." I said to the officers out of anger.

They just looked at each other as if they still had something else to tell me; quickly I dismissed the looks on theirs faces. I was furious, but somehow his wrongdoing seemed to have balanced my sadness. I couldn't give him a child; perhaps he felt he needed to have his own blood son to carry on his family name? Why in the world was I standing there trying to give justification to his actions, I couldn't understand! Finally I came to my senses, there was no need in me justifying his infidelity, when we could have adopted a kid. I begun to think he was just like the typical man, only his ticker had ran out on him in the heat of passion.

"Are you all right Mrs. Hamilton?" The policeman asked.

"Yes, I'm okay."

"Mrs. Hamilton, I don't know how to tell you this but there is more concerning your husband's death."

"What else could possibly be worst? Lay it on me." I said thinking I've heard it all, or nothing could be anymore devastating. They both looked at each other and I was getting a feeling that the information the officers were about to tell me, somehow was about to change the entire ambiance of the morgue.

"Your husband was having sex with a lady by the name of Tina Suarez. When he was taken to the hospital, his blood had cocaine in his system. They were rocking it up and smoking it."

The shocking news left me with my mouth wide opened. Never would I think Carlton was doing drugs. After hearing the woman's name it seemed like I recalled meeting her before in the grocery store with about three kids. She was in line at the register while her kids were clowning around in the buggy. I stopped one of the kids from falling out of the buggy, and we introduced ourselves. Carlton was standing behind me. I assumed she was on Welfare when she presented this card with the American flag on it to the cashier. He actually found out who she was and was having an affair with her! That low life, I started hating him more and I'd wished I could get my hands on that hussy.

"Drugs, I didn't know he did that!"

"But there is more Mrs. Hamilton."

"More, what else could it be, don't tell me he was a bank robber or something like that."

"*Naw*, that's not it." The officer looked at the other officer, and a smile dressed both of their faces. The other officer held his head down trying to disguise his smile by turning away from us as if he could not hold back his laughter, knowing what the other officer was about to tell me.

"Mrs. Hamilton not only was cocaine found in his blood stream, but there were large amounts of Viagra also. You see Mrs. Hamilton, when *folks* use cocaine a man can't get it up. They will do any and everything to get their nature back to engage in sexual activity. We suspect your husband was using Viagra to counter the effects of the cocaine." The officer stopped for a moment and stared at me while the entire time my mouth was opened wide. Then he continued.

"When we brought him down the effects must have still been in his system. His male organ was erected and stood straight up in the air. We couldn't push him into the drawer, he stayed out of the drawer until the doctor came and gave him a shot to relax his muscles. In all of my ten years on duty, I've never seen nothing like this."

"I guess that explained why he always had trouble getting it up with me?" The whole thing began to be kind of comical at that point. I just shook my head and walked out of there. I never told his folks what truly happened to him. I just let them think it happened at home. They wondered why I wasn't excessively crying at the funeral, and acting so pleasant at the house when the funeral was over. Truth was, I was going to be loaded. I found all kinds of investments he had, and a safe deposit box that contained his insurance and pension plan. He left me for good and it was *all good*!

A couple of days after everyone left I sat outside in my Jacuzzi, sipped on some wine and thought about how I was going to spend all of my money. The first thing I wanted to do was to move out of that big house and buy me a condo, something that didn't require a lot of work. I didn't work anymore after I cashed in those stocks. Carlton had thousands of shares in some large computer company. The stocks had split so many times since he'd purchased them and they closed everyday in the hundreds. I was rolling in dough, but no one knew it except for me, the same for the situation with his death. I kept both of them a secret.

I moved next door to Candice Albright, and we became good friends. She was a single parent when we first met, but later she married this fool that I did not like. How she was attracted to him I could never understand. He was attractive and all that, but he was too much of a street guy for me. At times when he would beat the crap out of her, I felt sorry for her. After Carlton, my tolerance level with men was short and sweet. They all could kiss where the sun don't shine!

Candice was a sweet country girl, a little naive I thought. But she was my friend. Emanuel Albright was the thug's name, if a person didn't know him they could be attracted.

Our walls were connected together and I'd call the cops on him every time I'd hear him beating the daylights out of her. Candice and I would party on the weekends, she was pretty; she sort of reminded me of Sheila.

After a few years in the condo, loneliness started to get the best of me. I was beginning to drink myself into a frenzy with so much idle time on my hands. One night sometime after Candice came home from the hospital with her second child, Emanuel knocked at my door. After peeping through the peephole, I thought that perhaps he was drunk and just came to the wrong house.

"Let me see what this fool wants." I said to myself as I opened the door.

"Hey, what's happening?" He said, looking me over while I was a little tipsy with my bottle of Hennessey in my hand and the ashes from my cigarette hanging in suspense.

"What you want Emanuel, your house is next door."

"I want to talk to you. I know you know how I been looking at you for the longest."

"Man, I *ain't* thinking about you. You know you're my girl's husband. Now take your *drunk self* home. Talking about you want to talk to me. You wouldn't even know how to handle a woman like me."

Now why did I have to say those words? That Hennessey must have been talking. I knew I hadn't had *none* for a while, it seemed as though that liquor just elevated my desires.

"I know I can handle a woman like you, I really don't think you can handle me. Word is, it *hasn't* been hit for a while. I just wanted to know if you were up for the ride?"

He should have never gone there; it just seemed like all of my juvenile instincts just road my desire. I couldn't turn down the challenge. I invited him in thinking I would just tease him as I done in the past. But, it went a little bit further and before I knew it we were sharing passion. It seemed like I hadn't been drinking at all, once we were in the mix. This guy was really turning me out. Never had I every experienced the sexual freakiness this man displayed. His broad shoulders and unblemished skin made me act like a maniac. Not to mention the size of him. Wow! He brought the freak out of me. I knew now why Candice took all of the abuse, I couldn't take any abuse from any man though, that was out!

But the way he was royally abusing my female organ, I'd needed it so badly. All night with only water breaks in between, I knew this man was going to leave me sore for a week and walking bow legged like a cowboy.

The next morning like a fool, I accompanied him to my door and kissed him goodbye; what in the world I was thinking about, I don't know. Knowing Candice was next door made no difference, we weren't going to have an affair or nothing like that. It was more or less a goodbye kiss, actually I wanted to sort of thank him for the best I'd ever had. He knew he wasn't my type of guy. I always knew if a man cheated once, he would cheat again, I didn't want him.

We were kissing when her door opened and she saw us. Candice went into a rage that was out of this world, she chased him and then she came to beat me down. I ran inside listening to her rant and rage making a total spectacle. Then I slipped out of my back door while she was still up front.

Grabbing my purse with my money I made a quick get away through the back yard and then to a hotel. I must've stayed in the hotel for two weeks while trying to let things cool down. Most of my meals I called for delivery; it was like vacationing for a while but then I needed to go home, or at least find out what was going on. Candice my best friend wanted to kill me, but I knew I was safe at the hotel.

Finally, one day I went out to the grocery store to pick up a few things. There I meet Debra. I was kind of skeptical about meeting someone at the grocery store again after that Welfare queen zoomed in on my husband there, but I gave it another shot with Debra. We talked on the phone until the *wee* hours in the morning. She was cool.

Later on I built up enough nerve to try and find Emanuel to get the low down on what was going on with him and Candice. I knew he hung out at the pool hall off of Monroe Avenue; all I had to do now was to find the telephone number. Looking through the yellow pages I found the low life pool hall's number. Anxious to call, my hands began to tremble after knowing I would be talking to this man again.

"Eman, it's for you." The gentleman at the pool hall said, I could only imagine he handed him the telephone.

"Hello, this is Eman." His hard voice vibrated through the fiber optic lines.

"Eman! Is that what they call you? This is Belinda."

"Oh hey babe, how you doing?"

"Fine, just called to see what was going on in the neighborhood, and what you and Candice was up to."

"Oh girl, Candice went back down south. Took the kids, and she's selling the house. You know it was in her name. Yeah, she's gone now. I'm just chilling. What are you doing?"

"Nothing, I had to get away from there. I'm in the hotel now, I guess it's cool to come home now."

"Yeah, I think it's cool to come back. Candice is gone now, *gonna* miss her though."

"Now how are you *gonna* miss her when you were always beating the daylights out of her? You could never be a man of mine. You hit it good, I won't tell *no* lie. But that's all it was. I'm glad I helped her realize you *ain't no* good, but for one thing. You just a good lay, Eman!"

"So what are you saying, it won't happened again?"

"Not in this life time! It was a mistake and you know it. I was drunk."

"You sure didn't act drunk."

"Just put it in your memory bank, or another notch in your belt."

"Hey, why all the hostility, don't be so mean girl. I thought we had a good time?"

"I did, it's just the after effects weren't cool. I had to hide out because of you, the so call player!"

"It was good though, wasn't it?"

"I don't know why you need so much reassurance. You don't know if you did it right or something?"

"*Naw*, I'm just asking, 'cause I want to hook up again with you. You were so expressive and you made a whole lot of noise like those white girls."

"Forget you! I just wanted to know what was going on in the neighborhood!"

"*Click!*" I hung up the telephone and was mad at Eman. I hate to be compared to anyone; he was turning my emotions into something comical. He just brought out the worst in me.

Finally, I checked out of the hotel and returned to my condo. Things didn't seem right there anymore. Now I had no friend to talk to and share my thoughts with. Candice was gone and so was Carlton. My home was no longer impressive to me, I made my mind up to move. I was indecisive as to where I was going, anywhere would have been better I thought.

After about a week of soaking in my thoughts, there was a knock at my door. It was Emanuel. I knew I shouldn't have let him in, but I did. Loneliness had overcome my better judgment, all that was on my mind was how he had rocked my world the first time. So I let him put forth the effort to do it again. When they say it's never as good as the first time, I had to find that out the hard way; it wasn't. I was disappointed with the feeling of being treated like a piece of meat or a slut; I deserved more. After bidding him farewell he knew we weren't going to be getting together again. I guess I wasn't like his other *girls* that were in the streets. I never had any kids and I wasn't loose.

During the intimacy *I felt it all*, there was no need for the pounding and brutal efforts he was trying to put on me. I needed tenderness, gentleness and definitely some slow motion. This was not Eman's style; well endowed didn't mean a thing to me if he didn't know how to use it. I wanted to get away, somewhere far from Rochester. Too many bad things were happening. My husband died, I lost my best friend and I was tapping her old man and didn't really want to. Now, here I am just thinking about who to call and drinking this cold hot chocolate. I'm glad I only have one more day here. I was pleased when my girlfriend Veronica said I can stay with her until I find a place. I didn't know how I would like Brooklyn; she said she enjoyed it, so I assumed I would too.

My boxes were packed and waiting for the movers, tomorrow would be a better day, I thought. Although, the adventure with Eman, wasn't what I expected, I did manage to get fulfilled until the next time I could get a fix. I guess the remote control to the wide screen was my only friend, so I flicked the channels until I stopped. I was thinking my mind would be at ease until I listened to the drama that was going on the tube. Some talk show just made me laugh until my jaws ached.

This guy and his wife lived in a trailer park and they drank excessively. After a night of drinking, he woke up the next morning trying to satisfy his hangover by popping the top off a can of beer. His brother in-law was spending the weekend with them and was passed out on the sofa. The husband stepped outside of the trailer to get some morning air. When he stepped out of the trailer the center blocks that were used for steps were missing and he felled flat on his face. The brother in-law was using the blocks to fix the raggedy car that sat in the yard. The husband smashed the beer can with his face and he began to bleed excessively.

When he stood up the small dog that his wife had recently bought was underneath him, he had crushed the dog. The dog was lying on the ground whimpering with his intestines hanging out of him. The husband felt sad for what he had done and he wanted to take the dog out of its misery.

On the side of the trailer he retrieved a baseball bat and commenced to beat the dog to death. His wife was arriving in the car and saw him beating her new pet. Immediately she ran to stop him. They began to fight before he had a chance to explain to her what he was doing. By this time a noisy neighbor looked from her kitchen window and saw them fighting and she called the police.

The police arrived and found them fighting and placed the husband in the police car and drove away. While in the police cruiser the husband explained what had happened when they were a couple blocks away from the trailer park.

They stopped the car and told him to get out. They said he already had a rough morning. Later the man found out what neighbor had called the cops on him and he confronted her. They began to have a love affair. He was making love to the neighbor that had called the police on him. On the talk show he wanted to tell his wife about the affair, but he had some more startling news. After having the affair with the neighbor, he also was making love to her eighteen year old daughter and they made plans to run off together; he was sixty years old.

Whoa! This is some crazy stuff, and I thought my life was crazy! How in the world do they put this *stuff* on TV? Let me get up out of this chair and get ready for my move. I'm *gonna* miss Sharon, but I'll stay in touch with her. I think I'll call my mother, haven't talked to her in a while.

My mother, strong, attractive and caring, she's always been a good ear for me. Whenever we were together guys would asked if we were sisters. I knew their harmless *come on* were delivered to both of us. My mother would just smile and laugh at the flirtatious remark, while I merely said she was my mother.

Her hair had the sheen of silk, most of the time she'd have it curled inward and let it hang. Thick, full and shinny, I only wished I had hair like hers. Each day I counted the new strains of gray that would appear. She'd quickly dye it back to black when too many gray strains appeared. I rationalized now why she kept all of my secrets away from Daddy. I shared everything that went on in my life with her, including the situation with Emanuel.

I think my mother also had some dark secrets she kept away from my dad, although, she never share them with me. I could sense my mother was doing something when I was younger. Sometimes we would go places and she would meet people, as a child I could never understand why she would always tell me, "now, don't tell your Daddy, he would just get upset. And we don't want to get him mad, now do we?"

"No Mama, I won't say *nothing,*" I would respond.

I should have known something was wrong even back then. Especially when my *father; with his everlasting always do right self,* would give me those long speeches.

"Now Belinda, if anyone ever tells you not to tell me something, it's only because they are doing something wrong. Never feel like you have to lie for anyone! When they tell you not to tell me, they are doing something bad, always be able to talk to your dad, regardless of what anyone else may say. I'm here for you baby girl."

With Mama hiding where we'd been and all of the uncles she'd introduce me to that Daddy didn't know. I knew between the two of them they were putting me in the middle of some *stuff* I really didn't want to be a part of. It was too heavy of a load for a young girl I thought. I dismissed it all! Mama grew out of it; I think. They had an argument in the middle of the night that woke me up. Since, she'd become a loving wife and the mother she is today. I think Daddy gave her an ultimatum. Perhaps, from my mother is where I received most of my thinking of being so tough, maybe her flirtatious ways were in my x or y-chromosomes.

Everyday it seems she needed someone to pay her a compliment, telling her how beautiful she was. I didn't need that; I guess from my father side I had that confidence within myself. At times I would think my mother needed to have other men drooling over her to feel desirable. At forty-seven she could pass for twenty-nine. My dad was fortunate to have her, although he too looked young for his age. I guess that's why they hung in there with each other and overcame their differences. After that night they argued Mama stopped telling me not to tell Daddy where we'd been, or who she talked to. But, she kept my secrets when I asked her not to tell Daddy something because he would get mad, or did she I wondered.

She taught me to always say thank you whenever someone would pay me a compliment and never let it go to my head. She'd say there's always someone prettier and beauty can be a gift or a curse. I rationalize with those words, for sure, being conceited would have put a damper on my social life. It seemed as though ups and down had become a part of my life, in more ways than one.

On the phone my mother would just say, "It'll be alright, you just sad from loosing Carlton, people make mistakes. You just *gotta* learn from them and move on. Don't let them get you down honey. We all make mistakes, some folks won't talk about theirs, but they too make mistakes."

I always felt better after I talked to my mother. To her I could do nothing wrong, it was as if she'd been there and done that, when it came to me. How she could have possibly experienced anything I had and be married, I never understood. It was just so overwhelming to have my mother always sympathizing with my numerous situations. She'd always delivered that awe feeling as if she experienced whatever it was I was talking about. *Naw,* I think I will talk to Mama tomorrow. All of this mental stress has taken its toll on me today. *Better* finish getting ready for my move to Brooklyn. I sure am glad Veronica said I could stay with her until I get settled in.

Chapter Two
No More Drama

The quaint and serene beaches of Lake Ontario I'll certainly miss, a new destination will give me the opportunity to refocus and get my life back on track. Perhaps the presence of a new environment would be the solution to all of the madness. My mind has to be completely clear if I'm to move on with my life.

All of the mess I've gone through over the past several months has become mind boggling. I feel as though my brain is about to malfunction, and cause me to have a nervous breakdown. I'm confused and really don't know what to do, this life is about to drive me crazy—it's so off balance. It's more than I need to be thinking about right now.

The troubles of my past are going to consume me if I'm not careful, that's definitely one thing I can't afford to happen. Disastrous would be an understatement for how my path has ended up. I believe I need some professional help.

Staying in Rochester will be as if I'm being held hostage while trying to escape the demons of my past. Life has become nothing but a constant struggle for me. There are just too many reminders of the bad things that have happened to me in this city, many of them I'm guilty of causing to myself. I think my relief and solution to the hurt my actions have caused, to myself and to others, is to get a way from here and I must do it now!

Tomorrow the movers will come; afterwards I'll take a long walk along the beach, stick my feet in the sand and think of my new destination.

It was a beautiful fall day; the temperature was in the mid seventies while I drove down the Interstate towards Brooklyn. When I told Veronica I thought about leaving Rochester, she invited me to stay with her. I didn't have to stay there; I could've bought me a lakefront home and just chilled. But, I thought it would be best to take Veronica up on her offer, just to relax and have some fun; it would be a way to get my mind off of things.

The wind blew briskly through my hair; the top on my convertible was completely laid back. The sound of Jay-Z from the CD player helped change my mood, quickly I shifted into high gear and swerved around some old folks that seemed to be out for a Sunday drive—nothing else seemed to matter, but my Mustang and the highway.

The traffic jams were thick when I approached the outskirts of Brooklyn. Everyone was driving as if they had taken an excessive dose of Ritalin. A fool in the left lane swerved around me in a fancy sports car, shouting as if I had stolen something from him.

"Get the out of the way lady, can you drive?"

"Kiss my black a..." I said, after he made me a part of his road rage game.

"Show it to me." The stringy head blond guy shouted back.

How could I resist the challenge? Immediately, I stopped at the nearest intersection, shifted my car into park, and lifted up my dress. I proceeded to drop my gold Victoria Secret panties and boldly displayed my perfectly sculptured God's gift to any man's dreams. He was horrified to say the least. By this time, the traffic had completely come to a streaking halt. Horns honking, fingers pointing and whistling sounds ranged in the air from the other motorist while they watched and stare.

What a relief, I told myself. I didn't care about the trivial matter—too busy trying to escape the reality of my past? Brooklyn, New York, the place I wanted to be. After carefully maneuvering through the traffic for about 45 minutes, finally the charade subsided. My car came to a halt and my convertible top was in the locked position. 50 East 51ˢᵗ Street, I noticed it was right down street from Utica Avenue; the ladies of the night there were more than vivid.

Veronica had arranged for me to chill out with her for a couple of months, to see if I wanted to live in the Big Apple. After talking with her over the phone, I knew I didn't want to live on the north side, she said it was filled with hoodlums.

I arrived in front of her building the same time she was coming from the grocery store with bags in her hands. Our eyes met, instantly we greeted each other with joy.

"Veronica! Girl, it's good to see you!"

"Belinda, my God look at you! You haven't changed a bit. Just look at you, *all tiny*. Here I am *done* gain a few pounds."

"I can't tell, you look the same to me."

"*Yeah, right!* Whatever! I'm glad you made it. I had to slip out and get a few groceries. I was hoping I'd be back before you got here, how was your trip."

"Awe, it was cool girl, just can't take anymore of that drama up in Rochester, you know what I mean."

"Yeah, I know, girl you've been through it."

"Tell me about it!"

"Girl, just get your stuff and come on up."

"Okay."

Veronica stood patiently while I retrieved my luggage out of the trunk. Most of the time I'd travel light on weekend getaways. Since I knew I was staying for a while I had my two black sturdy Samsonite suite cases for the trip. They were heavy, and I was glad they had rollers.

"Girl come on, and what took you so long anyway? I've been waiting on you for two hours since you last called."

"You really don't want to know, but let me tell you anyway. On the outskirts of the city, this guy almost ran me off the road. I told him to kiss where the sun don't shine. He told me to show it to him, and you know me!"

"No you didn't girl?"

"Like Hell I didn't, mooned him and whoever was passing by, got a few whistles in the process too!"

"*In the middle of traffic?*"

"Yes!"

"Girl, you are still crazy as ever. I guess that's why we can kick it together."

"I know that's right."

Veronica's apartment was spotless, a bar sat in the corner of the living room and she had what looked like an eight-piece sofa set that almost covered the entire room. Exhaustion was creeping into my dwellings. After putting my luggage away in the spare bedroom, restlessly I sat down on the comfortable sofa and kicked my legs up on the ottoman.

"Let's have something to drink. You still drink Hennessey?" Veronica said as she wondered over to the stereo and put on some music. I could see she still had it going on, even with the extra pounds she hadn't lost her shape at all—the girl still had a small waist line.

"Is there another drink?" My lips smirked in total anticipation. I could hardly wait after the long stressful drive.

"*Well* then, lets get our drinks on!"

"Veronica, where is Ike?"

"Girl, I told you I kicked him to the curb a longtime ago."

"Why is his ugly *mug shot* still on the mantle then?"

"I just keep it there for a reminder not to run into anyone like him again.

You know, he was like someone you ran into that you told me about, that *thuggish* guy."

"Don't even go there? I came here to get away from all of that drama, please don't remind me. Put on some jazz. I'm tired of listening to *all of that* rap. Make it a little Kenny Lattimore, or something mellow."

"Girl the last time I heard some Kenny Lattimore, Kelvin was riding this pony."

"Kelvin who?"

"Kelvin Barker, you know I told you about him while you was still in Rochester, remember?"

"Oh yeah, you said he was the old man of an associate of yours at work. Christina,—that was her name, her old man right?"

"Yeah that *heifer*, and she didn't even know it."

"Girl seems like your scheme is habitual. You have to be the Queen of Betrayal. I hope you know getting caught comes with a heavy price to pay."

"Like you the leading authority on being a do right woman."

"I'm just saying, 'cause you know I've been there. Like they always say, 'you reap what you sow!' Retribution for all of the stuff we've done may cost us our lives."

"You *just tripping*! I'm not messing with him anymore. He stopped bringing the cash and that's when the booty calls stop! I do miss him though."

"You just watch what I'm telling you. There's no way you're going to get away with the undercover dirt. You told me when Christina walked out of the front door, you were walking in the backdoor undressing her man. Girl we played those scandalous games when we were kids in Boston, remember."

"Those were some fun times, huh Belinda?"

We both laugh while Veronica passed me my first glass of Hennessey straight on the rocks. My first sip went down smoothly, and my pumps lied on the floor while I stretched into a relaxed mood.

"Believe me Veronica, manipulation and deception can cause an ultimate downfall."

"What do you mean? It takes two to tangle. If an available Boo considers himself to be the Maintenance Man servicing women, why can't I be the Maintenance Woman, I need to be service too!"

"I'm just saying..."

"Girl *don't* even say it. I just know the lifestyle of the men I deal with, reflects a life of Milk and Honey. The women they selects, gets showered with the finest of all amenities; whatever their heart's desire. Now, if it's good enough for them, why shouldn't I be able to benefit from the same game? They're certainly no better than me!"

"Girl, you are *gonna* have to pay someday. Just remember that payback is a mother."

"Like you don't have plenty of dirty laundry?"

"Yeah, in my past and besides, I only slept with one person other than Carlton."

"Hey, at the rate we're going, one of us will be wearing those short little black dresses to our funeral, huh?"

"You know at lot of the women would love to spit in our faces while we're lying in that coffin."

"I hear you, 'cause you sure do lack empathy for another woman's man."

"Look who's talking. I don't know how you can even live with yourself?"

"Girl, it sure ain't easy. Now, where were we?"

"We were talking about Kelvin."

"Oh lets not talk about Kelvin anymore, that's foul territory."

"Okay, I'll leave it alone."

"Now don't get me wrong Belinda, it's just that I couldn't help it. I was obsessed with the thought of making love to another woman's man, like you were with Emanuel."

"Nah, it wasn't obsession with me, maybe that bottle of Hennessey brought the beast out of me!"

"I think you were just horny."

"Yeah Girl, you know a little of that had something to do with it." We laughed and poured another drink. Veronica was my girl, it had been a while since I saw her. To be exact it was at my wedding with Carlton. I could have sworn I saw Carlton eyes and Veronica's locked together that day, but instantly I dismissed the thought.

"Belinda, at the rate we're going sleeping around with our friend's old man, there's no need for them to create enemies."

"Speak for yourself girl, one time don't make me a bad person! But, it haunts me though."

"You talk like you need to see Dr. Ruth. They say she's the leading sex therapist in America."

"Veronica, I just told you I slept with Emanuel only once. Well I take that back, it was twice. It's not like it's some kind of bad habit or anything."

"Belinda you're as guilty as Hell, I can tell you're lying."

"So what are you saying, I really need to go see Dr. Ruth?"

"It certainly wouldn't hurt."

"All I need to do is to find me a man. Why don't you search in places other than another woman's bedroom?"

"Look whose trying to give me some lessons in morality, Miss Goodie Two Shoes. Girl, *pleazzzze!*"

"At least I know how to pick my man, and not his wallet."

"Is that so, like Carlton?"

"Hey, you can't talk. What about Ike?"

"That's enough. Now out of all the people you could've chosen to talk about, you definitely know not to go there. Like I told you, Ike is like a bad nightmare that will never go away. Girl, you know I told you he almost killed me!"

"I know. I was just kidding. Veronica, don't take things so seriously. Give me another hit of that Hennessey. What do you have in *the frig* to eat? I'm about starved to death, you know we have to feed that liquor."

"There's nothing, except some leftover pizza from last night. And you know if we eat that stuff, it'll give us a bad case of diarrhea. Let's go out to eat. It's on me since you are my company. Let's celebrate a new beginning. I owe you one, I had a good time at your wedding."

"That's fine with me."

"What do you have in mind?"

"Some prime ribs."

"Sounds like you want to eat the whole cow."

"You know it girl!"

"Girl, let's go. I'll take you over to Morton's of Chicago. They have some of the best prime ribs in Brooklyn, not to mention how fine the men are there."

"Whose car are we taking? Let's ride in your Benz, it'll give me some time to relax and enjoy your system."

"Okay girl, Morton's right across town on 31st.street."

"Hurry up girl, I'm starved."

"Are you starved for some food or for some sex?"

"Veronica, you know me too well, but, to answer your question, both. Girl seems like I stay horny all of the time every since I let Emanuel tap this *thang*. It's like I can't get enough of good loving."

"Girl you don't know what good loving is. You need to get laid by one of the men in my stable."

"*Yeah right!* I've had my share of the prime beef. Let's change the subject."

Veronica new E-series Mercedes was plush, the wood grained dashboard and leather seat set the tone of elegancy. I have to give it to the girl, although she was a Little Hot Mama, she did have style. Her men of choice may have been someone else's, only because she would only give it up to the men that would give her something. If they didn't have money, she wouldn't be bothered with them.

Veronica was a high maintenance woman, from her hair to her toes. Her hair was cut in a short fashionable style—thick but lean she was; with a rear end that could hold an ashtray and a drink on it, without spilling a drop. She had magnetism eyes, a hazel brown look, most of the time they would leave men speechless. She was my girl from the old neighborhood, and there was nothing we could say or do to each other to loose our friendship. We were so tight that if she was to come in and find me in bed with her old man, he would be out and we would remain friends. We knew where we stood!

"We are here already?"

"I told you Morton's wasn't too far from the house. Let me pull over to the valet parking guy, he's standing by the curve."

Veronica slowly steered her foreign driving machine closer to the front entrance. She stopped the car and stepped out in her short tight skirt. Slowly she exited one leg after another exposing her thighs for attention. Somehow I knew she wanted the guy's eyes to droll over her and follow her every movement.

"Hello, my fine Nubian princesses," exclaimed the Valet attendant.

"Hello," we shouted in unison to the Valet.

"Let me have your keys," he responded in a low baritone voice while holding the handle to Veronica's door. "I like the color of this fine driving machine. What color is it?"

"It's metallic gold." Veronica responded proudly.

"Quite unique, it definitely speaks of royalty, a nice chariot for two lovely Nubian princesses. Oh, by the way I'm Mike and I'll be watching this beautiful piece of machinery for you. Enjoy your evening of fine dining at Morton's. You couldn't have chosen a better place to eat. It doesn't come any better than this!"

"Thank you, dark and handsome," Veronica said with a genuine smile, she was flirting in a humorous way.

"You're welcome, enjoy your evening."

"Girl, he's *finnnnee*," I said.

"True. But he's also a parking attendant. *Gotta* admit though, he's a parking attendant with class."

"He's a man, that's all that counts!"

"I guess? He could also be gay. You know those gay men be looking good."

"Could be? I still think he's fine." I said.

"Okay, come on lets go inside," hastily, Veronica hurried me on.

The aromas from the restaurant permeated our nostrils when we entered the establishment.

"It sure smells good in here." I said as I glance around the elegant restaurant. Just from sight it had expensive in the air. It was totally my type of place.

"Girl, take a quick look to your right. That's some kind of presentation the waiter is making at their table. He must've brought everything out of the kitchen for them to see, except the sink."

We stood in amazement at the array of food being presented. A young handsome waiter quietly stepped up behind us.

"Good afternoon ladies, my name is Terrance may I help you? Did you make reservations?"

"No, we decided to come here at the last minute. Will that be a problem?" Veronica said with confidence and a quaint smile, displaying the attitude of a woman that was use to getting her way.

"Of course not, just wait a moment and I'll get right back with you."

"Thanks darling," Veronica said in a seductive voice while gazing up and down his body.

"Girl, you're always flirting!" I shouted.

"I just know how to handle these men in the city. They look at a fine lady as if we are a piece of meat; I just use it to my benefit."

"I feel you Veronica. I guess you know what you are doing."

"What are you trying to say? It's not like I'm throwing myself on anyone, these African Princes deserve this finest. All I want to do is get my groove on."

"I hear you." I responded in kind.

"You know I'm no different from most women."

"Awe Veronica, you know you be digging for gold." Gingerly, she pushed me on the shoulders and we laughed.

While still in the midst of our crazy conversation, the waiter approached for the second time and signal for us to follow him.

"What shall it be smoking or none smoking?"

"Nonsmoking." We spoke in unison.

"Thanks. Then nonsmoking it shall be. Will this corner booth be okay?" he pointed while looking at both of us. His stare was deep; for sure I knew if he wasn't in a waiter capacity his quest to get to know us would have been revealed.

"Yes. This will be just fine." I responded, while Veronica continues to observe our surroundings.

"Make yourselves comfortable. Here's the wine list; I'll get back with you shortly."

Abruptly I turned facing Veronica. "What will it be, a little red wine or white?"

"I think I'd like to drink a little red tonight." Veronica hesitantly responded.

"Me too, a good vintage bottle from Napa Valley would suit me just fine. They say it's where some of the best grapes are grown in the country. Make it an odd year; I hear they are the best. I've been keeping abreast of that type of thing. I've experimented with so many Vintage wines lately."

"Sounds good to me, let's go with it. Wine from the Napa Valley it shall be."

The waiter approached the table and asks. "Have you beautiful young ladies made your selections?"

Peering into the waiter's big brown eyes, assuredly I responded,

"Yes, I believe we have."

"What shall it be then, red or white?"

"Red." Veronica intervened.

"What brand can I bring to you lovely ladies?"

"Anything from the Napa Valley will be fine, make it an odd year though." I said, while still staring at the menu.

"May I suggest a bottle of Ferma Blanch? It has a rich flavor and goes down with ease."

We said okay and the waiter turned and walked away, Veronica nodded her head in a fashion indicating for me to look at the plumpness of his rear end. I couldn't help myself but to look. Shapely his behind was, we laughed and before we knew it he had returned with a white towel place on his forearm. He began to take the cork out of the bottle with pure expertise. His charm was truly one to be reckoned with.

"Let me have your glasses and I'll pour you a sample. Take a sip and tell me what you think."

"Hum, it smells good." Veronica said as she put the huge glass to her lips. "Taste a little sweet though, what do you think Belinda?"

"I love it."

"I'll be back to take your orders shortly." Once again he gracefully walked away. Veronica attentively watched the waiter walk away. She took note of his finely sculptured body. It was apparent he worked out on a regular basis. His chest protruded through his shirt, but his buns really spoke for themselves.

"This wine is probably as sweet as the waiter."

"Girl, I know what you mean. Y'all have some good looking men here!"

"I know girl, it seems like the cute ones are always in a domestic capacity though."

"Veronica, Veronica," I said in astonishment.

"What, now girl?"

"Is that one of the pro football players sitting at the table in front of us?"

"I don't know. You know I don't care about sports."

"Neither *do* I just the players girl!"

"What's his name?"

"How should I know? If you really want to know go ask him, after all this is your town."

"I will."

She ran behind my chair almost making me spill my drink.

"Veronica! You don't have to run all over me. He's not going anywhere."

"Sorry, he's just so fine."

Veronica hurriedly approached the table to talk to the well sculpture gentleman sitting all alone.

"Yes, may I help you," the gentleman responded in a deep voice.

"Aren't you one of the New York Jets?"

"Yes, I am. Who are you, a reporter or a real sports fan," the gentleman said with a snarl.

"Neither, I'm just simply an admirer."

"Are you like most women? Once they see all of this, they think they are obligated to get it. You seem to be no different than the rest of them, approaching me like this."

"Now don't categorize me. I'm not just any other woman. I am 'The Woman.' It's more to me than my superior appearance. I possess style and charm among many other hidden treasures. If you dig deep enough, you might find pure gold. But, I know your type. They only talk a big game."

"If you say so, you seem to be full of confidence young lady. I may have to take you up on the challenge."

"If you act right, Sir, I just might break you off a little *sompum, sompum.*"

"Girl, you're crazy!"

"Maybe so," Veronica turned her behind in the direction of Mr. Jones face.

"If you're sure you can handle all of this," referring to her sexual prowess.

"Have a seat." The football player waved his hand towards an empty chair.

"I would, but as you can see, I'm dining with my friend. Won't you come and join us?"

"Okay, but I'm waiting on another player."

"Don't worry; he can join us at our table when he arrives."

Veronica grasp his hand with confidence and lead him to the table, I was waiting with a charming smile on my face.

"Waiter."

"Yes Sir, Mr. Jones."

"Let Dommincee know that we'll be dinning at the corner booth with these two lovely chocolate drops."

"Yes Sir Mr. Jones, I'll let him know."

As Mr. Jones slowly approached the table, easily I could assume him noticing me peering, sizing him up. Then Mr. Jones looked intently into my eyes.

"Hello," sprouted from his full shaped lips in a seductive and smooth voice. "Now, you are?"

"Belinda. Belinda Norris and that is Miss Belinda Norris. I'm sorry; I didn't get your name. And you are?"

Thank goodness I started using my maiden name again. I didn't want any reminder of Carlton, I was in a new world now, and besides it seemed like Veronica had hit the jackpot with this one.

"Just like the rest of my admirers. They're so busy looking at my manhood that they become mesmerized—their thought processes completely fades away."

"I certainly would like to test your manhood," Veronica interjected.

This guy was bursting with conceitedness, he began to turn me off, but it was kind of cute watching his confidence level. I began to wonder if all of the men in Brooklyn were as such.

"You can," responded Mr. Jones in an even more sensuous tone than the first.

"I will!" Veronica shouted. Then she reached underneath the table and rubbed Mr. Jones thighs.

"Stop, girl! Get your hands off of my leg. Are you sure you are all right?"

"Yes. You have nothing to be afraid of. I'm not going to hurt you. I just wanted to feel the total package, if you know what I mean?"

"I see."

"Belinda."

"Yes, Ms. Fancy Pants."

"What do you think?"

"Think about what?"

"This big Mandingo player."

"Girl your mind stays in the gutter."

"Now don't try and pretend that you don't know what I'm talking about. I saw you sizing him up when he first approached the table. I think I'm going to have him for desert tonight."

"Mr. Jones, would you please excuse her? They just let her out of the state's mental hospital today."

"It's okay. I understand. Most women can't resist all of this."

"I see. So what position do you play?"

"Middle linebacker, do you know what position that is?"

"No."

Mr. Jones stood up and turned toward me, as if he was about to physically demonstrate.

"Let me show you." He pulled my chair out and stood in front of me as if he was a bull about to charge me. Quickly he grabbed me in front and twisted my body around holding me in a bear hug fashion. We were pressed against one another, I could feel him, I felt him real good. Veronica was right!

"From here I can through you on the ground and tackle you!"

"Oh okay, well just don't hurt me now." I said in a lady like soft tone, generating and delivering a smile all the while.

Veronica became agitated at the two of us and told us to stop, in an abrasive and loud voice. "Just wait a minute," she said in a disgruntled tone." I brought him over here for me Belinda, not you."

"But, you said you weren't interested in sports."

"I'll tell you anything."

"Yes, I see."

"Just get away from him. Remember, he's my dessert. This six foot five, 285 lbs. of muscles is just what I need to rock my world, right about now!"

"Girl, you're so nasty."

"Not nasty, just real. You know I get what I want."

"I know, and me too!"

"Yeah, that's why your ass is here with me now."

"Let's not go there."

"What's that all about?" said Mr. Jones.

"Oh, nothing, just girl talk, that's all."

"Mr. Jones, have you ordered yet?" I asked trying to change the subject. Veronica was getting on my nerves, acting all desperate.

"Yes. Look to your right, I believe our food is on its way."

"I believe that it is."

The waiter approached the table with food in both hands.

"Excuse me I believe this is for you," he placed my food in front of me. I was impressed he had remembered who ordered what.

"Thanks." I responded with a smile displaying all thirty-two.

"And this is for you." Gently he sat Veronica's plate on the table.

"Thank you Terrance." Veronica said. "Girl everything in here is fine as hell." The waiter smile knowing Veronica was talking about him also, it seemed as though he needed the compliment when she said it. I think it kind of made his day.

"Mr. Jones, here is your lobster tail cooked just the way you like it."

"Thanks Terrance. Don't forget to send Mr. Dommincee over to the table when he arrives."

"I'll do that Mr. Jones. Is there anything else I can do for you at this time?"

"No, thank you."

"Don't hesitate to call on me. Enjoy your meal."

"Let's eat up young ladies."

"I can hardly wait," Veronica responded. "I'm so hungry I can eat a horse."

"Veronica where's your manners?" I retorted.

"Girl I can't help it. I need to hurry up and finish this main course. I can almost taste my juicy dessert."

Veronica then took a quick glance over towards Mr. Jones with her tongue licking the strawberry held between her fingers, all covered in whipped cream. Each lick was more purposeful than the preceding one. She made certain Mr. Jones didn't miss the show. Veronica received his undivided attention and loved every bit of it. She wasn't going to allow me to take center stage anymore this night. Her ability to captivate a man with her seductive ways was far superior to most women, and she knew it.

Mr. Jones grinned at her as they began to enjoy their meals. She knew he couldn't take his eyes off of her after such a display of erotic foreplay with the strawberries. What man could resist the thought of her tongue entering into the arena of his most private world? Veronica realized they couldn't, and Mr. Jones was no exception to the rule. This was all her game; she made the rules and broke them at will. She was the one in control and she enjoyed every moment of it.

Mr. Jones had become a hostage to her seductive ways. Soon, Veronica would have Mr. Jones eating out of the palm of her hands. He completely forgot about his meal and began to concentrate on how to lure her into his net. Little did he know, "The Black Widow Spider" was spinning him into her deadly spider web? He let his guards down and she couldn't permit him to escape her trap.

Suddenly, there was the shadow of what could have been a giant standing over our table. It was Mr. Jones's friend, Mr. Dommincee. He must've stood at least seven foot tall with huge arms bursting out of the sleeves of his shirt. He was well dressed and smelled like he was wearing some CK Seven. Mr. Jones introduced us and Dommincee joined in the fabulous dinning experience. I was happy Veronica had brought me to Morton. It was *all that* she said it would be and more.

Mr. Dommincee had preordered his dinner and Terrance had it waiting on him as he sat down with us. It was a feast fit for a king. Lobster tails, filet mignon, shrimp dipped in a delicious French sauce. There were several bottles of Pierre water sitting on the table to wash it all down. What a meal! It was awesome.

Veronica had begun to flirt with Mr. Jones at the dinner table a little more. She took her shoes off and caressed him with her toes. Mr. Jones had a huge grin on his face and seemed to really enjoy Veronica's flirtatious ways. His pants were now beginning to bulge from the excitement. The pressure from Veronica's flirtatious ways had him in a massive heat. His macho image had completely diminished. Everyone at the table was aware of their ungodly activity.

"Veronica," I exclaimed. "What in the hell do you think you are doing? Girl you have no manners whatsoever. We are trying to enjoy our meals, aren't we? Why don't you just stop until we finish with our meal? Girl, the night is still young and if you want to go get your groove on, I'm sure Mr. Jones will oblige."

"Belinda, please leave me alone, I can handle this. I'm a big girl now."

"You are one foolish one too!"

"Who cares? Mr. Jones doesn't seem to mind. As a matter of fact I think he is just about ready now."

Everyone let out a big chuckle.

"Girl, you just don't know when to quit. Why did you have to call the brother out like that?"

"I told you that I was going to give him some of my Nubian love nest."

"No, you just want some of his Mandingo power driver to break your membranes."

"Whatever. What's your problem? Are you jealous?"

"Jealous of what?"

"That I'm going to get my rocks off tonight like never before."

"Maybe you will, so what!"

The waiter came over to ask if we needed anymore service. Then a beautiful six foot tall blonde approached the table and gave Mr. Jones a wet juicy kiss directly on his lips. To everyone's surprise, he introduced her as his wife Melody. Veronica had been so busy trying to get her grove on for the night; she completely forgot to ask him if he had a significant other.

Unfortunately for Veronica, her bubble just burst. Melody had come to take him home. Instantly there was an *awe hell no* expression on Veronica's face. The element of anguish and surprise surrounded her with total disbelief. Veronica had been played and the joke was on her. She was supposed to be the player; instead she had become the *playee*. She couldn't bare the embarrassment but she played the hand that had been dealt to her like a true player.

Mr. Jones, whose first name was Stevie, Dommincee and Melody quietly said their good-byes, leaving us bewildered.

The fun and games were now over and reality had sat in. Veronica no longer desired to have an intimate moment with Mr. Jones, but only to go home for a peaceful night's rest. What had been intended for a night of fun and games had now turned into a complete disaster.

Veronica called for the check. Terrance approached the table and informed us that Mr. Jones had taken care of everything on his way out. Terrance also told us that we could stay as long as we pleased.

Veronica told him, "thank you." Then we quietly removed ourselves from the table. We went into the ladies room and Veronica vented with a few choice words about Mr. Jones. Shortly thereafter, we exited the dining facility, signaled for the car and the Valet responded accordingly. I gave him a twenty-dollar bill for his service and we relaxed in Veronica's driving machine and drove towards the Brooklyn Bridge. On the bridge we were able to catch a breath of fresh air and allow time to forget about the dreadful scene of horror in the restaurant.

There was total silence as we began to cross the bridge. Only the sound of Veronica's engine was heard as we cruised across the bridge. From the bridge the city presented a beautiful view, the lights flickered against the backdrop of the buildings in the far distance across the river. It was picturesque scenery that should've been painted by a great landscape artist.

Finally the silence was broken when I busted up laughing uncontrollably; she knew I was laughing at her. I just couldn't stop. Veronica started laughing too, and gave me a gentle shove while she drove across the bridge.

"Girl, I had him!'

"Yeah, you did until the white girl showed up." I laughed some more until my rib cage began to hurt. I couldn't stop, she had me rolling. It was so funny to me.

"Girl lets go to a strip club and get our minds off of that fool."

"Okay," I was still laughing, I could barely get words to come out of my mouth. "I haven't been to one of them in so long." Tears started flowing from my eyes from laughing so hard.

"Girl why don't you shut the f.... up!" Veronica yelled at me. "You make me sick! How in the hell did I know he had a woman, brothers be tripping!"

I was still laughing but I managed to agree to the invitation, and suddenly we were in the midst of about 100 other desperate women at Little Al's, in the Crown Heights neighborhood. It wasn't a safe place but, it seemed to be a good place to relax and forget about what had happened earlier.

The Crown Heights district was widely known for a multiplicity of criminal activity. Veronica parked her car in the back parking lot and paid an attendant twenty bucks to pay special attention to it. At the front entrance, a couple of men gradually approached us, one asking for some loose change. We told him we would on our way out.

"Belinda, get a grip girl. You act like you never been to a strip joint before."

"I'll be all right. Just get me a double shot of Hennessey from the bar while I go freshen up in the ladies room." I said to Veronica, but the entire time I was a little apprehensive of my new surroundings. The place was filled with *Hoochie Mama's*. Almost all the ladies had hair hanging down to their backs. Not that there was something wrong with it, for some of them it just didn't went well with how they were swishing their rear end all over the place. Finally I made it to the restroom, and it wasn't clean enough to put a couple of pigs in. Water or perhaps urine glazed the floor, the sinks were brown from rust and there was no running water to wash my hands. Quickly I ran into one of the open stalls for a little privacy.

"It's funky in here," someone shouted as the door to the ladies room opened.

"Girl, I'm going to see Big Willie tonight," a voice inside one of the stalls shouted.

"I think Chocolate Candy has the biggest," said another woman, from her voice she seemed to be in her late fifties. I wonder why she was in the club in the first place.

"Who cares," I shouted from my stall. "You see one, you've seen them all."

"That's what you think, honey!" The younger woman responded.

The ladies filled the restroom with laughter. I knew I was going to have a good time. Just goofing around with the other ladies made me feel like the strip club was exactly what I had needed after the incident at Morton's.

I left the ladies room and went straight to the bar where Veronica was waiting with her double shot of Hennessy. She quickly swallowed it down and danced to the old school sounds of the O Jay's while someone on the microphone summoned all the women towards the stage where the show was about to began. We rushed up to the stage just as the rest of them did.

"Belinda, how do you feel now?"

"I'm fine, what about you?"

"I'll get over it. He made a fool out of me didn't he?"

"Yeah girl, he sure did. Just forget it. You'll be alright."

We took a seat near the front and the MC announced the first dancer. He introduced the audience to Dolomite II. Dolomite was about 5 foot 11inches, 195 lbs, and he had one of the best six packs any woman would desire of a man. He danced to the sounds of "Mr. Magic," by Grover Washington Jr. The crowd went into frenzy. He shook his beautiful black rear end towards the crowd in an erotic fashion for approximately two minutes before he turned, and faced the crowd.

"I can't believe what my eyes are seeing!" Veronica exclaimed.

He had on a leopard colored *g-sting* and his area of operation was protruding as if it was going to break every thread that held it together.

The more he moved his tight body in a rhythmical circular motion, the more I became moist. Clinching and squeezing my legs together was not effective, I could feel a trail of warm secretion running down my thigh.

My Victor Secret undies were soaked, and I grinded my teeth trying to hold myself together. I was still squeezing, as if I was trying to choke my little man out of his boat; hoping Veronica wouldn't look my way. Sopped, aroused and uncomfortable at the same time; it had been just that long. I really didn't need to be in a strip joint, the level of excitement was getting the best of me.

Dolomite began to approach me, I had some idea he was going to do that—our eyes had locked in on each other like a sniper with a scope. He straddled me and I wanted to take the ten-dollar bill I was waving and wrap it around his well-endowed self. If Veronica hadn't grabbed my hands, I probably would've taken his alpenstock and place it between two of the most loveliest torpedoes he'd ever seen before, I thought. I was thrill after he dance for me and around me, but the night was still young. What else could be waiting behind the curtains I wondered? I needed another shot of that Hennessey and I needed it right away. I had completely forgotten about the horrible event that transpired earlier, and that was all good. Dolomite II made me think about grabbing the first decent man I could find and have my way with him.

"Belinda," Veronica exclaimed. "Are you having any fun now?"

"Girl, you know I am! Did you see him all over me like that?"

"Yeah girl, but you know they all about getting paid. I'm in the same game they are, I *want's* to get paid too!"

"I've never paid for it before, but if they got the time, I've got the dime." We laughed and took another sip of our drinks. Veronica quickly noticed they were about to send the next dancer out.

"Belinda, hold up, they are starting the show again. King Kong is next and he looks like a big black gorilla for real."

"Veronica, have you ever thought about inviting one of the strippers over after a show?"

"Nah girl, like I said before, we both are about that m o n e y! Which one were you thinking about anyway?"

"I don't know, you want to wait and see who is willing to come?"

"I know what you mean girl they have me squirming in my seat too."

"So let's do it!"

"Okay, but for now let's just sit back relax and enjoy the show."

"Next up," the MC announced. "Mr. Long *Stroker.*"

He was approximately the same height an*d* weight as Mr. Jones, the professional football player that we met at Morton's. He danced to the beat of Michael Jackson's hit song, "Thriller."

Mr. Long shakes his tail a thousand times a minute. I just knew what Veronica was thinking, she wanted him—badly. While the music was playing, she went totally hysterical. The stripper danced his way from the dimmed lights over towards us. He turn his face towards Veronica and to my surprise, it was Mr. Jones!

"You no good for nothing M......F....., not only did you embarrassed us at Morton's, but you have the audacity to shake yourself in my face! You can go to h... I don't care how big you are!" I shouted and made a scene when I thrust my drink into his face.

Because of the confrontation, they called for the bouncers. Security grabbed us firmly by our arms and leads us out of the club. The crowd went wild and Veronica and I left what was to be a perfectly good therapeutic session of fun, to another episode of horrific loneliness. Little did I know my life was completely out of control? I could've blamed it on the Hennessey or on my experience with my best friend's husband, but in reality, it was no one else's fault except my own. What a crazy evening it had turned out to be.

"Veronica."

"Yes, Belinda."

"What's really wrong with me? Why did I go off like that at the club?"

"Girl, I don't know. Do I look like a shrink to you? You were just defending my honor."

"Do you think that I need to go see a shrink?"

"You might."

"For real!"

"Yep, for real!"

"Do you happen to know a good one?"

"Now why should I? You're the one with the problem."

"I just asked. Why do you have to be so smart?"

"Okay girl, I'll call one in the morning. Now let's get out of here and go home."

"Sounds good to me."

"What about your big handsome piece of meat back there?"

"Forget it. It's just not worth it tonight. Girl, let's go home and get comfortable."

While walking to the car we met those same two guys we encountered on the way in. Again they walked towards us and asked for some change. Veronica reached into her purse, and she grabbed three dollars and gave it to one of them. They didn't harass us anymore and we walked quickly to the car. The attendant was still there watching Veronica's car as instructed; the parking lot was jammed packed with an abundance of the latest model cars. Veronica and I sit down, and wrapped the seat belts snuggly around us. She started the car and we slowly drove off as the attendant waved goodbye.

After driving for about five minutes, I took a quick peep at my watch. It was five o'clock in the morning.

"Time sure has flied by," I shouted.

"I know girl, and I'm tired as hell."

"Me too."

"I can't wait to get in the bed." Veronica exclaimed exhaustingly.

"I know that's right."

"Don't worry. It won't be long. The house is just around the corner. Just one more turn and we'll be there."

"Who's that standing in the front of your doorway," I asked while fear had started to overcome my mood. Things were happening, the city life was a fast pace, and I had only been in Brooklyn not even a day."

"I don't know. It's too dark for me to see his face."

"Were you expecting someone?"

"No. I don't think so."

"Drive around the block and see if he'll be gone when we get back."

"Okay, I'll do that. If he's there when we get back, I'll call the police."

"Yes, that's the right thing to do. I don't have any room for "No Mo Drama" tonight."

"Girl, I know what you mean."

"Veronica! Who do you think it might be?"

"Girl, I told you I don't have the slightest idea who it could be."

"Drive slowly. I hope that he's gone by the time we get back there."

"Me too."

We drove slowly around the block for a second time and when we returned the man was still standing at Veronica's door.

"Look girl! He's still there. Call the damn police. Hurry up."

"Belinda, I'm too nervous, you dial it."

"Okay, give me that Cricket and I'll dial them up. Veronica, stop being so scared." I said, although I was a bit intimidated also.

"Hello, operator?"

"Yes, how may I help you?"

"We need a police dispatched to 2223 31st Street."

"Do you have an emergency?"

"I wouldn't be calling you if I didn't!"

"What's your emergency, Mam?"

"There's a man standing in my friend's doorway and we have no idea who it is."

"Does he have a gun Mam?"

"How should I know, I'm not the police department? Am I supposed to go search him to see if he has a gun?"

"Don't get smart with me. You're the one that needs the help, so chill out!"

"Are you going to send the police to investigate or not?"

"Why should I? You don't seem to have an emergency."

"Go to Hell! I don't know how you got that job in the first place!"

'Click!'

"Oh no she didn't!" I shouted because she hung up the phone on me.

"Veronica, that ignorant dispatcher hung up on me."

"I kind of figure that."

"What do you mean?"

"You provided her with no pertinent information to help us. No one needs your nasty attitude when you're the one who needs the help."

"So it's like that now. Huh!" I retorted.

"Girlfriend, I call it like I see it."

"Okay, I get the message. But he's still standing in the doorway."

"Let's go see *who* the hell it is we're so afraid of."

"Let's do it. By the way, do you still carry that nine?"

"You know that I don't leave home without it. This Smith and Weston is all of the protection I'll ever need."

"Let me have it."

"Here." Veronica passed me the shinny weapon. "Be careful with that thing. You probably don't even know how to use it."

"Don't bet on it."

"Take it."

"Let's go. Open the car door slowly."

"I will."

"Hey!" shouted Veronica. "What are you doing in the front of my door?"

"Waiting on you," the stranger answered in a deep baritone voice.

"I don't know you, do I?" Veronica said while still trying to see who he was in the darkness of the night.

"Yes, Veronica, it's been a longtime since we last met."

"Who are you?"

"I'm Nathan. Don't you remember me?"

"Nathan Johnson?"

"Yes, Nathan Johnson, Veronica, it's been a long time since I last seen you girl. You are still as fine as ever. May I ask who the fireball of a lady holding the nine is?" I had the gun about waist high, hoping he didn't see me shaking like a leaf with it.

"Oh, that's my friend Belinda. She came down from Rochester to get a fresh start. Step to the side, let's all go in."

"That'll suit me just fine. By the way Ms Belinda, you can put that gun away. I'm not a threat to either of you two Nubian Princesses."

"Nathan, you are still as flirtatious as ever."

"I know no other way to be, than to be myself."

"I know that's right," I said while looking at the fine piece of specimen Veronica had at her front door.

"Step to the side and I'll let you in. Let's go up stairs."

"Sounds good to me."

"Belinda, go fix us all a drink. Nathan, do you still drink Royal Crown?"

"Girl, you mean Crown Royal, don't you?"

"You know exactly what I mean."

"Belinda, make one Crown Royal and two Hennessey's."

"They'll be right up."

"Veronica, what are you two lovely ladies doing coming home at this time of morning anyway?"

"You really don't want to know."

"Out chasing guys I would suspect. What else could it be?"

"If you already knew, why did you ask?"

"Just conversation, that's all. No harm intended."

"By the way Nathan, what brings you to my doorsteps anyway?"

"I was in town for a few days on some business and I thought it would be good to look you up. You know how we used to kick it girl."

"Yeah, I know. You were so damn good to me. I miss you."

"I know you do! You can still get the royal treatment if you like."

"What about, Belinda?"

"Let her join in and we can all get the thrill of our lives."

"I don't think so, she is not like that, but it must be my lucky night. Who would've ever thought that you'd be willing to share yourself with my friend too?"

"Baby, I'm down for it. It's all-good!"

"Hey Belinda, did you hear what Nathan proposed?"

"Yeah girl, your friend is off the hook. You know I've been horny as hell all night long, but I think I will pass on that one."

I sensuously walk towards the bathroom knowing that Nathan's eyes were following my every move, I left the door opened for him to see; Veronica was at the bar fixing some more drinks. While in the bathroom I discarded my outer garments to put on my silk short cut nightgown. First to fall to the floor was my blouse, exposing my voluptuous breast. Then I unzip my trousers, seductively shedding them giving him a taste of the Game we used to play. Fully aware that Nathan couldn't take his eyes off of me, I turn to see him watching me as I prepare myself to exit the bathroom. I returned to the living room and plopped myself on the sofa with my silk round cut nightshirt gown on. Veronica returned with the drinks, while Nathan was trying to get a glimpse of my now nearly starched from being wet so many times, Victoria Secret *undies.*

"Alright girl!"

"What Veronica, I'm just getting ready for bed. Y'all go ahead and do what you have to do." I said that, but in the back of my mind I knew when they would be handling their business, it would only remind me of the times when Candace could hear me getting my world rocked.

"Damn Veronica, your girl Belinda is hot, and fine as Hell!"

"Yeah, but she's a good girl. And besides you're mine tonight?"

Veronica started a fire in the fireplace and the three of us sat around talking for a while. The Hennessey was going down smoothly and his conversation was quite intriguing. I could see the eagerness in Veronica's eyes to get him to her bedroom. But, Nathan was trying his best not to be rude in front of me. It was getting late so I thought it would be best to let them know I would be alright.

"Hey guys, go lay down. I'll be alright. I'm just going to watch the fire, look at the tube and have me a drink; don't mind me. Have a good time. 'Cause if it was me I know I would."

"Awe no, it's not like that Belinda. I'm really enjoying your company and your conversation." Nathan said.

"Yeah, well you better *un-enjoy*! You're from out of town and I don't get to see you often. So, come on here and let's go into the bedroom before I get too sleepy."

I smile at Nathan while he shrugged his shoulders with his drink in his hands, as if he was saying 'a man must do, what a man has to do,'—although I knew he wanted to just as bad as she did. They went into the bedroom and soon I had to turn the TV up to equalize the noise. Veronica had dark curtains and blinds; she was able to keep the place dark even with the raising of the sun. A couple of hours must have passed, I felled asleep with my drink in my hands on the sofa, spilling the little that I left in the glass on me. When I woke up Nathan was standing over me, bare to the bone. And I do mean bone.

"Do you want me to sop that up for you, or perhaps we should *lay* next to the fireplace and let the heat dry it off?"

I was slightly delirious, but my mental faculties were in tact. Veronica was knocked out, and this fine specimen of a man was only inches away from me. Unlike with Candace, I knew Veronica wouldn't mind. For sure I would tell her at breakfast what had transpired, so I just went with the flow.

After hearing the seductive tone in his voice and seeing the look in Nathan's eyes, I willingly succumbed to his love command and immediately flung myself on the floor by the fireplace. It led to the most rewarding and irresistible encounter of my life. There he grabbed me from behind as I pretended to escape from his grasp. Then he thrust his arms around my waist, and turned me gently over facing him, and he began to caress my breast. Chills ran up and down my spine as my body went limp, and I fell spellbound to his erotic foreplay. My desire for him was intensified even more as I was completely engulfed by the passion of the moment.

Never before had I experienced the aurora of such sexual pleasures. After what appeared to be an eternity of heaven's pure delight, between my sweating thighs he continued, until finally I was able to release the passion that had been bottled up inside of me for what seem to existed my entire adult life. The climatic exercise rendered me helpless, not as a victim, but as a fulfilled woman.

I had needed a man to quench the red-hot fire that was burning on the inside of me, and Nathan was the one who managed to accomplish the spectacular feat. Even the tone of his conversation during foreplay was like a fresh breeze fanning embers that had been about to die. My inner joy, which had nearly been extinguished, had suddenly rekindled.

If there were ever the ultimate act of lovemaking displayed to a woman— this was it. It was as if I had been transported onto "Paradise Island," with all of its welcoming overtures. Bombs bursting in the air, stars falling as if it were from their starry sockets and a kaleidoscope of colors were dancing off the backdrop of the sky. Never before had I obtained such climatic fulfillment from the cumulative sexual experiences of my past.

My body, my mind and my soul had been drained of their spirit. I found myself lifeless and it was as if I had entered into the "Pearly Gates of Heaven." A journey into this world could only be traveled once in a lifetime. Experiencing this form of ecstasy ever again would have contributed to my death without question. Therefore, I must cherish the moment forever. I thanked him a thousand times for a job well done. He said, "It was all his pleasure." Then I went into the spare bedroom to get some well deserve rest.

It must have been around twelve o'clock when the smell of bacon entered my room. It was bright and I could hear the sound of voices coming from the kitchen. The aroma of coffee jolted me out of the bed. The retrospect of what transpired filled my dwellings with happiness. I felt good! Quickly, I dashed to see what all the commotion was. Veronica was standing at the stove with an apron on, her and Nathan were laughing and talking at the same time. I surprised them in midstream of their conversation, rubbing my eyes but feeling at ease.

"Good morning," Nathan said, while smiling at Veronica and making me feel that I missed an apparent joke.

"Good morning to you two." I responded only to wait and hear what it was they were discussing before I entered the kitchen, although I could tell Nathan had already told Veronica what happened between us while she was sleep. Instantly, I knew he had beaten me to the punch.

"Girl that was some night, or shall I *say* some morning, huh?"

"Awe Girl the whole entire day was a trip." I responded, only to notice the big smile on Nathan's face.

"I know that's right. Nathan should feel good as hell, he better be feeling lucky huh, hitting two fine sisters in one night!"

"I was going to tell you Veronica."

"I know you were. You know how we roll. Oh, he don't mean *nothing* to me. Nathan *knows* it. But *ain't* he good girl. Don't want to fill his head, but I *gotta* give credit when credit is due."

"Yeah child, since you brought it up. Old boy hit it nice huh."

"I felled asleep on him, I knew his old tired butt was going to wonder your way. Come on and sit down and get you some breakfast. You my girl, we go way back. What's mine is yours. Glad you got relief, 'cause you was stressing something serious."

"Hey how are you two women talking about me like I'm not even here?" Nathan asked in a playful manner.

"Just *be* quiet Nathan. Can't you see grown folks are talking. And besides, you are one lucky brother, hell you should be fixing us breakfast." Veronica and I started laughing.

"Awe come on, y'all knew what time it was. I think y'all was trying to play me."

"Play you, and for what. You are 'bout the *brokest* guy I've ever been with. Don't let your manhood go to your head." Veronica shouted, and then smile while shaking her head back and forth. I stood still; I had no complaints about the brother. I was glad he was a good time and came with protection.

"It was nice; I have to get out of here now." Nathan began to depart. "Nice meeting you Belinda and I had a great time with you. Bye Roni, you know how we roll, I'll call you from the Waldorf Historia, and I'm on the fifth floor there. Hope to see you the next time I am in town Belinda."

"Yeah, but I don't think it will be like last night though."

"Hey that's cool. I'll just be a friend, use me anyway you like. Veronica does."

"Get out of here Nathan, with your crazy self. Be a good-boy now." Veronica interjected.

The door slammed and Nathan was on his way. It was two more notches on his belt or maybe another one for Veronica and myself. However things may have went, the three of us were satisfied with what had occurred. Strangely, Veronica and I didn't go into details about how we both had shared him, so I just dismissed the idea of sharing the moments with Nathan. We both knew that as long as she didn't love him it was cool, but if she loved him it would have been hands off completely.

"So what do you want to do now Belinda? I took a week of vacation to help you settle in."

"Girl lets go shopping."

"Oh that sounds, great. Let's go to Manhattan around *Forty Doo whoop.*"

"I guess you mean forty second *street*?"

"Yeah Girl, you've got to get with the lingo."

"*Alrighty*, let me get dress."

"Later on I'll find a shrink for you."

"That's fine. Maybe the both of us can get some relief."

"Hey he's already done everything; he's going to do for me, if you know what I mean."

"Veronica, you dog, not the shrink too."

"I'm God's gift to men!"

"Your name is going to be all over this city."

"Nope, it's too big and too many men out there. I'm just having fun."

"I hear you. Let's get ready to go. I came to Brooklyn to get away from all of the drama. It seems as though it has followed me here as well. I have to put a lot of stuff behind me girl or I'm going to lose my mind—what little I have left."

"Like I said earlier, I'll get you some help later on today."

"I sure hope so. This is definitely no way to live."

"Girl you know that it could be a *helluva* lot worst."

"That's what I hear, but what kind of a fresh start is this?"

"Don't worry Belinda, it's going to get better, just trust me."

"Girl, right about now, I *have* no other choice but to trust you."

ℰℬ

Three months had now passed since I moved to Brooklyn. Not that I needed one, but I landed a job on Wall Street with the Wang Corporation as the manager over the computer analysts. My education at Columbia University was worth its weight in gold there. A sense of relief from all of the stress related issues that I'd been facing during the past year started to subside. The incidence with Candace's husband Emanuel had caused far more anxiety than I could've ever imagined.

With confused mind and other issues that I was relaying to my therapist, I manage to buy me a home. Now with the opportunity for some upward mobility in my new environment in Hempstead, Long Island, I took a break from all of the chaotic circumstances that had consumed my life during the past year. It had overshadowed me like a violent thunderstorm of dark clouds stationed upon the Eastern horizon after a sunny afternoon. As difficult as things have been for me, perhaps for one brief moment I can find some peace and tranquility and begin my life all over, I thought while sitting in my new home.

The phone rang and it was Veronica.

"I hadn't heard from you in about a month," I exclaimed.

"I know girlfriend. Things have been little hectic for me. I knew you would needed some time settling in at your new crib. By the way, how are things coming together?"

"Wonderful! Just wonderful it's so nice out here."

"That's good to know girl, particularly after all you've had to encounter over the past several months."

"Yeah, I know. Please don't remind me. I'm trying to get all of that mess behind me."

"That's good, I know that moving and settling in on a new job is enough to wear anybody down. Although, you have enough money not to work, I admire you for putting your skills to use. I guess it's a nice position to be in. At least it'll keep the stress off of you."

"I'm so glad that you know exactly how I've been feeling."

"Trust me girl, I know."

"Thanks for the empathy."

"You're certainly welcome."

"Since the move to my new home in Long Island, my time has been thoroughly consumed. It gives me little time for devilment, if you understand."

"You don't have to tell me. Been there, done that! I can feel you child."

"Veronica, it's a pleasure just to hear from you since you were so kind to give me a place to stay until something nice became available for me."

"Don't mention it."

"Also, Veronica thanks for the recommendation to go see Dr. Ray Stallings. He's good girl. He's making me feel better already. Matter of fact, he's helping me to find my "authentic self." Although Dr. Stallings is helping me get through my mental lapses, reconstructing my life has been more difficult than I could've imagined. I didn't realize the amount of guilt I had stored up inside of me. It wasn't until my ninth session that I realize the magnitude of it all. Dr. Stallings says, 'I'm on my way to full recovery, but it's going to take time to heal.' I wonder why I still feel a little depressed now. It must be from the stress of the situation. I still see some progress."

"Girl, I told you he was the best."

"You didn't lie about that. He's very deep. The introspection exercise he has me involved with at this time has permitted me to develop some positive female relationships on the job already. It's been a while since I've opened up to anyone besides you. I felt too vulnerable and didn't feel like being disappointed again. It had been difficult for me to even hold a ten-minute conversation with people I didn't know. Now things are a little different. I've even decided to invite several of my co-workers over to my place for a game of spades in another week or so. You know you're always welcome."

"I know. That's good girl. You need to expand your social group."

"That's exactly what I've needed all along. I wonder why in the world *did it take* me so long to find this out."

"Only you and the "Good Lord" know the answer to that question. You know that you have always been a little slow." Veronica laughed at what she said.

"Girlfriend, you are still crazy as ever. All that I can say for sure is that for the first time in years, I'm feeling as if my life has real meaning and purpose."

"It's good to hear you say that, Belinda. I'm so glad your life has turned around for the better. At the rate you were going, your life was coming to an abrupt ending."

"I know girl, I know. That's why I will always be in debt to you. Sorry, to carry you through my life's story. Now why did you call me?"

"Belinda, I just thought we could get together this weekend and go have some fun. It's been awhile since we have done that."

"You're right."

"So what do you think about it? Are you coming with me or not? Let's just go hang out."

"Maybe?"

"What do you mean maybe?"

"Girl, I've been so busy over the past several months attempting to get my life back on track, I thought I was going to have a nervous breakdown. I even had to call on my former pastor for some advice. It was so embarrassing to speak with him about my issues, especially after not attending church in the past three years. I believe the last time I stepped foot in that church was at my Grandma Jessie's funeral. Dr. Solomon can really preach child. You would've thought he was going to bring her back to life. My counseling sessions with him were wonderful. He had just the right words to say. His ability to connect the problems of the average person is astounding. He almost persuaded me to get back in the church. Now, it's a good possibility I might just do that, and soon."

"Yeah, I know. That's the main reason I decided to call you. We need to just relax together this weekend. Just get away from the rat race. You know what I mean? Maybe a little church on Sunday won't hurt."

"Girl, let me think about it. I know it can't hurt."

"Belinda, what's there to think about? Just don't plan anything for the weekend. I'll be over to pick you up at 10:30 Saturday morning. We will go shopping at Macy's. Girlfriend they have an awesome two for one sale going on this weekend."

"Yeah, I heard." I said laughingly.

"It'll be nice."

"If that's true, then I'll see you at 10:30 on Saturday. Maybe we can find us a new outfit to go to church in. You know how we do."

"Yeah Belinda, I know. It's a date."

"Belinda."

"Yes, Veronica."

"Before I forget, there's a letter for you that was delivered to my address on Tuesday."

"Who is it from?"

"It has no forwarding address. It's simply addressed to you. I'll bring it over on Saturday."

"That'll be just fine. See you Saturday."

"Later."

Now, I wonder who in the world could have sent a letter to me at Veronica's. There were only two or three people from Rochester as I can recall that knew my destination. I know it couldn't have been from poor Candace because she didn't like writing letters. Mistakenly, I told that sorry ass husband of hers Emanuel about my initial plans. I also informed him about my relationship with Veronica, but he's too stupid to write–I think. The only other person that's aware of my whereabouts is my former pastor, Dr. Solomon.

While I'm sitting here contemplating who it could possibly be that would have sent me an anonymous letter, I'm going to call Veronica right back. Let me see, it's Tuesday now and I believe that I'll stop by on Thursday evening instead. I'll try and surprise her, but my ulterior motive is only to retrieve that letter. Damn! I hope that it's not from my x-best friend Candace.

I can imagine the nature of its contents if it's from her. She definitely will be justified in giving me a piece of her mind. Just look at me. That's exactly the demon that I've been trying to be delivered from. I'm always thinking the worst about a situation. I guess that's one of the reasons that I've been so depressed lately. Now if it had been from Dr. Solomon, he would've sent it on the churches' stationary. This thing is tearing me up. Now *who* could it be from? I can't wait; I must go over to Veronica's now. I'll call her back and let her know I'm on my way. Hesitantly I picked up my cell phone.

"Ring, ring."

Hurry up and pick up that damn phone, Veronica.

"Hello."

"It's me again."

"Yeah Belinda, how can I help you this time?"

"Girl, I need to come over now."

"What's the urgency?"

"That letter. I need to know who it's from tonight. It's burning me up on the inside."

"Since it's like that, come on over."

"Girl I'm on my way. Just let me find my keys and I'll be there shortly."

"Girl, please be careful. You know that there's a bunch of fools hanging out this time of night."

"I know. Maybe I can stay over."

"I doubt it. Girl, I'm expecting a little company tonight and I don't plan for you to mess up my evening."

"Okay, I understand. I'll just pick up the letter and leave."

"You can stay a little while."

"We'll see. Girl, let me go since it's so late. I'll see you in a few."

"Girl, please be careful."

"I will! I'm getting in the car as we speak."

"Come on."

"I'm driving out of the driveway as we speak. Give me about twenty minutes or so and I should be at your door."

"Okay. Bye. See you shortly."

"Bye."

That sneaky Veronica, who in the world she thinks she is getting a booty call from before the week gets started, I bet its Terrance from Morton's. She said as soon as her calendar was clear that she was going to break him off some. Let me stop speculating, I'll see once I get there, I thought. Five minutes later I was at her front door. Traffics wasn't that bad after all. I had to locate a suitable parking space close to her house. I can't be caught walking the streets alone at night. Somebody might try to rape me. Finally, I was at her steps, with my cell I called her to open the door so I wouldn't have to wait.

"Hello."

"Veronica, it's me. I'm walking up the steps now. Let me in."

"Okay. I can see you through the curtain. Give me a second while I find me keys to unlock the door."

"It's about time."

"Girl, why are you panting so hard? Did you have to run from anyone?"

"No. I'm just tired, that's all."

"I feel you girl. Have a seat and I'll bring you the letter."

"Thank you."

"Here, open that thing now! I can't wait to find out who it's from."

"Just a minute, give me time. Stop sweating me anyway. Why do you have to be all up in my business anyhow? You've always been so nosey!"

"I'm just as inquisitive about it as you are, that's all. What does it say? Who is it from?"

"Girl I said, *give* me time! Now let me see."

"Hurry up, Belinda."

"Veronica! Veronica!"

"Yes, I'm waiting."

"Whoever it is says that I better watch my back. And what's this that's wrapped up in the brown paper? Veronica! It looks like a bloody chicken's heart. I wonder what all of this could mean. Girl I'm scared! Please help me!"

I was almost on the verge of a serious breakdown.

"Belinda! Belinda! Get yourself together! Whose husband have you been sleeping with lately?"

"Don't even go there, I told you I don't do that anymore."

"*Since when?*"

"Never mind, I can't think of who it is that would do such a vile and cruel thing as this."

"Somebody really has it out for you girl. They are messing with those roots and *thangs*. It could have originated from one of those Voodoo Doctor's down south."

"Girl, please stop talking like that. Shut up and just help me. Call the police and call them now! And I thought all of this shit was behind me."

"You are dealing with an entirely different element of personalities in the City. These people will get rid of you in a heartbeat. They are not like those folks up in Rochester. You have to watch *your* back at all times down here. Girl, just be careful. I'll dial the police now."

"Veronica, what's taking them so long to answer the phone? You can never get one when you need them. As far as me watching my back, I have no other choice but to do that. I see that these shelled folks down here don't give a damn about anything or anyone. Hurry up and get them on the line!"

"I'm trying as hard as I can."

"I know. I'm just scared that's all."

"Me too girl, now come on and answer the phone. Seem like I've been waiting for 30 minutes already. These sorry ass cops, I bet if I call in a terrorist attack they would send in the US Army. The entire military would knock down my door. Are we still on high alert status since the 9/11 disaster?"

"I don't know, but you're right. We are not at the top of their priority list. Now answer the damn phone!"

"By the way Veronica, who did you say was coming over tonight for that booty call?"

"None of your business!"

"It's Terrance, isn't it? I know it is."

"Keep guessing. By the way, he should arrive in a few more minutes. I think that it's about time for you to leave. Girl, you know that I need to set the tone before he gets here."

"While you're worrying about having sex with some young punk, my life has been threatened. What kind of concern is that for your friend? Just give me the phone and I'll talk to the police myself."

Chapter Three
The Visitor

Sheila

I could hear voices in the background, but I was unable to make out specific words at first. One thing I did know-they were talking about me. I wasn't sure where I was or why I was there. Everything seemed so distant. It was as if I were stuck in some kind of bad nightmare, a nightmare I couldn't come out of. Those voices sounded more like a tape recorder with bad batteries. The words were alien to me. Voices, only voices-where were the pictures I wondered. I was living in a world of inaudible words and unseen sites-a state of animation. Or, I questioned, was I really living at all? What if I were…? No, I can't be, I tried to reason. But, how else could I explain my predicament. I, I, I-who the hell was I anyway? Funny, I couldn't remember.

My eyes opened, and I found myself in some kind of room. I didn't seem to be able to move. My body didn't respond to any orders from my mind. My eyes were the only part I could control. I slowly scanned the room, searching for any clues-any clue to help me figure out what was going on.

As my eyes roved around, someone walked into my room. It was a nurse. So that's it, I reasoned. I'm in a hospital.

"Hi there sweetie," the nurse said smiling. "You gave us quite a scare young lady, but you'll be alright now." She flipped through my bed charts and wrote down some notes.

"Your parents sure will be happy to hear that you're back with us," she continued. Parents, I thought. I hadn't even thought about parents. It was reassuring to know I belonged to someone though, even if I didn't know who that someone was.

I quickly realized I was bandaged from head to toe. Whatever happened to me must have been pretty severe. I must have looked like a mummy. My right leg was suspended at a forty-degree angle, attached to a wire at one end and a supporting bar at the other end. The rest of my body was covered with bandages and metal objects. I wondered if I was run over by a car or something.

Judging by the looks of things, a truck would be the more likely suspect.

"Suddenly my room door opened. Two people entered, a man and a woman.

"Hi baby," the woman said.

"Hi Shelia," the man added. So, my name was Sheila. It's a start I thought. Now if I could figure out the rest of the story.

"You had us so worried baby," the woman spoke again, brushing tears away from her eyes.

"Your Mama was worried, but I wasn't, the man said. "I told her that you would be okay. I told her. I knew you would come out of that silly coma." Now things were beginning to make a little more sense. I had been in a coma, and these were my parents. My father began to speak again.

"Sweetie, the nurse said you probably wouldn't be able to talk with us just yet. I'm going to ask you a few questions darling. If you can understand what I'm saying blink your eyes once for yes and twice for no. Can you understand me?" I blinked my eyes once. You would have thought someone had won the lottery judging by the responses.

"She understands, she understands," my mother said elated.

"Do you know who we are," my father asked. This time I blinked my eyes twice, and the jubilation which filled the room moments earlier, quickly dissipated.

The nurse, standing on the sidelines, gave encouragement to my parents.

"That's quite normal in these cases," she reassured my parents.

"She's under some strong medication, and it's probably affecting her memory. She'll get better," she promised.

This disclaimer seemed to pacify my parents, and their smiles returned slightly. In the back of the room, I saw a shadow. It was a man, and he freighted me. I don't know why he did, but he did nevertheless. He was a tall elderly white guy with stringy hair. What he was doing here, I wondered. His mere presence was enough to send my vitals into an uproar.

Suddenly the machine started beeping. "What's going on?" my mother yelled.

"I'm not sure," the nurse promptly replied. "But you'll have to leave now-please."

My father ushered my mother out of the room, and the nurse injected something into my arm. The room began to get dark again, and soon I was back into the other world, or at least I thought I was.

"Do you remember me Sheila," someone said. From behind my room petition, the white man appeared.

"No, should I?" I asked. At the same time, I felt a deep unbridled anger return. Sensing my anger, the man shot back.

"Oh, I like it when you're angry cause when you are, you're at your best."

"What!" I snapped. Who are you, and what do you want?"

"Don't you know darling," he said smiling like the cat's meow.

"Get out of my room now or I'll scream," I threatened.

"Go right ahead," he bluffed. I screamed as loud as I could.

When I awakened, the nurse was standing beside me. Apparently, I had been having a bad dream.

"Now, now darling, it's alright. You were just having a bad dream." I searched the room for the white guy, but he was gone. Still, he was familiar, and I was sure I knew him. It would come to me in time, I reasoned. Everything would come to me in time. But how long would I have to wait, I wondered.

"Your parents and a few other friends will be by to see you shortly Sheila," the nurse told me.

"In the mean time, you just take it easy young lady." Take it easy? How did she expect me to take it easy? I was glued to my bed and I didn't know who I was, but she wanted me to take it easy. Right now, I'd take it anyway I could get it. Lying in the bed all wrapped up like a mummy, an oldies song suddenly started playing itself inside my head.

"*Here I am in the hospital, bandaged from feet to head, in a state of shock, just that much from being dead. Here I am in the hospital. I guess actions speak louder than words. It's a thin line between love and hate. It's a thin line between love and hate.*" Maybe my husband beat me up in a fit of jealousy. If I had a husband, why hadn't he come to see me? Maybe he was in jail. Maybe I killed him. There were just too many questions for me, but not enough answers. I didn't know how long I had been in the hospital.

Around 10:00 a.m. my parents came to visit me. Mama brought some pictures with her. I guess she thought the pictures would help me recover my memory.

"Hi Sheila," Mama said entering the room.

"How are you darling?" My father was out in the hallway talking to the doctor. I could hear his voice in the background. Mama pulled up a chair and started flipping through old photographs.

"This is you when you were first born," she said while showing me a toddler picture.

"And this is you when you were five years old. This is one of my favorite pictures; it's you when you were sixteen. Do you remember the other girls standing beside you?"

The other two girls looked familiar, but I couldn't name them. Sensing my frustration, my mother interrupted my thoughts quickly.

"The girls are Veronica, Celeste, and Belinda." As soon as my mother mentioned the name Belinda, a light went off inside my head. Belinda, I knew that name and that face. Veronica and Celeste, yes I knew them all. And now I looked at Mama with new eyes because I finally recognized her. Tears started flowing out of the corners of my eyes. Just about then, my father entered the room.

"What is it *baby*?" my mother questioned me.

"What's wrong?" My father jumped in the conversation.

"Are you hurting sweetheart?"

I blinked my eyes twice. Then Mama made the connection.

"The pictures, did you recognize someone in the pictures?" she blurted out. I blinked my eyes once.

"That's my girl," my father said proudly. "Do you know who we are?" he asked slowly and cautiously. I blinked my eyes once. Mama started crying and daddy hugged her. I had finally figured out who I was, but I still did not remember how I ended up in the hospital. My parents yelled for the nurse, quickly she came and grabbed my charts from the foot of the bed.

"You're a real trooper," the nurse said while looking over the data on the machines. "You're making remarkable progress; you are a strong young lady."

My parents and the nurse left my room within a few minutes. I could hear them talking in the hallway. I couldn't quite make out just what they were saying, but I could hear a few words.

The door opened back again, and I thought the nurse was coming back in. To my surprise, it wasn't the nurse. It was the white guy again. Oh no, I must be dreaming again; I must have fallen asleep.

"Hi Sheila, I'm back," he said as he stood in the corner of my room. "I heard that you got your memory back or something. Tell me dear, do you remember me?" I tried to tell him to leave my room, but I couldn't speak.

This meant I wasn't dreaming because I could only speak when I was dreaming.

Oh my God! This guy was real and he was in my room. I felt my heart starting to pound wildly- due to fear, anger or both. This man had some guts. He knew exactly when to show up and leave. I wondered if anyone else knew who he was.

"Tell me darling, do you remember me? You should. You and I are very good friends."

It was then I noticed a nurse-paging device close to my right hand. The nurse must have just placed it there recently because I hadn't noticed it before. Reaching for the device, I also discovered I was regaining some use of my arms and hands.

"That's not nice," he said as he saw me attempting to grab the panic button. "I'll be back," he promised.

I grabbed the paging device and pushed it hard. The man slipped out of my room, waving at me and smiling.

A nurse came into my room about a minute after the man left.

"What can I do for you missy?" she asked as she approached me.

"Are you in pain?"

I mistakenly blinked my eyes once.

"You're close to medication time anyway. I'll just give you a little something to ease your pain." The nurse slid a syringe into a tube, which seemed to be dangling from my left arm. A few moments later, I was back into *never, never* land. Only I didn't expect to find Peter Pan.

"Hello darling, I'm back." I opened my eyes and found the white dude standing in the corner again with his arms folded. Oh no, not him again I thought.

"I told you I'd be back, and here I am. Do you remember me now?" he questioned me.

"No, but I wish you would get the hell out of my room man!" I told him.

"Why? Don't you like me anymore? You use to love me. Don't you remember?" He went on.

"Remember when you use to give it up to me for a little cash? Remember how I used to have my way with your sweet young body? You made me feel so young. Remember? You remember me don't you Sheila? My name is Freddy."

"Freddy who-Freddy Kruger?" I asked.

"It's good to see you haven't lost your sense of humor Sheila," Freddy said approaching me.

"Stay away from me, and get out of my room!" I demanded.

"Don't act like that Sheila. That's no way to treat your sugar daddy. You used to love the way I touched you. I made you moan with every stroke of my fingers."

Freddy started to lift the covers over my feet and roll them back toward my waist.

"What the hell are you doing?" I yelled at him. Sliding his hands between my bandaged legs he whispered to me.

"You know you like it Sheila. It's just like old times darling."

I screamed as loud as I could.

I woke up sweating. I must have had another nightmare. I looked around the room, but there was no Freddy. Good, I thought to myself. At that precise moment I remembered the real Freddy. He was Freddy McLemore, and I had done a few *tricks* with him to earn some fast cash. Oh my goodness, I started to remember the gang again.

The gang was responsible for my behavior with Freddy. Playing all those tricks on the guys had gotten me caught up in it. One day Freddy had approached me at the supermarket, and asked me if I were still playing tricks with the guys. I was totally stunned when he asked me this. I wondered how he knew.

"Don't worry, I'm not going to tell anyone about it," he promised me. Then he slipped me a business card, and asked me to call him if I wanted to graduate from baby dolls to men. Embarrassed, I took the card. I almost through it away several times, but something wouldn't let me. Why I was even thinking about doing such a thing, I thought. I wondered how much money he would pay to see my young black naked body. He looked like he was well off. I could probably get his money without giving him anything.

One day after school, I decided to test the waters. From school I called Freddy and asked him if he would mind me stopping by. Of course he said no. He asked me what time I thought I'd be there, and I told him around 7 p.m. or so. He lived about five miles from my house. It was a short subway ride. He had a big spacious apartment. I could tell he was loaded with cash. At first I changed my mind several times before approaching the address. Then, I made up my mind to do it. I rang the door buzzer, and he answered through the intercom.

"Is that you Sheila?" he asked.

"Yes, it's me."

"Come on up," he replied. He opened the door and let me in.

"Can I get you anything, a beer, a smoke or something?" he asked.

"No thank you," I said feeling anxious and nervous.

"I'm glad you came," he continued as he fired up a joint. You don't mind do you?"

"Not really," I said.

"So, tell me Sheila, what brought you here today?"

"I don't know," I said honestly. I really didn't know what I was doing there, and I was beginning to wish I hadn't come at all.

"Are you sure you don't want a puff. It'll loosen you up and make you more comfortable. I know you're nervous but you needn't be. I'm not a pervert." He stuck the joint over to my lips, and I took a hit off of it. He was right of course; it did make me feel better. I took another hit, then another. Soon, the nervousness had completely vanished.

"Now tell me Sheila, what brought you here today?"

"I was thinking about your offer," I said. "Is it still good?"

"Yes it is," he said smiling. "What do you have in mind?"

"I need a hundred dollars to buy a new dress," I said without hesitation. I wanted to know how serious this man was.

"It's yours," he said without giving it a second thought. This was a chess game, and I was up for the challenge.

"What do I have to do?" I asked.

"What do you want to do?" he quickly shot back. The way I figured it, I would get him so horny; he would blow his stack without me actually giving up anything. What I hadn't counted on was my own horniness. I should have never smoked the marijuana. I pulled off my blouse and exposed my bare breast to Freddy. I was just going to tease him, like I had with all of the other boys our gang had teased, but Freddy was no boy. Before it was over, he had tricked me, and I had not only lost the game, but something else too.

On my way back home, I couldn't believe I had done such a thing. I told no one, not even my best friends. Freddy started buying me all kinds of expensive gifts, and provided me with lots of money. I had become his private little whore. After about a month of these sexual encounters, I knew I had to get out of it. I told Freddy how I felt, and he was pissed. He said I belonged to him, and I would belong to him forever. This was the Freddy

I remembered. But was it he who was responsible for me being here in the hospital? I wasn't sure.

The doctor came into my room around noontime or so. He removed most of the bandages covering my body. He tested a few nerves and then left. Later my nurse entered the room.

"The doctor says you're doing well, and soon you will be able to begin physical therapy."

Finally, the nurse removed the long tube, which had been stuck down my throat. It had been there so long, I almost forgot about it.

"Now that should feel a better, huh?" She wasn't kidding. I felt a lot better. The nurse asked me to move my toes, hands, etc.

"Very nice," she said. "Everything seems to be working fine. You'll be up and walking in no time at all." The nurse removed my right leg from the trapeze it was attached to, and lowered it slowly to the bed. I almost looked normal again.

When my parents and a few other friends entered my room later in the afternoon, they were delighted to observe my progress.

"Hi Sheila," Mama said bursting into my room. "The doctor says you are doing great."

"Hi Mama," I whispered. The room went deadly silent before everyone burst out into tears and laughter.

"She's talking, she's talking!" Mama cried. You'd thought I was a toddler just learning to speak. In a way, I was.

"Ah baby," this is the best news we've had all month," daddy shouted.

"How long?" I mumbled.

"How long what baby?" Mama asked.

"How long have I been here?"

"You've been here a little over a month Sheila," daddy said getting back into the conversation.

Soon after I was able to speak again, I started physical therapy. It was slow and painful, but it was the only way to get out of the hospital. I also started to have regular chats with the shrinks. According to them, I was repressing the memory of what happened to me. As they explained it, it was too painful for me to remember, so repressed the whole incident. It may or may not return, they warned me. Only time would tell.

In my own heart, I knew my current predicament had something to do with Freddy and the gang. How much it had to do with one or the other, I wasn't sure. But I was bitter. I was bitter about the gang, bitter about

Freddy, just bitter about everything. One thing was for sure; I would have to put an end to this nightmare in order to move on. This was about the only thing the *shrinks* and I agreed on. So, during my long rehabilitation, I made a plan to find my old friends Belinda, Veronica, and Celeste. My physical therapy lasted for two more months, and finally it was time for me to leave.

The big day had arrived, and I was ready to leave the hospital. My parents would be arriving shortly, and I couldn't wait to leave.

My clothes were all packed, and all of my paperwork was completed. I was ready to leave.

I was taking a walk around the hospital. Suddenly Freddy appeared out of nowhere. As soon as he saw me, he tried to walk away. I was infuriated.

"Hey!" I screamed," and started to walk towards him. He started to pick up his pace. I started to run after him. Freddy started running. I pursued him as fast as I could, which wasn't fast. Freddy ran out the door with me in hot pursuit. By now, we had gained the attention of the nurses and the security guards. Freddy quickly disappeared in the crowded streets, and I fell to the ground, panting. The nurses caught up with me and carried me back inside. My parents were coming to the hospital at the exact moment.

"What's going on!" daddy yelled.

"Your daughter's trying to kill herself," my nurse sarcastically said as the other nurses placed me in a wheelchair.

"What?" my father said confused. "Sheila, what's going baby?" Still out of breath, I answered.

"Nothing daddy, I was just trying to get in a little exercise." Freddy was going to be my secret forever. I had made up my mind never to tell a single soul about him—ever. After this little incident, I was examined by the doctor and pronounced fit to leave. I was finally out of the hospital. Now it was time to find my friends—Belinda, Celeste, and Veronica. And, it was time to find the truth.

Chapter Four
A Good Night

Life can be like a Ferrari commercial, whereas I'm looking at something nice but knowing I cannot have it. Without a doubt the way I felt about the commercial described all of my past relationships.

"Belinda, how are you doing?" Barbara Williams shouted as we crossed path at the South Lake Mall. Barbara was from the neighborhood, daily from seven to eight o'clock in the mornings she would be out walking the streets of the neighborhood for exercise.

"Hi Barbara, how are you doing?" I surprisingly said.

"Girl, I've been alright, just busy you know, I'm so glad the kids are back in school," she sighed with relief.

"I *heard that!* You've got some time to *do you* now, right?" I replied while nodding my head.

"Yes! And *I'm loving* it. If they were here right now, they'd be *pulling all* on me, hollering, just *acting a natural* born fool," she grimaced.

"*Girl!* You are so crazy," a smile glazed my face as I waited to hear what she had to say.

Barbara was around 32 years old, five feet four with short dreads. She stood with broad shoulders, trimmed eyebrows with a tight six pack from working out. I never saw her in anything but athletic clothing. Even at the mall, she looked like a model in athletic wear.

"I'm serious girl," she paused and then continued. "Have you heard about Mr. Johnston?" Barbara tilted her head to the side, eagerly waiting for a response.

"No, what's going on?" I questioned quickly.

"Child, they found him dead yesterday morning in his house."

"What! Mr. Johnston? You are lying! I just saw him a few days ago," I said with grief.

"Yep, dead girl," she uttered.

"What happened?" I questioned sadly.

"The coroner says it was from natural causes, but Julie, that's his wife you know. She says she wants an autopsy done on him."

"Really, I don't blame her. He was too young for natural causes, right?" I responded in disbelief.

Barbara's hands were well manicured and her posture was straight even when she walked around the neighborhood. It seemed as though she practiced a walk ensuring her shoulders were pressed back and strolled with a flare. Her teeth were as bright as ivory, and evenly shape as if she wore braces her entire life.

"I know that's right," she shifted to the side and glanced around the mall. "It's been a while since I saw you Belinda, are you dating someone?" she gleamed while waiting on a response.

"Not really, I've just been taking it easy," I said with confidence.

"Girl, my husband has a single coworker that's just relocated here, I think you two may like each other," her eyes were filled with enthusiasm.

"Oh really?"

"Yeah *girl,* and he's cute," she proclaimed.

"Okay," I massaged her comment gingerly.

"We could have something over at my place, and introduce you to him."

"I don't know Barbara, it's been a minute. But, I've got to be honest I could use some male entertainment," my eyes sparkled as my body shifted side to side.

"I'm not a match maker or nothing like that. I just think you might like him," she exclaimed.

"I hear *you*, it's just that I've been on some crazy blind dates in my times."

"Girl, I know what you mean. But, I think you will like him," her forehead creased as she raised a brow.

"Okay, I'm going to take your word on it. Let me get your number," my mouth curved into a smile while getting my phone out of my purse.

"Great! When you call me I'll have your number."

"Alright Barbara, I'm trusting you on this one, what's your number."

"I promise you, there's nothing to worry about. If I was single, I would be all over him. The boy is fine!" her eyes blazed with excitement.

After I received Barbara's number, we said good bye, and she left the mall with her bags in her hands. During the time we were talking, I couldn't help but to think, did loud mouth Veronica tell this woman any of my business.

An hour had pasted and my therapeutic shopping came to an end. Outside of the mall a huge waterfall was flowing in front of the entrance, a few feet away was the valet stand with the attendant and my car keys. I had on a two piece short set, sandals, a sunhat and sunglasses. A simple *fly* look for the mall, and for the men to hawk over.

"Can you get my car for me please?"

"Yes and how are you doing today? Did you have a good time shopping?" he glistened.

"Oh yes I did, thanks for asking," I responded with eagerness to get my car from the valet attendant.

৯০ ৫৩

After an intriguing day at the mall, relaxation was on the agenda. The sun began to diminish through my living room window, a constant reminder bedtime would be near, and male companion-ship was non-existent. I only wished I had someone to call, but thinking about the end results became annoying, feeling used like a piece of meat. But, on the other hand I would get what I wanted in return. Stevie came to my mind, we always had a good time, although I knew he was some sort of a player, it didn't bother me. There was a choice in my life, freedom or loneliness, and it seem like freedom always won the race.

"Hello Stevie?"

"Yes, who is this?" his deep voice penetrated my phone.

"This Belinda, Stevie."

"Oh wow! It's good to hear from you," he sounded surprised.

"You acted like you didn't know who I *was*, my name didn't appeared in your 'Caller ID'?" I questioned, wondering how can anyone not keep my name on speed dial.

"Na girl, I lost my phone at six flags on a roller coaster, this is a new phone, I'm glad you called. I lost all of my contacts."

"Didn't you have them stored?"

"I thought I did, they told me I didn't, something about a sym card or something," Stevie said reluctantly as if he was clueless how a cell phone works.

"I'm glad I called you, I probably would have never heard from you."

"Na, that's not true, sooner or later I would have bust up there and knock on your door," he chuckled.

"Unannounced?"

"For sure!"

"You may have seen something you don't want to see," I snapped.

"Hey, if you had company I would have just stayed at the door, you know how we *roll*," quickly, he massaged his ego.

"So, what woman you *was* with on a roller coaster? You know you're getting a little too old for the roller coaster!"

"Girl, now you trying to get all up in my business, you know how you and I do."

"You are so right, my *bad* for asking you that."

"So, what's been going on Belinda?" he questioned not in a concerned way—but a noisy way. Instantly, I knew Stevie was just trying to *get all up in my* business.

"Oh, just taking it easy. I needed to hear from you, I know your life style is more fascinating than mines."

"Girl, I'm glad you called, I've been waiting to share with someone. My life was a spinning wheel, I'm glad things has finally calmed down."

"Wow! I can't wait to hear," anxiously I waited for the *periling* story I knew Stevie would deliver.

"I met this chic, a Puerto Rican girl in the club, and we started *kicking* it. You know having some fun. She had a 14 year old daughter."

"You were dating someone with children? I thought you would never do that?"

"I know right? But I did. Belinda, I swear she must have put voodoo on me or something. I couldn't even think right. All I know *is* I wanted to be with her every moment of the day."

"Are you sure you didn't just fell in love?"

"Na, it couldn't have been love, *'cause* I still had some friends on the side. You know how I *roll*, that's why you and I can *kick it* the way we do."

"So what happened?"

"First of all, how we meet wasn't too strange, she mistaken me to be a famous ball player in the club."

"Yeah, you get that all the time, I used to hate it when we went out, and you got all the attention."…….

"She bought drink after drink and one thing lead to another."

"She found out you were broke and not a ball player?" a smile and laugher seeped from me, I couldn't help myself but to laugh.

"Hold on Belinda, let me finish," you always starting something. "I told her my admirations were to be a lawyer, but the basketball scholarship, and partying lead me down a different direction."

"Okay, can't wait to get to the good part of this story."

"Oh, it gets better," he paused. "Anyway, she accepted I wasn't the ball player."

"And so did I after I started talking to you for the first time."

"That night at the club, I became a little tipsy, and so did she. I guess she wanted me to see what kind of car she had 'cause she wanted me to walk her to her car," he paused. "Being a gentleman I did."

"A little shivery going on, okay," I softly interjected.

"Yeah, but I shouldn't have, because when we got to her 911 *Carrera* Porsche we said good bye to each other and her car wouldn't start," he sighed.

"*Damn, how embarrassing.*"

"Not really, it worked out into my favor. I took her home; she said she would take care of the car the next day. I guess she felt it would be safe in the parking deck," he exclaimed. "Her daughter was spending the night over some friend's house, so we had the place to ourselves."

"Okay, a Porsche that didn't started?"

"*Right?* That's what I'm saying! I should have just called her a cab or something and ran!" at this point his voice became filled with sadness. "After a while of seeing each other, I noticed I wasn't seeing my other friends, but it didn't bother me."

"I was *kind' a* wondering why I hadn't heard from you."

"It gets *juicier,* I found myself stalking her everywhere she would go. When I would come over at night I would place my hand on the hood to see if she went somewhere after work. Belinda, I was going crazy over this Puerto Rican chick."

"Dag! Sounds like you had some roots put on you. But, they say the girls from Louisiana and the Dominican Republic are the only ones working roots like that. Maybe Jamaica too, I really don't know."

"I don't know, because whatever it was had me going crazy. I started being overly jealous, accusing her of seeing someone, we began to fight!" reluctantly he admitted.

"What! I don't recall you being the type to put your hands on a woman!" I retorted.

"That's what I'm saying Belinda, that's not me, the police came to the house seven times,"

"So, what happened?"

"She took out a restraining order on me, and I had to go to anger management after she dropped the charges," sadness and disappointment saturated the phone.

"Are you okay now?"……..

"*Yeah; but there is more to the story.* I began to have knee problems, it would hurt real *bad*. And one day it was difficult for me to breathe when I was getting *in* my car. *Felt like I* was dying girl."

"What!"

"I drove myself to the emergency room, and when I told them I was having chest pains and it was difficult to breathe, they started running like chickens with their heads cut off, trying to take care of me."

"*Oh my God!*" I became discombobulated. "What did they say it was?"

"*Come to find out,* I had blood clots behind my knee that moved up to my lungs."

"*Really?*"

"Yeah, and all off my friends had brought me flowers. My room looked like a flourish shop," he chuckled. "She tried to get into my room, but my man Scottie stopped her, but she pushed him aside and barged into my room."

"He was trying to keep her out?"

"Yeah, 'cause he knew she would go ballistic! She came into the room and *just went off!*"

"Damn!"

"They had to drag her ass out of there. *Yelling and screaming at me 'cause I had friends that cared about me.*"

"Wow!"

"I'm okay now, just chilling out, trying to find myself. You know what I mean, right?"

"Of course and I do understand."

"I'm sorry Belinda; I just have to take myself off of the dating scene after seeing what it is doing in my life."

"Oh Stevie, I do understand. You take care, and we will talk soon."

"Okay Belinda, thanks."

ℰↃ ℭℛ

Wow! What drama is going on with Stevie? Damn! I was glad he couldn't come over. After talking to him I felt as though I was being used as a human dumping zone. The nerve of him thinking I wanted to hear all of that when I just wanted to get laid. He had a lot of things going on.

The tea kettle on the stove whistling sound was familiar indicating my tea was ready—I needed a hot cup of tea after listening to Stevie. I really think he had on an ankle brace and didn't want to tell me. That's probably why he didn't ask me to come over to his place. If I would have gotten there and he had on an ankle brace, it would have put me over the edge, I would've *went off.* An ankle brace is something I just don't want to see during intimacy.

It was definitely time to call someone else. Derrick was next in line. Derrick, didn't like talking on the phone, therefore, I knew our conversation would be short and sweet.

Derrick, was a ghostwriter, he always kept my interest with his stories. Unlike Stevie, he would avoid the ghetto drama. Most of his stories had a positive ending, unlike Stevie, but I always had a great time with them both.

"Hello?"

"Derrick?"

"Yes."

"This is Belinda."

"Hey! How have you been?"

"Oh, I'm alright. Just strolling through my phone, and realized how long it's been since we talked," slithered words generated from a lie.

"Yeah, it's been a minute, you *alight*?" he questioned with eagerness.

"I'm okay, *just* wondered what you were doing this evening?"

"I really don't have any plans."

"Me neither, I thought maybe we can take in a movie at my place, with some wine and pop corn?" my eyes sparkled with anticipation for a response.

"Okay, I noticed you didn't mention food," Derrick quickly negotiated; I could easy expect something like that from him.

"I sure didn't, I don't feel like cooking!" I retorted.

"*How 'bout* I order some Chinese to be delivered before I get there?"

"Oh, that would be nice of you," my entire face brighten, Derrick knew exactly what to say and to do.

"What time?"

"Seven will be fine, if that's okay with you?"

"Sure see you then."

છ૭ ૦ૅ

At six forty five sharp, Derrick's shinny black 740I BMW pulled into the driveway with its peanut butter leather interior. I just loved his car and the way it smelled inside. While riding in his car I felt like I was on a magic carpet floating, the comfort was fantastic.

He exited the car; I made sure he couldn't see me peeping out of the window. It was difficult waiting on the six one full of fun man; at least the evening won't be filled with drama, like with Stevie.

When the door bell rang, I didn't want him to think I was *thirsty* by rushing to open the door, so I waited.

"I'll be right there!" I yelled as I bumbled my way out of the bedroom.

My hair was in a curly style with jewelry on my hand, wrist, neck and ears. I didn't want him to think I was desperate, so I threw some jeans on with my OGG boots, sweater and a vest. I wanted him to work for the treasure by disrobing me.

"Wow! Don't you look delicious?" his whole face brightened up.

"Thanks Derrick, come on in," my eyes glinted just to tease him.

"The place looks nice," his head glance around the house and up to the ceiling.

"Thanks Derrick," I whispered apprehensively, not knowing what his next compliment was going to be. Derrick was good, and he knew why he was here. We both wanted to get laid, but keep it with a little class and not treat each other as if we were just a fuck.

"You keep it so clean and neat."

"I try; let me take your coat."

"I see the food arrived."

"Yeah, and you knew exactly what I wanted," instantly, I thought that could have came out in the wrong way.

"How can I forget, Magnolia Beef, side of fried rice, sweet sauce on the side, and a black stallion standing in front of you."

I was confused; did he catch on to the statement or what?

"Come here girl!" his manicured hands reached for me.

"Oh big daddy, since you put it all like that," lasciviously I glided into his arms.

Derrick caressed me in such a gentle way, a different kind of hug. His arms enveloped me, I felt safe, as if for the moment—time had stood still. He was gentle and warm; with my head laying on his chest the wonderful

80

smell of Versace Eros permeated my nostrils. Wow! He made me feel special, like a little girl in her daddy's arms. I wanted to call him daddy and repeat it all through the night!

"Okay, have a seat dude. I like that sweater, half turtleneck, okay *I hear you*."

"Thanks, *what up lady?*" empathically he inquired. "I can go on and on about myself, but you know I'm not like that. I want to hear what's been going on *wit-cha* girl?"

"Nothing much, just the same old thing, I've been waiting to hear some of your stories, they be exciting."

"You think so?" he plastered a smile on his face.

"Yes, really," my eyes bored into his.

"I just got finished with a project I really enjoyed."

"Tell me about it," I beamed excitedly.

"You know I'm a *Ghost Writer*?"

"Yeah, you write other people's stories and get paid for it, I know."

"Well, the project I just completed was the wife of a professional basketball player memoir."

"Really?"

"Yeah, one time when I was conversing with her over the phone he got on and said he just wanted to talk to the person who his money was going to."

"Okay."

"I told him, '*he is I and I is him,*' and laughed," he gave a half smile. "Anyway, she told me when the season was over they would like to spend a weekend with me. I said okay sure."

"Hold it right there Derrick, this sounds like it is going to get juicy, let me pour us some wine first."

The bottle of *Beringer* White Zinfandel awaited me. Slowly, I poured us some wine, and knew after a few glasses we both would be in a desirable mode. Good food, wine and sex—an enjoyable evening I deserved.

"After the project was over she had an agent and a publisher on standby. The book took off and they came to visit. Her picture she sent me didn't do her justice, she was a knock out, and he was six feet eleven. He had to bend his head coming down my staircase from the guest room."

"Wow dude, really?"

"It was a Saturday night and we all were getting ready to go out partying. I asked her what kind of club they would like to go to. She said, 'Derrick I want you to take us to a strip club,' I was surprised," his jaw dropped. "She wanted to take her husband to a strip club."

"Wow Derrick, can't wait to hear how that turned out."

"I waited patiently downstairs in the living room for them. After about two *'beautifuls,'* Hennessey, Liqueur and cranberry juice, she came walking downstairs one step at a time with a sway as if she was on a runway. The girl was fine and all of her back was out—she had everything in the right place."

"So what am I 'chop liver'?"

"Now Belinda, you know you got it going on, I'm just trying to paint the picture for you," he snapped back.

"Alright then, but don't paint it too well, I'll get a little jealous," I sneered jokingly.

"Yeah right, you get jealous, stop playing and listen."

"Okay, I'm sorry," I rested my shoulders back on the sofa, sipping on my second glass of wine by now.

"Her husband the ball player came down and we got into their SUV and drove to the strip club. She sat in the middle of us at the strip club. His wife—my client, motioned for a stripper to come give her husband a lap dance. I heard her told the stripper, *'and bitch do your job on my husband,'* she didn't play no games."

"While the stripper was giving him a lap dance what were you doing?"

"I called me a stripper and got me a lap dance too," his eyes flickered with a lustful glow.

"Okay, when in Rome do as the Romans right?"

"Strangest thing, while I was getting my lap dance she turned and looked at me and said, 'I know you! You are the author I met at the convention center, you wrote that book?'

"That's weird."

"Well I was tired of playing the third wheel with my new friends, so I invited my dancer over to my house after numerous lap dances."

"That was mighty friendly of you, didn't know you do strippers."

"No girl, she was a fan. And she was married. She just wanted to talk about how she had to go to another job after the strip club closed while her husband sits at home and not working."

"You don't get it do you? That's how *women of the night* will reel you in."

"If that's the case I wasn't buying whatever she may have been selling," he chuckled. "She followed us and in the driveway I notice her car was filled with cleaning supplies. Apparently, she cleaned an office building after she would leave the strip club."

"Wow, and her husband, is at home while she is out in the streets?"

"I guess so, we just talked and drank some champagne before she went to her second or third job, and the conversation was stimulating."

"Sounds like a fun night, I hadn't had that kind of excitement," I went poker face on him.

"And you don't need to Belinda, I'd like to be your excitement this evening," he gave me a nice, but dirty look.

"*Really?* And how would I be excited?"

"By letting me touch you gently," he touched my face gently along my cheekbone.

"Like you are doing now?"

"More than gentle strokes on the skin, I'd like for you to feel me inside of you."

With one hand he gently rubbed my forearm and with the other he slithered his index finger alongside of my cheekbone down to my chin. Thoughts of the stripper straddle on him entered my mind. I wanted him, but I couldn't rush it. I wanted the night to last forever.

Derrick sat back and sipped on his wine. The pause gave me a little time to inhale and exhale, he was moving fast and I was letting him get me to the point of needing and wanting him. Derrick knew what he was doing and didn't need any instructions nor coaching—my type of a guy.

He sat his drink on the end table; I waited patiently for his next move. His arm envelope across my shoulders and he pulled me closer to him, our eye balls stared at each other. We were so close I thought my retina was going to burst. He had me in *any way* possible.

Closer his lips came to mines until they touch, and I embrace a nice soft kiss from him as he held my shoulders tightly. I was at my boiling point and couldn't hold back any longer. Without thinking I slowly lower Derrick down to the sofa and became the aggressor.

"Wow!" he whisper.

Hastily, we began to remove each other's garments to bareness. I was anxious and wetly out of control. We made love, passionately and endlessly. Derrick had quenched my thirst for sex, with a sigh of relief I knew it would last me for a little while and if not, I would have to rely on *'old faithful'* my toy.

৸ এ

The sun shone in through my bedroom window, and there he was lying in my bed as if he lived here. Derrick was a peaceful sleeper, handsome and with a lot of things going on professionally, no baby mama drama—he was always a great lay and I had no problems exploding for him until I was completely drained.

His eyes slowly opened as if he could feel me breathing over him as he sleep.

"What's going on baby, good morning to you," his eyes widened.

"Morning, how did you sleep?" confidently I ask, 'cause I knew I *put it on* him.

"Like a baby!" he yawned while stretching his arms.

"Awe okay, cool, 'cause you sure didn't act like *no* baby last night. You really threw it down," I gasped from the thought of last night.

"How sweet of you to say that, I've got no complaints about you either," excitement overtook his face.

"Thank you baby," warmness lathered my body as I leaned to kiss him, bad breath and all. "You got time for some breakfast?"

"That would be nice, let me put my clothes on and I can help you."

"Na that wouldn't be necessary, you just bring your handsome self to the kitchen and get a cup of coffee, I *got* it."

"I'll be on my way."

Collective memories some stayed in my mind others faded away. Last night memory, for sure, would stay with me forever. Although, I would be a shame to say it to my girlfriends, but I've had some one nightstand I can't even remember their names. Perhaps they were meaningless, wasteful and were meant to be forgotten.

Chapter Five
Nothing Stays the Same

Another night of giving in to my sexual lusts proved to be less than satisfying. I may have gotten some much needed sexual release, but what did that prove? That I could sleep with whomever I wanted to whenever I wanted to? Which proved nothing, except I was a…well never mind.

I paced around the house, thinking about the untold number of men I'd casually slept with. I know my beauty and youthfulness attracted men like flies to sugar but looking in the bathroom mirror under my makeup light, reminded me time was moving forward, not backward. I wouldn't be young, beautiful, and sexy forever. Well, maybe I would. I couldn't help but smile at myself.

Needless to say, on a more serious tip, I chastised myself for all the years of foolish, self-centered, and selfish mistakes I'd made in my life. Of course thoughts about my betrayal of Candace surfaced. How could they not? No matter what I did, where I went, who I slept with, how much I shopped, my mind always came back to Candace.

Sometimes I don't understand myself. I go around bragging about my beauty, the way I dress, the money I have and of course the way men drool over me. With someone like me, who could have any man I choose, why on God's green earth did I betray my friend? How could I sleep with Emanuel and all but flaunt it in Candace's face.

Okay, my shrink keeps telling me to let bygones be bygones, but how can I? I mean, I had no good reason for some of that senseless, stupid stuff I did. My behavior at times was unacceptable. Sleeping with Emanuel was one of those times I regretted forever. No way could I truly call myself a friend, not a real friend anyway, when I went behind Candace's back and screwed her man. Of all the available men walking on this earth why in the hell would I sleep with hers? But I knew why I did it. I may not have admitted my truth to anyone else, but standing in the mirror, I admitted it to myself. I always felt the need to prove I was desirable and wanted. I guess it is a psychological thing of some sort. I don't know, but it is what it is. It's like I'm always trying to prove to God knows who I have what it takes; I'm the cat's meow. I sort of laughed at that thought. *"Cat's meow*? Wow, Belinda, you're losing it, girl," I said aloud to my reflection.

I finally got enough of arguing with the girl in the mirror. I know it was early in the morning, not even quite nine o'clock. Some would say it's too early for a drink, but after Derrick left I needed a *pick* me up. A mental *pick* me up. The only thing that could do that was a good stiff drink of Vodka.

I went in the kitchen, over to my mini bar that had every kind of delectable liquor a person could want, at least a person who liked to drink like I did. I studied the bottles of alcohol like I was choosing something off of a food menu before deciding on my favorite—vodka. I went and got a glass out the cabinet, went to the fridge and put some ice into the glass, and then proceeded to open the bottle of vodka and pour myself vodka on the rocks. No chase.

The ice cubes clinked in the glass as I turned up the glass to my mouth and took a deep swallow. *"Ahhh."*

I had on my cherry red robe that I put on after Derrick left this morning. Last night, while Derrick entertained me, I have to be honest; there was no need for clothes. That's what had me laughing. We spent the night in our birthday suits frolicking around and making love from room to room. I laughed again as I swallowed the last shot of vodka before pouring me another round.

We showered together sometime during our night rendezvous, but that session of love making he put on me this morning before he left warranted a long bath in a hot tub of water.

I took another gulp as I walked with the glass and the bottle of Vodka up the hallway toward my bedroom. In my bedroom, I placed the vodka on top of my dresser drawer, while I rummaged through the drawers for underwear. I settled on a baby blue silk panties and matching bra set. I laid the items on the bed and then proceeded to go to my walk in closet. I looked through it while nursing my drink. I took a swallow only to find the glass empty—again. I moved some items over and set the glass on the shelf in the closet.

After choosing a revealing over the head dress and matching heels, I placed the dress on the bed and the shoes on the floor next to my bed, and retrieved the empty glass.

I refilled my drink, this time all way to the top. There was only a piece of an ice cube left. I started to go back in the kitchen for another couple of cubes but changed my mind. The lukewarm liquor would hit just right. No need to add any more ice.

Relaxing against the tub with my bath pillow underneath my neck, fragrant bubbles covering me like a blanket, and my bottle of Vodka sitting on the tub's edge, I replayed the previous night…and morning with Derrick. Dang, that boy had serious moves and the perfect equipment to go along with those moves. I laughed at the thought of his skills, while taking another drink. If I was the typical kind of woman, I would have caught feelings for him, but for me, it was the other way around. It was the men who were always catching feelings for me although time and time again I made it clear I was not the one to give in to love. Not just yet, at least. I had too much living to do as a single female. Plus, when that time came, if it ever came, I wanted my life to be together. Along the way, I'd hurt too many people, including myself. Things would only be complicated if I added love to the equation.

My promiscuity, and I cannot lie, my excessive drinking too, had been the cause of too many breakups, mess-ups, and trip-ups in my life. I was grateful so far I had not contracted any STDs although I practiced safe sex—well at least most of the time that is.

Ahhh, the water feels so good. It's relaxing me. I close my eyes and allow the vodka and the water to take me away.

I woke up splashing my arms and legs in the tub. Dang, I almost drowned myself. Thank goodness, I woke up. I was gasping, spitting, and reaching for air as my head came up out of the water. I obviously had fallen asleep. Guess one too many drinks, good sex, and a hot bath sent me into oblivion.

Almost panicking after having almost drowned myself, I climbed out of the tub, allowing the water to drip freely from my stallion like body. I reached for my bath towel, drying off as I went into my bedroom and fell across the bed. I lay there staring at the ceiling until my eyes grew heavy.

I woke up in a sweat, looking around confused. I sat up in the bed. It took me a minute to realize I must have fallen asleep. I had no idea what time it was, or if it was day or night. I searched for my phone. Found it under the covers. I looked at the phone screen. It was almost noon. I must have been more exhausted than I realized.

I saw my clothes at the foot of the bed where I had placed them earlier. Throwing the cover aside, I sat on the side of the bed, reached for my panties and bra, and started getting dressed. I had to hurry up; I had wasted so much time sleeping the morning away. I had an appointment at the beauty salon and nail shop in an hour. The morning binge drinking was slowing me down considerably. Usually I was able to bounce back after a night of binge drinking. This morning, or should I say, this afternoon I felt different. I was queasy, sluggish, and I did not feel well at all. I had to make a change. I couldn't keep going like this. Oh well, maybe tomorrow. For now, I needed to pull myself together and do what I needed to do—get beautified.

෴ ෴

The past two months have been crazy. My life changed on the drop of a dime. I don't know when my drinking became so out of control. All I know is for the past few weeks, I've been having black outs, periods of time where I would sometimes lose memories of things I'd done, people I'd hung out with, and places I'd gone. But tonight was the last straw when I woke up in a filthy, stinking room next to not one, but two scrounge looking men. The one on my right was snoring, had a gray over grown beard, and a hairy chest. He was naked as a jaybird with a protruding belly. The hair on his head was salt and pepper gray, and it too was unkempt, like he hadn't seen the inside of a barbershop in ages. I was almost afraid to look to my left but I slowly turned my head. The other man had bleach blonde hair with black roots. He was a white man, clean-shaven, with deep potholes all over his face.

I stirred in the bed, trying to ease up from between them. I managed to sit up on the mattress, which was on the floor. There was nothing else in the room other than the thin mattress and a rickety looking chair and table sitting in a corner.

I looked at the men again then eased my naked body to the foot of the bed, got up, and that's when I saw the litter of empty liquor bottles strewn across the small dark, foul smelling room.

I looked around for my clothes. I found my dress on the other side of the mattress near the salt and pepper haired man's side. I grabbed my dress, slipped it over my head, and then looked for my phone and purse. I didn't see anything else but my shoes. I slipped into them, looked back over my shoulder one last time at the two strangers, opened the door, and took off out of there like a bat out of hell. I ran up a hallway, until I saw a door. I ran to the door, opened it, and took a deep breath when I met the cold burst of air outside. I had no phone, no money, no purse, nothing. I had no idea where I was or how I got there. I walked up the dark street until I saw a street sign. I learned I was in an unsavory part of the city. God, what had I gotten myself into? With my arms folded, trying to keep myself warm from the cold night air, I kept walking until I saw a corner store.

I entered the store. The person behind the counter looked at me like I was a piece of garbage. When I caught a glimpse of myself in the surveillance mirror hanging in the store, I immediately understood why he looked at me like that. First of all, my dress was on inside out, my hair was all over my head, my mascara had made streaks along my cheeks, and I smelled like a whisky still.

Excuse me, sir," I said to the man. "Can you let me use your phone? I... someone stole my purse with all of my money. I need to call someone to come and get me."

"Get out of here!" the store owner yelled. "Get out of my store. NOW! I'm sick of you homeless people coming in here. All you do is steal get out!" he yelled.

I took off out of that store like a bat out of hell, afraid of what he might do to me if I stayed. I ran up the street until I saw a McDonald's. I begged people going in and out of the restaurant for money. Most of them turned me down, but after a few hours, I managed to collect enough coins to catch a bus and make it close to where I lived. Here I was, I had plenty of money, yet I was begging on the street like I a bum. At that moment I felt humiliated and embarrassed.

When I did make it home, it was daybreak. I searched for my extra hidden key that I kept in a small container buried underneath a bush by my front door. I couldn't wait to get into the house, get out of my filthy clothes, and take a hot shower.

While I showered, I noticed bruises between my thighs and on my breasts. I felt myself becoming physically ill as I thought about what those men and I did in that room. Did I actually have sex with them? The evidence was written all over my body. Memories began flashing as I scrubbed the filth of the night before away. I could see one of the men, the big belly one, bouncing up and down on my body while I performed despicable acts with the other one. What was wrong with me? I needed help. I needed help badly. I needed to make a change.

After I scrubbed my body until the water turned frigid, I got out of the shower, dressed, and then climbed in my bed. I didn't bother to eat or do anything but go to sleep. This time when I woke up, it was night time—again. I looked at the clock on the nightstand. 9:15 p.m. the clock read. I had been sleep for over twelve hours!

I slowly climbed out of bed. My belly was rumbling. I couldn't remember when I had last eaten a good solid meal. I went into the kitchen and opened the refrigerator to see what I could put together. I didn't see anything appetizing. I opened the freezer. I had a few frozen dinner bowls. I took one of them out of the freezer and popped it in the microwave.

After eating the food and drinking two glasses of ice water, I went to the living room sofa and laid on it. I picked up the remote and turned on the television, scrolling through channel after channel until I saw something on BET that caught my eye. I watched the movie until the urge for a drink hit me.

You would think after waking up in a strange place next to those two bums would be enough to make me never want to take another drink. And I did feel like that, but my body said something different. I craved a shot of Vodka. *Just one shot,* I told myself. *I'll have just one drink.*

I got up off the sofa and went back to the kitchen, retrieved the bottle of vodka and a glass, and returned to the sofa.

I woke up and the sun was beaming through the window. It had happened again. I was confused about the time of day or what day it was.

This time I got up, *squint* my eyes against the sun, and went to the bathroom to brush my teeth, urinate, and clean myself up.

My phone started ringing just as I came out of the bathroom and into my bedroom.

"Hello,"

"Hey, girl, Where have you been?" asked Veronica on the other end. "I've been calling you for days. I was about to put out a missing person's report on you." Veronica laughed.

"Hey, Veronica," I said, less enthused because I was still feeling discombobulated. "Girl, you won't believe what I've been through. But anyway, what's up?"

"I wanted to see if you wanted to get together later this evening. I'm meeting some friends at that new club on Farmington Boulevard. You know the one we were talking about a couple of weeks ago. It's supposed to cater to a more selective crowd of people. You know, people like us who have it going on." Veronica laughed again.

"I heard that, but I don't know, Veronica. I've had a rough couple of days." I didn't want to tell her I had been laid up with two homeless men. The thought of what I'd probably done with them almost made me physically ill again.

"Girl, please, you have all the time in the world to get your beauty rest. You're a woman of leisure, with not a care in the world. Now, what do you say? I need you, Belinda. There's someone who's supposed to be coming that I think will be the perfect match for you."

"I'll think about it, but I can't promise you I'll be there."

"Okay, call me later. You're starting to worry me though, Belinda. First I can't reach you for days, and now you're turning down a chance to turn on your charms to a hunk of a man? What's wrong with you?"

"I don't want to talk right now, Veronica. I have an appointment I have to make it to," I lied, hoping it would be enough to get her off the phone.

"Okay, then. Call me though. Okay?"

"Yes, I'll call you later, promise." I told her and hurriedly ended the call.

Next thing I did was make myself a big breakfast of eggs, biscuits, bacon and a fruit cup. I ate every last drop of that food and I even wanted more, but I didn't give in to my cravings. I had to keep this fine figure of mine intact.

After I finished breakfast, I went to make myself a glass of vodka, but stopped myself.

"What are you doing?" I said aloud. "You have a serious problem, Belinda. You need help, girl." I kept talking to myself until I convinced myself I could at least talk to my shrink. Maybe if I talked to a professional I could get some pointers as to what I could do to stop my excessive drinking. Not that I considered myself to be an alcoholic, but I knew I had some issues, some real serious issues I couldn't seem to shake on my own. That's why I figured I drank like I did. I was always consumed with guilt about the choices I'd made over my life. Sleeping with other women's husbands or their boyfriends and I didn't care if the girl was my friend or not. If I saw a man I liked, I had to prove I could get him in my bed in which I managed to do easily at least 99% of the time.

But that was playing out. Shucks that had played out after I woke up in that filthy room with those nasty men. *'Lord, please don't let me get a disease or worse yet something like HIV or AIDS. How could I have been so stupid? And why don't I remember meeting those men or going off with them?'*

I shook my head, trying to get them out of my mind. I cleared the kitchen and then went to the living room so I could go online and see about finding someone I could go talk to.

I ended up finding a counselor who had some pretty decent reviews online. I didn't want to see the one I had seen before because he was old, antiquated, and his counseling left me feeling like I should have been counseling him. I called the number and made an appointment. Luckily, he had an opening for later that afternoon.

Talking to a counselor actually felt pretty good, probably because white boy was *fiiine*! I left his office determined to get him to lay me down on the blue leather sofa in his office. All while he was so called counseling me, I was thinking about how I wanted to rock his world.

I made another appointment to come see him the following week. I was going to be dressed to seduce the pants right off of him too.

After my session, I called Veronica to see if she still wanted to hang out and she did.

I went home, changed into a tight fitting designer dress with the perfect matching pumps and jewelry. I arrived at the club ready to slay.

"Belinda, over here," I heard Veronica calling for me almost as soon as I stepped foot inside the jazzy club.

I rushed over to her, meeting her halfway across the club floor. *"Hey, girl!"*

"Hey, chick. Come on," Veronica said, grabbing hold of my hand and leading me across the dance floor to a private VIP section upstairs.

When we got up there, it was like we were in a different space and place. Even the servers were dressed different than the ones who were downstairs in the club. These servers were in outfits that almost looked like fancy tuxedos and the women were dressed in all black above knee skirts with black tank tops, and tasteful. As soon as we made it upstairs, Veronica led me to another section of the club that was even more private. We went through double doors and entered an area that looked like a whole new club.

There was a group of people who I recognized as some being Veronica's friends. There were some other people she introduced me to that I didn't know.

"I want you to meet my friend, Belinda," Veronica said, as a very tall, handsome, dark skinned men stood from the table where he was seated and extended his hand toward me.

"Belinda, this is Malik. Malik, this is Belinda."

"Nice to meet you, Belinda."

I blushed when he flashed a hypnotic smile at me. His voice was deep and captivating. Brother was fine for days. I already knew how the night would end—with him in my bed. It was inevitable. No way was I going to let a good looking brother like him walk away without a taste from my cookie jar.

Malik and I had a blast at the club. We laughed, got to know each other more, and danced all night long. By the time I left the club, it was almost three a.m. I was lit. I had more than my share of drinks. Thanks to generous Malik I didn't have to open my purse and spend one single cent.

"I don't think you should drive, Belinda," Veronica cautioned as she and her man and friends got ready to leave the club.

"I'm good," I told her, knowing full well I was feeling good, real good. But I still wasn't worried about whether I could drive or not. I'd driven my car home or to wherever else I wanted to go on occasions when I was sloppy drunk. I know I was wrong for the times I got behind the wheel and drove while drunk but what can I say. Tonight I wouldn't say that I was sloppy drunk, but I felt the effects of the vodka, no lie.

"Don't worry about her. I'll make sure the lady gets home safely," Malik assured Veronica, while placing his arm at the small of my back and pulling me close to him.

I laughed. "See, Veronica. I'm in good hands."

"Take care of her, Malik. Make sure my friend gets home in one piece."

"No problem. I've got her," Malik assured Veronica again.

"Are you ready? I'll drive you home and send for your car in the morning. *How about that?*"

"Uh, I guess so, but I'm telling you, I can drive. I'm not that wasted," I tried assuring Malik.

"Okay, look, I live like seven minutes from here. What do you say we go to my place? Keep the party going?" he suggested.

"I'd like that," I said, almost swooning into his muscular arms.

℘ ℭ

Malik and I barely made it into his apartment before he pulled me into his arms and started kissing me. His hands caressed me all over as he walked me backwards to his bedroom.

He swoop me up into his arms, laid me across the bed and climbed on top of me, all while unbuttoning his shirt.

"Let me help you with that," I said in my drunken state of mind. Quickly,

I began helping him remove his clothing and he began helping me out of my dress.

His kisses were hot and fiery. His moans of pleasure rang throughout the room, mixed with my own groans of sexual satisfaction. Brother had mad skills.

When the sun came up, true to his word, Malik drove me to pick up my car.

"I enjoyed you," he said as he opened my car door.

I smiled. "So did *I.*"

"Maybe I'll see you around sometime," he said.

"Maybe you will," I countered, noticing he didn't ask for my phone number. I knew right then and there this was just another one night fling. Oh well, that's the way the cookie crumbles sometimes.

I got into my car. Malik closed the door, not bothering to give me a peck on the lips or cheek. Instead, he stepped back from the car and threw up a hand.

"Be safe."

"Sure," I said, as I turned the ignition, put the car in drive, and sped off.

As I drove home, my mind was encased with one thought after another. I needed help. I kept telling myself that, but I hadn't done anything about it. All I knew was that I needed to make a change in my life. But where would I start?

When I got inside the house, I immediately pulled off my clothes and took a hot shower. I was a little hungry too, so when I was done with my shower, I made myself a spinach omelet and drank two cups of coffee with just a couple of shots of vodka in it to give it a taste.

My phone rang.

"How did it go with Malik last night?" Veronica asked.

"He was all right. I've had better."

"You are something else, Belinda." Veronica laughed into the phone. "Are you going to see him again?"

"I doubt it. He didn't ask for my number and I didn't ask for his. But who cares? Girl, there are too many other fish in the sea for me to be worried about whether I'm going to see him again."

"He's a good catch is all I'm saying," Veronica offered.

"I'm a good catch too, you know. I mean any man would be lucky to have a woman like me on their arm."

"Well, I hope you two hook-up again on a more serious note. I want you to find love and happiness. *Know what I'm saying?"*

"Yep, I hear you. And thanks for being a good friend, but I can look out for myself. I can get any man I choose and lock him down, if that's what I wanted to do. I'm just not ready to settle down with one guy just yet. I did that and look where it got me?"

"I say you came out on top," Veronica laughed. "I'm not making fun of you being a widow, but I'm just saying you're still in the land of the living and he's….well…"

"Six feet under, serves him right for screwing around on me. I mean what man in his right mind would cheat on a woman like me? You see where it landed him. God don't like ugly."

"I guess you're right about that. What are your plans for the day?"

"I think I might drive to Lakeland to that new outlet mall for a little retail therapy. You want to tag along?"

"I wish I could," Veronica answered, "but I already made plans with *my boo."*

"I heard that. Well, have fun. We'll talk later."

I ended the call with Veronica and then went to my closet to find something to wear. I picked out a printed romper and a pair of open toed sandals. It was supposed to be a hot one today, and I was going to dress accordingly.

I looked at my phone. It was still early. I had plenty of time to do whatever I wanted to do and for now, I wanted to crash. I hadn't had but an hour of sleep, if that much.

Foregoing my bed, I went into the living room, lay on the couch, grabbed my purple throw off the back of the couch, and curled up in it. My eyes suddenly felt like a boulder was pressing down on my eyelids, forcing them to close.

ₐₓ

I woke up in a daze. Shaking my head, I looked around a room filled with darkness. To my right and ahead of me, I caught a tiny stream of light. I got up from the couch. Shivering, I hugged myself. That's when to my amazement I realized I was naked. When did I take off my clothes? I distinctly remember having on my bra and panties. Looking over my shoulder for the purple throw or my under garments, I couldn't see a thing.

"Where is my phone?" I asked myself. Taking a few steps forward I reached for the wall and allowed my hand to travel up the wall until it landed on the light switch.

I exhaled, "Thank you, Lord," and turned on the switch."Light! *Yess!*" My big smile turned into a huge frown when I followed the burst of air into the hallway. I rubbed my eyes and shook my head, hoping my eyes were fooling me. They weren't. The front door was wide opened. I ran toward it while looking around me, afraid someone would jump out and attack me at any moment. I reached the door, looked outside briefly, and then closed and locked it. Leaning against it, I inhaled and then released a long torch of air. Shivering, but not from the cold this time, but because of fear. I walked up the hallway, back to the living room. I paused at the entrance to the kitchen when I saw two empty liquor bottles on the counter. Next to the bottles were two glasses.

Now I was really growing worried. Who had been in my house while I was asleep? How did they get inside?

I tiptoed into the kitchen, looking around the dimly lit space. I usually kept the light on the over the over on because I had a tendency of getting up during the night and rambling in the kitchen for a snack.

I studied the glasses. Had I blacked out again and perhaps invited someone over? What was going on? I looked at the time. It was five thirty in the afternoon but it was already dusk outside.

I decided to do a walk-through of the house just to be sure I was alone, but not before pulling a knife out of the knife holder to carry with me. Just in case.

The house was all clear, but in my bedroom, my covers were pulled back, half hanging on the hardwood floor. The bed pillows were on the other side of the bed and the outfit I had laid out earlier was nowhere in sight. It looked like I had been in the bed and more than likely I had company with me. *But who*? When? Oh, God, what is happening to me? On the nightstand was another bottle of liquor. This one was half full. But what was even more interesting was what was next to the bottle of alcohol—a toothpick.

Who was in here? That thought kept rushing through my mind. I was growing terrified, panicking even. I sucked in deep breaths, holding one hand against my upper chest. I went to the living room and sat back on the couch, leaning my head back.

No matter how hard I tried, I couldn't recall what had happened. One thing I knew for sure was that I had had sex with whoever it was that was here. That much I was certain of. The evidence was on my body and in my surroundings. I saw my romper lying on the nearby chair like it had been tossed there.

I got back up, ran a hot bath, and climbed inside the tub. I stayed in that hot tub of water until it turned cold as ice.

Next, after my bath, I put on a thick pink terry cloth robe, wrapped my hair up in a do, and went back to the living room. I would have to tackle changing my linen and cleaning up behind whoever I entertained, but that would have to come later. For now I needed help. I thought about calling the counselor again, but the more I thought about seeing him, the less enthused I was about it. I knew if I saw him again my mind would not be on therapy. Well, I take that back. It would be on therapy—sex therapy that is. My God, was it him? Had I invited him over? I couldn't think straight.

I decided to bite the bullet and contact Alcoholics Anonymous, before I talked myself out of it. The person on the hotline sounded like she was genuinely concerned about me. I talked to her, told her I was afraid I was having blackouts. She said she was a recovering alcoholic and she had experienced blackouts before becoming sober ten years ago. She encouraged me to talk, and I did. I was on the phone with her for almost an hour. At the end of the call, I knew her name was Peggy. She put another AA counselor on three-way. Her name was Lucinda. Lucinda was going to be my temporary sponsor until I could get involved with an AA program near me. We exchanged phone numbers. When I hung up from the hotline, Lucinda called me.

Lucinda and I talked and I became comfortable with her. So when she suggested coming to my house so we could meet and talk face to face, I readily agreed, and without prompting, gave her my address.

Lucinda arrived within fifteen minutes. She explained AA wanted counselors and sponsors assigned to individuals who lived within close proximity. That was designed in case a client was in a dilemma or having a crisis, like I was, and needed someone to come to their aid quickly.

"Come in," I offered when I opened the door and Lucinda introduced herself. She had an identification badge to assure me she was legit. Not that I was worried. My only concern at this point was to see what was going on with me. I hoped I wasn't going crazy.

"Have a seat," I told Lucinda and led her into the living room.

"Thank you, Belinda. You have a lovely home." She took a seat in the turquoise chair.

Her compliment brought a smile to my face, because I liked to decorate. It felt good when other people noticed.

"When was the last time you had a drink?"

"You're cutting straight to the chase, I see."

"I find that's the best way. So when was your last drink?" Lucinda pressured me again.

"Last night…this morning," I said in a barely audible voice.

"Do you have any liquor around the house?"

Why does she want to know that? It's none of her business. She's getting a little too personal. "Uh, no, but why do you want to know?"

"If you're serious about wanting to stop drinking then the first step is acknowledging you have a problem. Next, we need to make sure you don't have any alcohol around the house that will tempt you to take a drink. Shall we go to where you usually keep your alcohol?" Lucinda looked at me straight forward, not flinching.

"I'd rather we didn't. Not now. Not tonight anyway."

Lucinda exhaled, and then turned back toward the chair. "Suit yourself. When you're ready, give me a call. Is there anything you want to talk about? For instance, when your drinking began to cause problems in your life."

Almost without hesitation, I began talking. I told her about Sheila and what happened to her. How I blamed myself for the shape she was in and what was done to her. I told her about Candace and Emanuel, and my dead husband. I talked until my mouth was dry. I wanted a taste of Vodka so bad. I began licking my lips.

"Uh, can I get you something to drink?" I asked after I finally decided I'd shared far too much with Lucinda. But looking at her, she didn't seem to mine. She encouraged me to talk, and asked very few questions, which seemed to put me at ease. It was like she wasn't prying, and that I was willingly sharing things that were on my mind.

"You've certainly been through a lot, Belinda. We all have our reasons for drinking or doing drugs, including me. But that part of my life is in the past. I haven't forgotten it, but I refuse to allow it to dictate my future. You have to get to the point where you want to live more than you want to die, Belinda."

That night, after Lucinda left, I was tormented by dreams, horrific dreams about Sheila and Candace. They were stabbing me, and calling me names, telling me how I ruined their lives. Then it switched to dreams about the faceless, nameless men I'd slept with, like the ones I woke up in between a few nights ago. There were dreams of Emanuel and Malik and my new counselor. It all involved violence, sex, and drinking.

I woke up in a cold sweat, sat up in the bed, and then turned and placed both feet on the cool hardwood floor. I leaned down and to my left, opened the nightstand door, and reached toward the back of it. I exhaled in relief when my hands met up with the half pint of Vodka. I removed it from the nightstand, got back up in the bed, pulled the covers around me and then opened the bottle. I studied it for several seconds, inhaled it underneath my nose, and then turned it up against my thirsty lips. I knew I shouldn't have, but by the time I took the last drip of liquor out of that bottle, I wasn't thinking about whether I was right or wrong.

I threw the bottle across the floor. *"Ughhh!"* I got out of the bed, throwing the cover away from me as I stood up and then stumbled.

I needed more. Cursing out loud and continuing to stumble around, I looked through every cabinet in the kitchen. *Nothing!*

"What time is it?" The clock on the microwave said 10:33 p.m. "Better hurry up," I mumbled and grabbed my car keys off the wall rack next to the garage door.

"Owww!" I tumbled down the two steps leading into the garage. My knee and shin hurt badly. I saw blood and a nasty scrape. I couldn't let that stop me if I wanted to get to the liquor store before it closed at eleven. Thank God, there was one two blocks up the street.

I got in the car, fumbled with the ignition until I got the keys in it, pressed the overhead remote in my car, and put the pedal to the medal as soon as the garage door opened wide enough for me to back out.

If Lucinda, Veronica, anybody, saw me like this they would probably say I was wasted. And they would be right, but I had a lot on my mind. I deserved to have a drink or two...or three...or whatever. I had to get the demons off my back and keep them from wreaking havoc in my mind.

I made it to the liquor store just in time with five minutes to spare.

Before driving off the liquor store lot, I bust the cap on the pint of Vodka and pressed the bottle against my lips.

I sped off the parking lot, and up the street I flew. The first traffic light turned to red just as I accelerated through it. I came upon the second light or stop sign, whatever it was. I could have sworn I stopped or yielded. Needless to say, I drove into the intersection and suddenly just as I removed the bottle from my lips, I saw a truck, or SUV, appear out of nowhere. There was a loud crash. Where did it come from? What happened?

I looked around me. I saw smoke coming from my hood and a man racing toward me. He was screaming and yelling. At my window, he started pounding.

"Are you okay, lady? *Lady?* Are you okay?"

I looked at him. Somehow I managed to press the button to let my window down.

"Let me help you," he said.

I caught a glimpse of myself in the side mirror. Blood was trickling from my head and for the first time I noticed my airbag had deployed on both sides. My face was burning and tingling.

The man helped me out of the car. I was lightheaded, like I wanted to pass out. But was it from having had too much to drink or had I been injured?

I looked to my right as the man led me to the curb and helped me to sit down.

"The ambulance is on the way."

"Is that the man who hit me?" I asked my rescuer as I looked at the man standing near his car on the other side of the street. Sitting on the curb, near the man, was a woman. I guess that must have been the man's wife or daughter or girlfriend.

Traffic was beginning to stall. A few people gathered on the sidewalk. I guess they were spectators.

"That's the man and woman *you* hit," the man corrected me. "As you can see, she's pregnant. You sped right through a red light. It's a miracle nobody was killed. Looks like both of your cars are totaled."

"I hit *him*?" I asked to make certain I heard him correctly.

"Yes, and I understand why now. You smell like a whisky barrel and so does your car. You're drunk. The police are on the way. You're going to find yourself in a lot of trouble, lady. But thank God you're alive and those folks you hit are alive.

An ambulance and police car arrived within minutes. Paramedics checked the injured parties. The couple was transported by ambulance. I refused to go to the hospital. I felt fine, had I known what was about to occur, I would have opted to take an ambulance ride.

What happened next didn't faze me at first; probably because I was still drunk as hell. I was given a breathalyzer, then ticketed and carted off to jail. I was told my blood alcohol level was more than three times the legal limit!

I spent the first hours in the *drunk* tank before being moved to another holding cell. It was the weekend, meaning I would have to remain in jail until court on Monday morning.

It was the worst weekend of my life. I had to sober up in a tiny cell, lying on top of a steel bunk covered with a half-inch mattress and a dingy thin sheet.

Over in the night, I was transferred to a holding cell with at least thirty other women. It was nasty, roach infested, stinking and plain unsanitary. Some of the women looked like they were strung out on drugs. Others looked like they were street walkers, and others looked like and talked like being behind bars was a cake walk.

As for me, I was terrified. I'd never been in jail before. Who would I call? I didn't want to call Veronica or my daddy. None of my lovers would bail me out and if they would, I had no way to call them. I knew nobody's number by memory.

The more I sat there in the cold dismal holding cell, the more hours passed. I began to drift off. I was exhausted and I was also beginning to feel the effects of having been in a major car crash. My face was bruised up, my chest was sore and I ached all over.

The night grew later and I felt worse than ever. I called for help, but none of the guards paid me any mind. I stopped crying when I started getting dirty looks from some of the women in the cell with me. I curled up in a corner.

The next two days were just as bad. The food they gave us looked and smelled horrible. I couldn't imagine eating it. I did drink some water but that was it.

Monday finally came and I was roughly escorted to court with several other women like we were a herd of cattle.

The judge set my bail at what I thought was an unfair amount—$75,000. I was forced to contact my daddy. It was the only way for me to get out. He was the only one I trusted too. He got hold of one of his partners who knew a bail bondsman and I was set free until my future court date.

I got a good lawyer. Since this was my first DUI, he assured me he would be able to get me off with a fine.

The couple I hit turned out to be fine with just some bruising and no harm to the woman's unborn child. They were suing my insurance, but that was expected. I was just thrilled I would not have to spend another minute behind bars. That accident was another wake up call for me.

I called Lucinda and told her everything that had gone down.

"You need to get help, Belinda. Seriously, you could have killed those people. That poor woman could have lost her child. And you, oh my God, you could have killed yourself, Belinda! Do you understand now how serious this is? You are an alcoholic. You need help. Please, let me get you some help."

I was ready to give up. Everything about my life these past years had gone from living my best life to this person I was now. I didn't know how to describe the woman in the mirror anymore. I was still beautiful on the outside, but inside I felt like I was coming apart. I couldn't keep living this double life. And now that I was having blackouts, things were even worse. I almost killed a family because I couldn't control my drinking. I was my own toxic person.

"Thank you, Lucinda. Give me a few days. I'll be ready."

"A few days may be too late, Belinda. Do not put this off. You already have a case pending. You could go to jail."

"I'm not going to jail. I told you, my lawyer says he can beat the case. God knows I'm paying him enough," I heard Lucinda sighing. "I'm going to talk to my lawyer first thing tomorrow morning, and let him know what I'm going to do."

"Which is?"

"Uh, which is I'm going into a rehab facility. I told you, Lucinda, I'm serious about this. If you don't trust me, you're invited to stay at my house for these next three days. I need to notify a few people I'm going to be out of pocket, and by few I mean my friend Veronica and my daddy. I need to make arrangements for a house sitter and some other personal matters since I'll be gone for at least a month."

"I understand. I also accept your invitation."

"What invitation?"

"Don't pretend like you forgot you invited me to stay at your house for the remainder of the week, until you're ready to check into the facility."

"Oh that, of course I didn't forget. Are you going to stay or what?"

"I am. I'm going to get my things together, take care of some things I need to handle here and I'll see you in a couple of hours."

"Okay. If you forget something, it's not like you live that far. You're fifteen minutes away."

"*Right.* Well, I'll see you soon."

"Okay. Bye."

"One last drink, just one last...drink. That's it." I poured myself a glass of Vodka, swallowed it down, poured another one, followed by another, and one long last one.

"*Ahhhh,* it tastes so good. I feel *soooo* good." I danced around and around the house until I was dizzy and sick feeling. I ran into my bedroom and fell across the bed.

I don't know how long the phone had been ringing or was it the doorbell I heard. I raised my head off the pillow slowly, looking around to focus on where I was. I was relieved that I was at home in my bed. I reached for the phone and at the same time someone was pressing down nonstop on my doorbell.

"Hello," I said into the phone while picking up speed and going to the door. I looked at myself to be sure I was dressed in something decent. Especially, because over the past few weeks I woke up only to find myself naked a couple of times and half-dressed other times. I was relieved when I saw I still had on what I had put on earlier. Everything looked in tact as I listened to Lucinda on the phone yelling for me to open the door.

"Stop ringing the doorbell. Dang, Lucinda. I'm coming," I yelled back. I don't know why I didn't hang up the phone since I knew it was her at the front door.

"You're drunk aren't you?"

"Nope, I'm not."

"You are. I smell you."

Lucinda closed the door behind her. She held the handle to a small piece of rolling luggage.

"Where do you want me to put this?" she asked.

"In the guest bedroom, follow me," I stuttered. I was trying to stay alert or be alert but the vodka was making it hard for me to concentrate.

"Come...come on," I said again.

Lucinda followed me. She placed her luggage and purse in the room.

"Come on," she said almost like an order.

"Where are we going?"

"We're going to go through every nook and cranny in this house until I find every bottle of liquor you have stashed."

"What? I...I don't have anything left."

"You always say that but you seem to manage to get drunk every single day, and you say you haven't been anywhere. Stop the lying. Now, come on. Let's get this house cleared out. We're not only getting rid of alcohol, we're getting rid of anything that has alcohol in it period, including mouthwash!"

103

Lucinda wasn't kidding around; she proved she meant what she said. We searched for any and everything that contained alcohol. When we were done, we both were tired and ready to call it a night.

After I was sure Lucinda had everything she needed, I retired to my bedroom, undressed down to my *undies,* and climbed in the bed. I whispered a prayer and then reminded myself of all the things I needed to take care of before I committed myself to treatment. The longer I lay in bed, the more apprehensive I became about the decision. Could I pull it off? Could my home, my bills, my personal business, all be taken care of while I was holed up in a *drunk* tank? I was sure Veronica and my dad would do everything they could to make sure my personal affairs were in order, but I was still having second thoughts.

I pulled the cover up to my chest and turned on my left side in a fetal position. One thought after another kept me tossing and turning until the wee hours of the night. I guess I eventually fell asleep.

The next few days without having a drink of alcohol, almost drove me crazy. I had no idea, until now, I was truly an alcoholic. My body proved to me in its response when I wouldn't give it what it wanted. I became physically ill, vomiting, nauseated. I had the shakes and sweats so bad until Lucinda had to take me to the treatment center after a couple of days of me almost *spazzing* out.

"Do you have everything on the list?" Lucinda asked me as I gathered my luggage and purse.

"Yes, I checked everything. I should be straight." I could barely speak. I was just that out of it. I needed a drink. I needed a drink, just one, real bad. Lucinda seemed not to notice or care. At least she didn't acknowledge how I was acting or sounding.

"Is your friend or your father coming to see you off?"

"No, I talked to both of them earlier. They know what to do including how to reach you, too," I whispered weakly.

"Good and I have their information in my phone as well. Okay, let's do this."

The staff at the treatment center was ready and waiting on my arrival. They had done a pre-check in. Almost as soon as I arrived, they were on it. They showed me my bed, told me what to expect while I was at the facility, and on and on they went. All I wanted and needed was a drink—something they wouldn't give me.

I remained in *detox* for three and a half days. It was pure hell! Getting through *detox* was not just a matter of willpower or stopping cold turkey; I needed medical help.

The doctor at the facility explained that withdrawal can sometimes put your life at risk. Even when it's not as serious, it's still a big challenge.

He thankfully prescribed me medicine to help ease some of my symptoms.

On day five of being at the treatment facility, I began to feel a little better, like maybe I was coming back to myself. I even had a bit of an appetite, something I didn't have when I first arrived.

I joined the other residents who had recently come out of *detox* like me. We gathered in the cafeteria for each of the three meals. We could get snacks throughout the day if we wanted to.

The first week passed without much incident. Again, that's because I was trying my best to get myself together. When I looked in the mirror, I was horrified at the woman staring back at me. I looked a hot mess! No way was this acceptable for me. Not when I was used to being the best and looking my best at all times.

That evening I went through my wardrobe and matched up my outfits and shoes, got my makeup bag with all of my goodies inside, and vowed to myself that it was time I pull it together.

The next morning, when I went to the cafeteria for breakfast, I know heads swiveled. I was looking good, dressed to impress with my make-up laid, and hair on point. Treatment facility or not, I was going to look like I had stepped off of a runway floor.

I wish I could say the next thirty days went smoothly. They didn't. After I got over *detox,* and started attending group therapy sessions, individual counseling sessions and one AA meeting after another, I was sick of the whole program. I didn't think I needed this. I wasn't like some of the other people who were in the program. Listening to them tell their stories, made me sort of turn up my nose at them. They sounded like deadbeat drunks, stupid drunks, and just downright alcoholic bums. That was not me. Okay, so I had a black out spell or two. Did that make me an alcoholic? What about sleeping with random strangers? My list of questions gave me pause rather than make me believe I wasn't an alcoholic. Quite the contrary, if I gave the answers to my own questions, I would willingly admit poor judgment on my part, but an alcoholic? No.

As much as I hated being locked away from my normal everyday life, I was feeling better. My desire for a drink was passing and my urge wasn't as strong. Attending meetings around the clock, learning the twelve steps, and intermingling with some of the other residents, helped me through the program.

It also helped when I met a cutie named Gerard. Gerard was in the facility as a resident before I arrived.

I first locked eyes with that hunk at dinnertime the second week I was there. He came and sat at the same table where me and two other residents were seated.

The other two residents already knew him. He introduced himself to me.

"Hi," he said, extending his hand for a shake. "I'm Gerard. You're new here, right?"

"Yes," I nodded and briefly smiled. "I'm Belinda."

"Belinda, it's a pleasure to meet you."

From that point forward it was game on. Listening to him talk and engage with us endeared me to him. I was getting hornier by the second. This guy was *all of that and a bag of chips,* and I wanted the bag!

That evening, before we left out of the cafeteria, Gerard approached me.

"Hey, what do you say we meet outside later, on the deck? I'd like to get to know you better. I mean, if that's cool with you."

"Sure," I told him. No way was I going to pass up the chance to get to know him better or vice versa. I wanted to see what he really had going on. I flashed a flirty smile at him and winked.

"Okay, meet me in an hour, at seven o'clock. That work for you?"

"It does," I answered. "See you at seven."

I swished off, making sure I put a little extra swish as I walked away, knowing he was looking. *What man could deny all of this? Not one.* I thought and chuckled as I went into my room.

My roommate was lying on her bed, reading a book. She and I didn't say a whole lot to each other. I mean, me and women didn't always see eye to eye. Most females were jealous of me 'cause I had it going on. My roommate was a dorky, older white haired lady. She was short and chunky, probably in her sixties. I can't be sure. Either way, her name was Judy. She said this was her third time seeking treatment for alcohol. I hated to hear that, but that was not going to be me. I was not going to end up being a sixty something year old woman addicted to alcohol or drugs.

I met Gerard that evening. It felt good to be able to sit down and laugh and talk with a charmer like Gerard. He was not only good looking, he had great conversation. I tried to get a sneak peak of his package but I couldn't without making it obvious. I would bide my time.

106

"So, what do you like to do when you aren't getting drunk?" Gerard jokingly asked.

"Oh, I like shopping. What girl doesn't? I like movies, especially thrillers and dramas, mixed with a little hot romance."

"Is that right?" Gerard countered, eyebrows raised. "Romance, huh? Hot, huh? Is this hot enough for you? Or am I being too presumptuous if I took the liberty to do this." He pulled me into his arms and pressed his thick juicy looking lips on mine. His lips felt like a soft cushiony pillow. His kiss was sweet and full of fiery passion. Before I realized it, I felt myself becoming aroused by his touch. I couldn't stop him; didn't want to stop him either. His hands traveled up and down the course of my body, my neck, and my breasts. When he dropped to his knees I thought I would pass out from the pleasure he was evoking in me. I wanted him so badly. He didn't deny me.

Gerard looked around as if he was scanning the outside space to see if we were being watched. He got up from off of his knees, and pulled me by the hand.

"Come on, I think I know somewhere we can be alone without anyone catching us. You game?"

"Yes, I'm game."

I followed him back inside. Gerard led me to an elevator, a freight elevator. Pressing the button, the elevator door opened. We stepped inside. Gerard pushed a button to the basement.

As soon as the elevator doors closed, Gerard scooped me into his arms again and resumed kissing me and arousing me to a fever pitch as he explored the crevices of my body.

I was growing a little bit nervous, but not to the point where I wanted him to turn back. The elevator came to an abrupt stop and the doors opened.

Pulling me out of his embrace, he took hold of my hand again and led me up the quiet deserted hall to another door. The door said PRIVATE.

"Where are we?" I asked.

"I found this place one night on one of my explorations. I know how to get inside," he assured me.

He pulled out a key from his pants pocket; and put it inside the lock, the door opened. He grabbed me again, like we were two little kids playing *hide and seek*.

Closing the door behind him, he pushed me up against it and started his passionate kisses and touches all over again, before suddenly stopping and pulling back.

"Wait here," he said, and dashed away and over to a corner.

I watched as he went to a cabinet that stood about five feet. He moved the cabinet back from the wall by a few inches. I could tell from the way he was breathing, the file cabinet was not easy to move. It shook a little, unsteady, but did not topple over.

Gerard, after pulling the cabinet out a few inches, bent down and reached behind the cabinet.

I gasped, throwing a hand over my mouth when I saw him standing upright and holding a brown bag in his hand. I already guessed what it might be. I was right. When he came over to where I was, he opened the bag and allowed me to peek inside. It was a pint of Hennessey. My eyes grew large with excitement and my mouth began to water.

He opened the bottle and right away turned it up to his lips and took a deep swallow before passing it to me.

I hesitated. I had come a long way, well on second thought, not too long of a way, but long enough. I'd gone through that nasty *detox* and here I was, clean and sober for the past eleven days. Did I really want to give it all up for one drink? Was I strong enough to take just one drink and not a second or a third?

I slightly turned my head away, surprising even myself. "I don't think so," I told Gerard. "I've come too far to turn around now."

"Suit *yourself,*" he said. "I'm definitely not one to force a lady to do anything she doesn't want to do," he said in a seductive voice, before he started kissing me again.

He momentarily stopped to close the bottle of Hennessey and put it back. Returning to me, he led me again by my hand and over to another area in the room where there were linens and blankets. This was the first time I realized that we were in some type of utility room or supply closet. There were a number of shelves with a variety of products lining them. This particular area where we were standing was where they had shelves and shelves, columns and columns of sheets, spreads, and more.

He pulled several sheets and blankets off the shelves and threw them down on the floor before refocusing his attention on me.

Gerard said little, but his actions said it all. "You ready for this?" he asked, talking to me in a husky, sexual tone, almost like a groan.

I answered with moans of my own. It had been a while since I'd had the comfort of a man, and so far Gerard fit the bill of just the kind of man I needed…and wanted.

His speech was muffled by the effects of the Hennessey but I knew exactly what he wanted without him saying another word.

He gently eased me down on top of the pile of linen. I trembled in his arms when he kissed the moist hollow in my throat. From there his lips touched mine, featherlike. His fingers fumbled with his *hoodie* as he pulled it over his head.

I felt the thundering of his heart pounding against my breasts. Next, he pulled my shirt over my head with one hand, using the other hand to tug at my pants.

Giving him help, I peeled off my pants and panties. I had on no bra so I was free when he pulled off my shirt. In return, I started tugging and pulling down his jogging pants until they were gathered around his knees. He kicked them off without missing a beat.

I released a faint cry, as the sensual heat of our naked skin meshed. He pulled me firmly into the spread of his legs. I arched my hips to meet him, as if our bodies understood the rhythm of our lovemaking.

Gerard and I continued our almost nightly rendezvous for the remainder of the time I was in the treatment facility. After that first night, Gerard never asked me if I wanted to sneak and drink with him again. I wanted to, I can't lie, but I didn't. After the first three or four times, and when he had finished off the bottle of Hennessey, he didn't go behind the cabinet again.

I could deal with that because the brother was laying it on me and made me forget all about drinking. I laughed sometimes at the thought of finding a master lover like Gerard in an alcohol and drug facility. That was something I could write a book about…if I was a writer, that is.

The remainder of my time came and went in a hurry. When it was time for me to leave, the facility made a big thing of it. We gathered in the auditorium. It reminded me of a high school graduation. It was enjoyable and fun, if I must say so myself. I had made it through the program. Veronica, my father and Lucinda were there. Gerard and five other men and women were seated on the front row with me. We were the honorees.

All in all, the program was one that I will never forget.

"The big test starts now," Lucinda cautioned me when I stepped outside the walls of the treatment facility.

I nodded in agreement. "Yes, I know. I hope I'm ready."

"Only you know the answer to that, Belinda. If you want to be ready you have to make sure you stay ready. Do not allow anything or *anyone* to steer you off track."

At that moment, I could have sworn I saw Lucinda give Gerard an evil eye. Gerard was standing nearby, but he was talking to someone who I assumed was part of his outside support team. Anyway, she looked over at him and then back at me. I said nothing about what I thought I saw. Instead, I let her keep talking. She always had positive things to say, and I listened to her as much as possible.

"If you ever need me, I do not care what time of day or night, you pick up that phone and call me. I know they told you that you should be attending an AA meeting every day, two or three times a day. Do you understand?"

"Yes, I understand, and I plan to follow every rule they've taught us. I have my Twelve and Twelve book, plus some other essential tools they told me to use."

"This will work, Belinda. You just have to work the program. The Twelve and Twelve book is your Bible. It lays out the principles by which A.A. members recover and by which the fellowship functions. It teaches us about our new way of life and the traditions of AA. I want you to succeed," Lucinda assured me.

"You ready, pumpkin," Daddy said as he walked up with Veronica.

"Yes, I'm ready."

I embraced Lucinda again before parting ways. "I'll call you later," I told her and walked away with my daddy and Veronica to his car.

At home, I couldn't wait to inhale the fragrance of just being home. The yard, I could tell, had been freshly cut and manicured. Inside the house I was welcomed with that *I'm home* scent greeting me. The house was immaculate. I went to the fridge; It was packed with all of the foods I loved. I walked through the house, slowly, like this was my first time entering it. I broke out in tears. I guess it really had hit me. I was home. Like Dorothy in *The Wiz* I'd made it full circle through some tough times, some dangerous times, even some life-threatening times, but here I was. I was ready for a change. This time I meant it. I was for real ready to make a new start. No one could stop me now, not even myself.

Chapter Six
Now or Never

The wind was nippy and blowing cold streaks which seemed to stage a personal war with my leopard print scarf. I knew this was one battle my scarf and I would have to win. The aroma of hot Mocha Latte permeating from the nearby Starbucks was too much for me to resist. Perhaps my favorite Arabian Mocha Java would not only warm my body, but maybe it could warm my soul. Wouldn't that be some kind of miracle? I couldn't help but smile at the thought.

As usual, the Starbucks was jam packed with people whose lives were busier or perhaps more complicated than mine, I assumed. Why else would we hustle and bustle to get to a coffee shop for a daily boost of Macchiatos, Frappuccinos or Espressos? There's just no explaining it. Now, just like the others, here I stood. There was a time I would be standing in a different line - the liquor store line. Lord, it's amazing my mouth still begins to water at the saying of the word liquor. Awe, yes, a nice tall vodka tonic would be great right about now; in my past.

"Excuse me please," a voice ahead of me in line, interrupted my devilish thoughts.

"I ordered a Frappucino with extra whip cream, but look at this. There's no whip cream at all." The mild mannered lady's voice sounded familiar to me but that wasn't unusual. I hear familiar voices all day and everyday from people I know. There's the all too familiar voice of my support group counselor, my Mama and some of my friends.

"Mam, I'm sorry," the gentleman behind the counter apologized with obvious sincerity. "Let me get you another one."

"Thanks a lot. I appreciate it." She answered without as much as a sound of irritability.

I know that voice. I strained to look around the crowd in front of me. I couldn't hear the lady any longer, but I saw the back of her head as she moved to the other side of the counter toward the checkout line. No, it couldn't be. My heart began to pace rapidly before I had my first Mocha

Java! The voice, the head, both equaled Candace. I inched closer toward the counter, patiently waiting for my turn.

When I stepped forward to get a better look, she disappeared. I looked carefully all around the busy coffee shop. To no avail, there was no sign of her. I only turned my head for a second and she was gone. That couldn't have been Candace, I tried to convince myself. Why would she be here in New York and of all places a Starbucks; Candace never cared for coffee.

After the thought of the possibility of running into Candace, my mind drifted back. I began to reminisce on our friendship. Candace, my best friend, my confidante, the one whom I'd hurt with my childish and immature games. It had been years since I last saw her. The last I heard she and her kids moved back home with her parents, years had passed since then. I destroyed our friendship, all because of my selfishness and my low self-esteem. How could I do her the way I did?

Finally it was my turn to order.

"I'll have a large Arabian Mocha Java please."

"Yes, *Mam*," will that be all for you this morning?"

I nodded my head in an up and down motion while taking another look around for the woman I thought to be Candace

"Here you go, Mam. That'll be $5.75."

I knew the exact price all too well so I handed the gentleman the exact change. The refreshing taste savored my taste buds. I scurried toward the door after pulling my scarf closer around my neck before facing the fierce cold again. I gave a quick glace behind to ensure I wasn't being followed; the city life can bring on paranoia. I felt the warmth of the Java spreading through my gloved hand, and slowly it circulated my insides as I gobbled a sip while walking to speed along the busy sidewalk of Manhattan.

A sense of relief and calmness began to overtake me. I knew a Mocha Java would never take the place of a drink of whiskey, but it satisfied me to the point where I began to feel relaxed. My counselor always said we should replace our addiction with something else, or we will open ourselves up for the addiction to come back, it will stage a war of greater force against our willpower. Arabian Mocha Java was my replacement. I don't know if it was the winy taste it had or it's bitter sweetness. All I knew it was delicious and it somewhat satisfied my craving for alcohol.

I'd rushed to Starbucks every single day. Some folks probably would say I'm still an addict; only this time my Mocha Java wasn't eating away at my liver or threatening my sense of reasoning. I glanced at my watch; it was

7:45 a.m. I was right on time with only about a half a block to go before reaching my AA support group meeting. I wondered if I'd always been a drunk or an alky as my fellow AA constituents identified themselves to one another. I refused to think that way. It was too scary of a thought. Labeling me as a drunk was something I didn't want to accept. I didn't know if I could face another label-not yet anyway.

"Hey girl, come on in here. I'm glad to see you," Tamara said. Tamara had been a recovering alky for over seventeen and a half years. She was one of the head counselors of the support group. Alcohol was the reason she lost her husband; six figure salary, and a luxurious home in Connecticut. Now she had dedicated her life to helping others get up on their feet and back to living a gainful and fruitful life without alcohol.

"I see you're holding on to that coffee aren't you honey?"

"Tamara, how many times do I have to tell you, this ain't coffee? It's more than that. It's Arabian Mocha Java."

"Call it what you want Belinda, but it's still coffee."

I laughed at Tamara's all too familiar, but incorrect observation. Anything that was hot and in a Starbucks cup was coffee to her. She never quite understood how Starbucks made itself a multi-million dollar industry by applying fancy names, and a sprinkle of chocolate or whip cream here and there to what was nothing more than coffee. She didn't care where the coffee beans came from. To Tamara, coffee was coffee.

"Good morning, Belinda," the rest of the group members called out one by one.

"Hi everyone."

We all chatted a few minutes while we waited for the others to drift in out of the morning cold.

"Good morning, all. Let's take our seats and get started," Tamara called out at exactly 8:30.

"Belinda will you lead the group in our mission statement this morning?" she asked.

"Sure thing, it'll be my pleasure. Let's stand."

In unison we began to recite our pledge:

Alcoholics Anonymous is a fellowship of men and women that shares their experiences, strengths and hopes with each other. We hope we may solve our common problems and help others to recover from alcoholism. The only requirement for membership is the desire to stop drinking. There are no dues or fees for AA membership; we are self-supporting through our own contributions. We do not engage in any controversy, neither endorse nor oppose any causes. Our primary purpose is to stay sober and help other alcoholics achieve sobriety.

"Now let us recite the AA prayer," Tamera gracefully said.

Again, I led the group in the prayer that had become an intricate part of living my life of sobriety.

"God, grant me the serenity to accept the things I cannot change, courage to change the things I can, and the wisdom to know the difference. You may now be seated. Thank you group, Tamara, it's all yours."

"Thank you Belinda for opening up this morning's group session. How's everyone doing this morning?"

Tamara always had a genuine concern for the group. When she asked if there was something she could do to help, she meant it with all of her heart. I don't think I could have survived without her support. I'd been to several group meetings in the Bronx, Manhattan and even in Long Island, none of them were quite as good as the group led by Tamara.

One by one we shared our stories and discussed the lows and highs of the previous week. When it came to be my turn, I don't know why I started talking about Candace. Something within my spirit took over and for the first time in my life, I released all the pent up emotions of anger, hurt and disgust I felt towards myself. I was pretty on the outside, but I felt ugly and evil within.

I had always used my beauty to destroy other people's lives. Once I began talking, it was as if I had unclogged my speech or something. I couldn't stop! I shared with the group my true feelings about my life. I don't know why it happened this Saturday morning at this particular AA meeting. All I know is it just happened. The *Well* had been burst open after all the years I tried to keep it shut down. I continued to talk. . .

"There's a girl back in my hometown. Shelia is her name. She was seriously injured because of the naiveté and vein games we played and because of the way we treated others." I went on, pouring myself out to the group.

"Just this morning I thought I ran into another old friend. Her name is Candace. She was my best friend and how did I repay her friendship? I'll tell you how. I slept with her husband. I had one too many drinks and I slept with my best friend's husband.

When I betrayed her, my life appeared to spiral downwards, and I blamed it on my drinking. But you know what everybody? I'm tired of blaming it on the alcohol. I did it! I ruined not only my life but hers too.

This morning, standing in line at Starbucks, I thought I saw her. I can't be sure because I never saw the woman's face but there was something about her voice and the build of the woman. By the time I moved closer to get a better look, she was gone. I know it is unlikely Candace would be in Manhattan in the same Starbucks I was in, but there was something unusual about the woman.

Maybe my higher power placed it in my mind so I could finally share my story with you. For the first time in a long time, I feel free. I feel cleansed. I don't look at myself the same way as I used to. I believe I can finally forgive myself and I couldn't have done it without each of you. Now, if I ever do see Candace again, I believe I can face her and truly ask for her forgiveness.

Alcohol had me blinded. Alcohol made me numb to the feelings of others. It controlled me, ran my life and finally ruined me. Now I've been given a second chance at living and I'm not going to blow it. I know I'm an alcoholic. I'll always be an alcoholic but I also know I'm a recovering alcoholic. It's no longer my God. It's not my friend. It's my enemy and I'll fight against it with every breath I have left in my body."

When I finally took my seat I felt exhausted. I felt as if I had been lifting hundred pound weights and was tired from carrying them around for so long. I couldn't wait to get back home and curl around the fireplace. I wanted to snuggle against my cat, MochaJa, who I had decided to name after my favorite cup of Java, and drift off to sleep. I had experienced an exhausting morning. After all, I had just released a heavy load.

ℰℭ

A few weeks had passed from the time I saw the strange but seemingly familiar lady at Starbucks. My mind had settled back on my everyday affairs. I felt a new energy after what I called my freedom speech at AA along with a new zest for living and loving. Only this time it wasn't a sexual loving I wanted to give, it was a spiritual love. I wanted to give myself to someone in a mentoring way, to help pull them up when they hit rock bottom like I once did.

I poured myself into my volunteer work and spent more time at the AA Center listening and counseling other recovering *alkys*. I'd even talked to Tamara about starting some type of self-esteem class at the center for the members who wanted to learn some beauty and fashion tips. Tamara thought it was a great idea. All I had to do was put it in the form of a

115

proposal and we would go from there she said. I made it one of my main projects.

Every night when I made it home, I'd fix myself a hot cup of latte, feed MochaJa, and take a warm, relaxing shower. Then I'd curl up in the bed and begin formalizing my proposal. I'd been working on it for a couple of weeks when I ran into a jam. I knew if I wanted this proposal to knock the socks off of Tamara, the other counselors and directors, I had to get help from an expert.

I thought about my old friend Jim Lassiter. Jim was a recovering alcoholic and had been sober for almost four years. I'd met him when I used to attend meetings in the Bronx. I began rummaging through my Rolodex searching for his number. He was a grant writer so I knew he was the one who could help me pull this off and make a dynamic impression.

"Hi, may I speak to Jim please."

"Yes, hold on," the teenaged girl said. "Daddy, it's for you," she screamed.

A few seconds later, the heavy charming voice answered the call.

"Hello. Jim speaking."

"Hi, Jim. It's Belinda. How are you man?"

"Belinda, it's great to hear from you. I couldn't be better. Things are really going great for me and the family. What about you?"

"I'm doing well myself, Jim. I hope I didn't catch you at a bad time but I really need your help." I could hear a heavy sigh over the phone. I knew Jim thought I was calling because I had a relapse. Things were just too quiet.

"Jim, don't worry. It's not about alcohol. I have two years under my belt now. Two years since I've taken a drink, Jim! Can you believe that?" I was ecstatic just saying it out loud.

"I'm proud of you Belinda. One day at a time. That's what it takes Belinda. One day at a time. I was getting a little worried when you said you needed my help. Of course, I would have been willing to help you if you were in a tight spot and having a rough night, but I'm glad that's not the reason you called. By the way, what is the reason you called, tonight Belinda? I don't think I've talked to you but a couple of times since you left the meetings in the Bronx. How has things been working out for you?

"Just great, I'm attending a fabulous support group here in Manhattan, which is the reason for my call. I'm writing a proposal and I need your help. Do you think you can give me a few pointers?"

"Why sure. Why don't you take my email address and send me what you have so far. I'll look over it and give you some feedback.

"Jim thanks so much, you're one in a million."

With Jim's help and advice, the proposal was a big hit. The directors and counselors loved my idea of teaching etiquette, fashion and beauty pointers to the women. I even organized a small aerobics class that met twice a week. For once in my life, I felt like I was fulfilling the purpose designed for my life. It felt good not to be using others, but instead helping someone else.

When I left the afternoon group session, I headed for my evening dose of Mocha Java. A mist was beginning to sprinkle over the congested streets and sidewalks. I wanted to hurry before a storm settled in. The air was well below the freezing mark. Al Roker had predicted a snowstorm and freezing rain for later in the evening. I had to hurry home. There wasn't going to be much time before the city would be pummeled with the beautiful, yet dangerous, beds of snow and ice.

I burst into the Starbucks, ordered my Java and bolted for the corner grocery located a block and a half away from my house. I was only going to pick up some cat food for MochaJa and get a few items to make a salad to go along with the steak I was going to prepare for my dinner. I could always call in and get some groceries delivered if I became snowed in. That's one of the great things about New York I'd come to love. It reminded me of a giant room service. If I wanted groceries or a movie or a gourmet meal all I had to do was pick up a telephone and order it and within a half hour or so, it would arrive at my doorstep.

"Hello Mr. Jerman."

"Hia, Beeleena. You're *cumeen* to *geet zum grozrees* before the blizzard *settlez* in, yeah?"

Mr. Jerman was of Mexican descent. His heavy accent made it difficult to understand him at times.

"Yes sir, just a couple of items."

I was distracted by Mr. Jerman and also trying to hurry along to get the items I needed. I also wanted to stop and get a couple of books to read since I may be snowed in. Reading was one of my passions. It allowed me to escape into worlds I'd often dreamed of, where life and love was grand and gracious. I grabbed my items and paid for them hurriedly. And then I went a couple of doors down to the Soul of Man Bookstore.

"Excuse me." I didn't mean to bump into the person on the other side of my two grocery bags but I couldn't see in front of me as I rounded the corner heading toward the fiction section of the store.

117

"No problem." Just as the voice allowed me to pass, I froze. That voice sounded familiar. It was the same voice I heard at Starbucks a couple of months ago. My heart began to palpitate loudly.

I was afraid to turn and look. It couldn't be her. It just couldn't be. I forced myself to take a step back before turning my head in the direction of the melodic voice. My mind raced back quickly and I could hear Candace screaming and yelling at me when she saw me and Emanuel embraced in a tight passionate kiss. I heard the screams of anger and hurt and disgust.

I grabbed my ears trying to block out the horrid and shameful sounds of the past. I don't remember dropping my grocery bags. The anguish was too much. Candace, I'm sorry. I could see myself pleading with her, begging her to listen to me.

"Excuse me. Let me help you." The voice was below me. I looked down and saw the petite looking lady with coal black hair bending down picking up my cat food.

"Oh, thank you. I feel like such an idiot. I knelt down to gather my other items. When our eyes met I thought I would pass out. Instead I froze. I don't know how long our eyes locked into each other's. I don't know how long we stayed there on our knees in the quaint bookstore. I could see the freezing rain beginning to fall as my eyes took in the figure before me. I could feel my pulse racing and my mouth drying. It was her; Candace.

"Belinda! Belinda, my God it's you!"

"Candace. I…I…don't know what to say. Except…maybe hel….hello. It's been so long since I've seen you." I couldn't help but stutter. Here we were, actually facing each other and I was speechless.

"I believe the first thing we need to be doing is getting the rest of your things back into your bag."

"Sure, you're…you're right." I gathered my other items while Candace placed them into brown paper bags.

"Thanks Candace. How…how are you and what brings you here to Manhattan?"

"We've been living in the Bronx for about three months now. My husband's family is from Manhattan, that's why I'm here today.

"I thought I saw you at the Starbucks at 112th and Broadway a few weeks ago. I just couldn't get a good look at the woman at the time. The woman's voice was so distinct just like yours."

"I'm sure it was me. Whenever I'm in Manhattan I go and get my father-in-law a Frappucino. He loves Starbucks and since he's 88 years old and not as quick as he once was, I like to bring him one of his favorite treats whenever I can. I've actually taken him there a time or two so he can sit and relax and reminisce about old times. My husband has such a wonderful family. How about you? How are you doing Belinda?"

"I'm…I'm fine Candace. I've been living here for the past four years. I have a home a couple of blocks over. I guess you can say I'm still loaded. I teach an aerobics class and a beauty and etiquette class too. I live with my cat MochaJa and I believe I can now honestly call myself a Yorker," I let out a nervous laugh. "Things are just fine for me. Oh, look; the storm looks like it's heading our way." I saw the freezing rain coming down harder.

"It sure is. I guess I'd better get going."

"Where do your husband's parents' live if you don't mind my asking?" Cautiously, I said to Candace. I didn't want to appear like I was prying. I thought I might be able to see her again so we could talk. I needed the chance to explain my past actions and win her forgiveness. I wanted to let go of the past and move on with my life.

"They live on 48th and Vine. I'm headed back that way now."

"I live at 52nd and Hepburn. Look, Candace. I'd really like a chance to see you again and sit down and talk to you. I have so much to say to you.

"Look Belinda. I hope you don't think you have to bring up the past because there's no need. As you can see, I've moved on with my life and so have you. I have a wonderful husband and great in-laws. The children are fine and I'm happy with my life. You don't owe me any explanations or anything so please…"

I quickly interrupted her.

"No, Candace I do owe you a lot…a whole lot. I need to be able to talk to you. I promise, if you'll just hear me out! Afterwards I won't bother you ever again. Please, Candace."

She hesitated for what seemed like an eternity to me. I didn't' blame her one bit. I had been the one to betray our friendship and our trust. I was prepared for her to tell me she didn't want to talk to me about anything and then she would bid me farewell. Candace hesitated as if trying to make sure she chose her words wisely.

"I…I guess it won't hurt to talk to you at least one time. I just don't want to get entangled in a lot of old memories Belinda. I hope you understand where I'm coming from."

She sounded so fragile. I could hear the apprehension in her voice. Yet, she wasn't cruel or mean to me. I wouldn't' have blamed her one bit if she had been.

"I know we both need to head to our destinations before we get snowed in at this bookstore." Candace allowed a smile to cross her round smooth olive face.

"You're right Candace. Let me give you my number." I tore a piece of the brown paper bag, grabbed an ink pen off the counter top and wrote down my number. "Here you go Candace. Just give me a call when you have some time. I'll even come to the Bronx if you'd like. We could meet over coffee or lunch."

"No, that won't be necessary. I'll just give you a call when I'm here in Manhattan. Then we can decide where to meet. Look, I'm sorry Belinda, but I really got to get going. It was good seeing you again."

"Yeah, it's been good seeing you too, Candace."

The bell at the top of the door rang as we both stepped out into the frigid New York air. Again we went our separate ways, in opposite directions.

I realized as I approached the safety of my home, Candace hadn't bothered to give me her number. I felt like I would never hear from her again unless we by chance bumped into each other somewhere. How could I think to blame Candace if she never wanted to see me again?

The New York winter passed and just as I expected, I didn't hear from Candace. For the first several days after our encounter, I continuously check my messages hoping she would have called. After the first week and a half, I felt she didn't want to have anything to do with me. It seemed like I wouldn't get the chance to tell her how sorry I was for messing up her life, but things were still going pretty good for me.

The Three E Class was going pretty darn good. I chose the name Three E that stands for Exercise, Etiquette and Esteem. The women at the AA support group loved it! We started out with seven members and in just a few short months the class had grown to over 35 members. Every week there was more signing up from various support groups throughout the city. Tamara wanted me to write another proposal to start a Three E class in the Bronx. I was ecstatic. Finally my life was coming together.

I remembered a counselor or recovering alky telling me long ago during my drinking days all things work together for the good to those who love God. I don't remember where the saying come from, but I think it's somewhere in the Bible. I didn't believe the person talking to me at the time had any idea what they were saying. Now things did seem to be working out for my own good. That's another thing I made up in my mind to do; get more involved in church. I had no idea where to go because it had been so many years since I stepped foot inside a church door. I decided the next time one of the group members invited me to church I would definitely go.

I heard the phone ringing as I was turning the key to the door. *If only MochaJa could answer my calls, she'd pay for her room and board*, I thought. Just as I sat the grocery bag down on the foyer table, the phone was heading into its fourth ring. One more ring and my answering machine would automatically pick up, and that's exactly what happened. I heard the sound of my voice and promised once again to change my message.

Hi, you've reached 555-4609. Please leave a message at the sound of the beep, and someone will get back to you as soon as we can. Beep.

"Hello, I hope I've dialed the right number. Belinda, this is Candace. When you have a moment, please give me a call at...."

I rushed over to the phone before the voice on the other end had a chance to finish.

"Candace...Candace, hi it's me!"

"Hi Belinda, I wasn't sure if I had the right number or not. I ran across this number on a torn brown paper bag and decided I would give it a call. I remembered you writing your number down but the message on the answering machine didn't sound like you."

"I know it. Several people have told me that," I said. "I keep telling myself to change it but then I get caught up in doing something else and never get around to it."

I don't know how I felt actually hearing Candace's voice on the other end. I felt awkward, nervous or just plain old embarrassed. What would I say to her, now that she had actually called but why did she wait so long?

"Candace, it's good to hear from you girl. Are you still in Manhattan? That's where you said you were living now isn't it?

"I'm in Manhattan on and off. We live in the Bronx. My husband's mother lives in Manhattan."

"That's right. I knew Manhattan came in there somewhere. Didn't you tell me that both of your husband's parents lived in Manhattan?"

"Oh yeah, I sure did, but I believe it was a couple of weeks after I saw you when my husband's father passed. That's one of the main reasons I didn't get a chance to call you. I've been quite busy getting things worked out with my father-in-law's estate, helping my mother-in-law plus helping my husband in his ministry.

I didn't recall Candace telling me anything about her husband being in the ministry.

"*Ministry?* I didn't know your husband was a minister," I responded with a bit of curiosity, I'm sure resonated in my voice.

"Yes. He started a youth ministry at a small church in the Bronx. We've been busy organizing youth sessions, bible study programs and several other activities for the youth in the community and in the church. The whole mission of the ministry is to reach youth who are not churchgoers and share the gospel with them. I'm sure I don't have to tell you; there are a lot of our youth today not only in the Bronx but all over the world who have gotten involved in gangs, drugs and violence. Just look at all the negativity we've been hearing about the violence in the schools. My husband loved young people and he feels like his calling is to help them make better lives for themselves."

"Candace, that's great to hear."

I could tell she was really enthused with the work her husband was doing. When we first met, Candace didn't want to hear anything about church, God or religion. She and Emanuel loved to party all the time. That was actually how she and I became as close as we did, partying, hanging out and just kicking it.

The only thing about Candace is she didn't allow the alcohol to control her like I did. I never would've imagined she would've made a 360-degree turn around and then to top of it all off, married a minister. Whew! Listening to her was mind-boggling.

"Thanks Belinda. I'm happy and I'm truly blessed. The reason I'm calling is to invite you to church, that is if you would like to visit with us."

I know I hesitated at her invitation. I've heard folks say God has a sense of humor. This was certainly one of those times since I had been telling myself to get to church. I just wasn't expecting to go this soon. How could I say no to Candace? I drew in a deep breath and let the words come out.

"Sure, Candace. I...I'd like that. Just tell me when and where and I'll be there."

"I'd like to invite you to come out this Sunday. Our praise and worship service starts promptly at 10:45 a.m. I promise we won't keep you there all day," she laughed.

"Okay. Tell me the name of the church and I'll see you on this Sunday."

"It's Golden Gate Outreach Ministries. I'll be looking for you."

"Candace, what's your last name now?" I didn't want to get to the church only knowing her former name."

"Karuso," she replied. "Candace Karuso. I won't hold you any longer Belinda. I have some things I must attend to. I'll see you Sunday."

"You sure will, Candace. Goodbye now."

When I hung up the phone, I glanced over at my caller ID. The box read, 'out of area.' Candace had done it again. She didn't volunteer to give me her telephone number. Maybe she forgot, I told myself. The other half of me knew it was intentional. Inviting me to come to church was one thing but trusting me with her phone number and address was stretching it just a tad bit too far.

I caught the subway to the Bronx. I was up at 4:30 in the morning pacing the floor. I tried calling information, hoping to get a number for Candace so I could back out of going to church. I just didn't know if this was the best thing to be doing. What if Candace had some ulterior motive for inviting me? What if she had some scheme arranged to try and pay me back for hurting her? I needed a drink. I needed a drink badly. I picked up the phone and called Casey, my AA partner.

"Casey, hi, it's Belinda."

"Belinda, tell me what's wrong, girl," she responded with sleep still in her voice.

"I want a drink Casey. I need a drink bad." Casey and I had been each other's AA support persons for over a year. I could rely on her to be there for me during those times I felt like I would give in to the call of alcohol. Like me, Casey would reach out to me if she needed a shoulder to lean on. She reminded me how alcohol had ruined both of our lives. She told me to focus on my future and look back on how far I'd come. I felt the urge to drink subsiding with each sentence she spoke.

"Look how well the Three E class is going Belinda?" Casey said patiently. "Think about what you've come through and how much you've persevered. You've given so many of us a positive outlet. We can't turn back now. We can't allow alcohol to take control of us-not ever again Belinda."

After talking and listening to Casey for almost forty-five minutes I felt I had crossed over the hurdle and the urge passed.

"Thanks Casey."

"That's what it's all about Belinda. You know it. Now go on to church and stop thinking about the past. Have a good time and send a prayer up for me." Casey said.

"I can do that, girl. I just hope it gets through. I'll talk to you later, Casey."

I hung up the phone, went over to my closet and grabbed the navy two-piece skirt set I had picked out the night before. I climbed in the shower and allowed the hot jet stream of water relax my mind and body.

When I made it to the church, my watch showed that it was exactly 10:47. I walked up the steps with a nervous precaution. As I pulled open the door leading into the sanctuary, I was greeted on the other side by two greeters or ushers.

"Come right this way," one of them said. "Would you like to sit up in the front?" she whispered.

I shook my head to let her know that I wouldn't. Instead I sat in the middle. I looked around for Candace but didn't spot her anywhere in the middle size sanctuary. Just as I continued to look around, I felt someone ease on the bench beside me.

"Belinda, I'm so glad you made it!" Candace's voice was the loudest I had heard her speak in some years but even then it was still soft and welcoming.

"Did you have a hard time finding us?" she asked.

"No, not at all," I whispered.

"Don't be nervous Belinda. Everyone here is quite nice and they'll make you feel right at home. I'm going to sit here with you, okay?"

"Good. Thanks Candace."

The organist began to play and a group of singers approached the pulpit singing "Lord we lift your name on high....Lord we love to sing your praises...I'm so glad you came to save me...."

Candace began to sway and clap to the music along with the other members of the congregation. Before I realized it, service had ended and several of the congregation came over to introduce themselves and welcome me. Candace introduced me as a friend of hers before she moved to New York City. I didn't believe she still considered me as a friend, until then.

"Did you have a good time, Belinda?" Candace asked me as she walked me outside into the sunshine.

"Yes, I most certainly did. The message was right on time for me too. I have been telling myself every day I was going to start attending church. When you called, I thought it was rather strange that you invited me to church. Then when I came today, the preacher was talking about giving our time to God and being active in church. I guess God does want me to get my house in order, huh Candace?"

"You're right about that. He sure does and this is the first step. I hope you come back to visit with us or at least find you somewhere close by in Manhattan where you can go. Since I've become a Christian, I can't tell you how much my life has changed."

Candace continued to introduce me to her friends as they came by hugging her and saying hello. Out of nowhere, a tall, muscular built man came up behind Candace and grabbed her around her tiny waist.

"Hi sweetheart," he said bending down kissing her on the side of her neck. Candace blushed and turned around toward him.

"Belinda, this is my husband...Elliott...Minister Elliott Karuso. Elliott this is Belinda. The lady I was telling you about from back when I lived in Rochester."

He stretched out his thick, olive skinned hands towards mine. I thought I caught a glimpse of uncertainty gleam from Candace's eye as my hand reached out to meet his. His hand embraced mine with firmness as he took his other hand and placed it over mine.

"It's nice to meet you Minister Karuso."

I felt like I was on stage for the entire world to see how I would react. I don't know how Elliott looked. I was too afraid for my eyes to meet his. I didn't want to give Candace any reason to think I would ever betray her trust again.

"Please call me Elliott. Did you enjoy the service Belinda?" His voice was strong and rang with confidence. His heavy northern accent reminded me of a professional radio personality.

"Yes I really did. I'm glad Candace invited me. Candace, I don't mean to have to rush off but I'm supposed to meet some friends later this afternoon."

"Oh, okay Belinda. We understand don't we Elliott?"

"*Of course.* Maybe you'll come and join us again and afterwards Candace and I could take you out for brunch or something."

"That sounds good to me," I replied sounding like a nervous little prude. I couldn't believe myself.

"Thanks again for inviting me Candace."

"I'll give you a call Belinda and maybe we can meet for lunch or something when I come to Manhattan."

"I'd like that Candace. Bye now." Man, was I glad that was over. I hated to lie right after coming out of church, but I knew I couldn't stay around them any longer without showing how uneasy I felt. I had to talk to Candace. I had to get the chance to ask her to forgive me. Somehow I knew that time was approaching quicker than I expected.

125

"Hi MochaJa baby," I crooned while she curled up around my ankles meowing, "Mama's home."

I fixed her a can of real tuna while I pulled out the makings for a salad for myself along with a diet Dr. Pepper. I curled up in front of the TV and began watching Danielle Steele's movie "Daddy," on Lifetime Television for Women.

The Three E class went off without a hitch. I had an all time high of 45 participants! I couldn't believe that this many women would actually get up on a Monday morning to attend a 6:00 class but they did. I decided to have an early morning class on Monday and Friday and an evening class on Tuesday and every other Friday. Casey and a couple of the other group members volunteered to help me.

"Belinda," Tamara stopped me in the locker room before I could get to the shower. "I thought you might want to know I spoke with one of the directors in the Bronx. They've given their stamp of approval for a Three E class at two of the support group locations. He wants to know a good time for the two of you to get together and go over the aspects of the program."

I let out a scream. I couldn't hold back the happiness I was feeling at the thought of the Three E program spreading throughout the AA family. I squeezed Tamara as tight as I could before doing a two step dance around the locker room! Tamara followed me laughing and screaming right along with me.

"I'll give him a call and make an appointment with him! I've got to hurry before I'm late. I have to take MochaJa to the Vet for his weekly grooming! See *ya*!"

I took a quick shower, jumped in my black linen Tracey Lee business attire and dashed out of the building to my doctor's office. It was that time again the old Mammogram and physical. I don't know why I dreaded going to the doctor so badly since it was for my own good. I wanted to make sure I remained in good health. I could've had a lot of things messed up in my body from all my years of alcohol abuse.

After my doctor's visit, I decided to treat myself to lunch at Tom's Diner. The restaurant owner was the real life inspiration for the character Cosmo Kramer on the popular sitcom, Seinfeld. There was always a tour of some kind going on at the restaurant. While approaching the restaurant I could see the crowd looked sparse. I thought I would try to see if I could waltz right in and grab myself a nice turkey on sourdough combo. I was halfway right. No tour was scheduled until three o'clock. I had more than enough time to sit down and have a somewhat satisfying meal.

"Are you ready to order Mam?" the young lady asked.

"Sure, let me have the number six, please. I'd like my turkey on sourdough with all the trimmings, except onions that is. I'll have a decaf, cold tea and what's the soup of the day?"

"It's chicken noodle, Mam. Can I get you some of that as well?"

"No, thank you, I'll pass on chicken noodle today."

While waiting patiently for my order to arrive, I did a little people looking. I had been careful to choose a seat next to the window. Looking out among them I saw people of all shapes, sizes, and of all nationalities. I began to imagine what they were thinking, what occupation they held. Had they faced problems like me? Were they happy or sad? Were they rich or poor? Thought after thought filled my mind.

The bell ringing over the entrance to Tom's Diner brought me back to reality. The lady who walked in was dressed in dark sunglasses, with a red and cream silk blouse and cream silk trousers in. Her matching leather flats appeared to confirm this more than likely was her first time in Tom's as she stood checking out her surroundings.

I raised my hand up in the air, "Candace, Candace," I called out to the perfectly dressed woman. "Candace, over here."

She looked over her shoulder and came towards me.

"Hi, Belinda. How are you?"

"Hi Candace. We meet again, huh?"

"Yes indeed we do. I thought I'd come in and get myself some lunch. I've been running errands for my mother-in-law most of the morning and now I'm starving."

"Join me, I just ordered a couple of minutes ago. I can give you the heads up on what's really good." I laughed.

"Okay." Candace eased into the chair in front of me. The waitress spotted her and came over.

"Hi, Mam could I get you something to drink?"

"*Diet Coke please.*" Candace always liked Cokes. I could never understand how she could drink them from the time she woke up in the morning until she went to bed. It never kept her from sleeping and she said it never bothered her kidneys.

"Let me know when you're ready to order." The polite waitress replied.

"What did you order Belinda?" Candace asked.

"I ordered the number six, the turkey combo. It's delicious too. It comes with fries and Cole slaw."

"That sounds real good. Miss…I'll take the number six with extra mayo, please."

"Your orders will be out in just a few minutes."

"How are things at church?" I asked Candace.

"Oh, everything is just fine. Elliott has been working hard with the youth ministry. He really has some great ideas and as for me, I love the church. I don't think God could have led us to a greater group of people."

"I don't see how you do it all, Candace. You're helping your husband with his ministry and then you're coming back and forth to Manhattan, what… two…three times every week to help your mother-in-law? You are one of those superwomen, girl. I don't think I could do it."

"I guess you have to love what you do. My husband is such a great guy and his parents, his mother now, are just adorable. Since my mother passed a couple of years ago, the Karuso's are like my family. There's nothing I wouldn't do for them."

"I'm sorry to hear about your mother. Was she ill?"

"Yeah, she had breast cancer."

"How are your kids, Candace? They're almost teenagers now aren't they."

"*Almost.* They're doing just fine. They don't give me or Elliott a moment's trouble. We're so blessed."

"Here you go ladies," the waitress interrupted.

"Now tell me about you Belinda. What's been going on in your life?"

"I've been living in New York for almost six years now."

I knew when I told her this she would remember it was right after the nasty incident with her and Emanuel. "I lived with a friend for a while until I found a place of my own. I'm still not married and I live a couple of blocks from here."

Things became quiet for a few minutes as we both enjoyed our meal. I think we were also afraid of delving too deep into each other's lives too fast.

"Candace," I began to talk. I couldn't help it. I had to get things out in the open. "I can't help it. I've got to tell you how sorry I am for hurting you."

"Belinda, please not now." Candace looked down, almost as if she was embarrassed to hear what I had to say.

"Candace, I have to say it. Look. There's a reason we keep on running into each other. Do you know how unlikely that is to happen to two people in a city as big and busy as New York?"

Candace shook her head in agreement. "You're right Belinda. I just didn't want you to feel like you owed me an explanation or anything. The past is the past. I'm a Christian now. I love the Lord. He has taught me how to forgive Belinda. I forgave you a long time ago, and I didn't have to see you in order to forgive you.

So much was going on back then. I wasn't exactly a miss goody two shoes myself. Our thing back then was partying, having a good time and doing our thing. Emanuel was a dog. I knew that and so did you. You weren't the first one he messed around with on me. I just didn't want to see it. I wasn't the best wife myself. You know that we spent most of our time drinking and clubbing, so what else could I expect."

"You should have been able to expect your best friend to be true to you Candace. I wasn't and I'm sorry. I'm so sorry."

I tried to hold back my tears but they still began to escape as if they had a mind of their own.

"Not here, Belinda. Don't cry here or anywhere for that matter. It's over. I'm glad to see that you're doing fine for yourself. I used to think about you and often wondered what happened to you. When I first saw you, I didn't know how I was going to react. I thought I would still be angry at you even though I prayed to God to help me forgive you and Emanuel, and he answered my prayer."

"Candace, I can't sit here and lie and tell you that it's been easy, because it hasn't. I had to admit a lot of things to myself. One of those things was that I'm an alcoholic. For so many years I denied it. I tried to hide it. I kept telling myself I could control my drinking. I have to admit I used drinking to shield me from all the stuff in my life that I didn't want to face."

"I understand Belinda."

"I always thought life would be easy for me because of my looks, but even thinking I could sail through life on of my looks was ludicrous. When I came to New York, I still refused to own up to my drinking. Sure, I had money but its true—money can't buy happiness. All it bought for me when I arrived here was more alcohol. I found out where all of the best bars were and I hung out in full force."

"You didn't have any positive friends in your life Belinda?"

"My so called friends were just like me, trying to hide their problems in a bottle. Those few people who tried to be my friends were the ones I messed over. When I wasn't drinking at some bar I was at home sprawled across my living room sofa fighting a hangover. Whatever didn't go right in my life, I used it as an excuse to drink. I keep messing up, Candace. I've ruined friendships and relationships."

"Belinda, we have to talk. I mean really talk. Now is not the time. Don't you see, Belinda? God will forgive you if you just trust him and ask him to forgive you. We have to get together when we both have more time."

"No! I want to talk now Candace. I have to get as much of this out of me as I can. I've held this back for all of these years and I can't hold it back any longer!"

I knew I had to tell Candace everything that was on my heart before I lost my courage to do so. I had to keep on talking.

"I was drinking so much that I began having blackout spells. There were days passed and I couldn't begin to tell you what happened. I remember one of my neighbors invited me over for a party to celebrate her husband's recent job promotion. I was always the one who had to get smashed. By the end of the night, this guy, who I didn't know at the time, literally put me over his shoulder, so I've been told, and carried me home. I was sloppy drunk, Candace."

"Oh my goodness, Belinda."

"When we made it to my house, he said I pulled off every stitch of my clothes and begged him to screw me! Thank God, he's the kind of guy he is. Instead of taking advantage of me, he put me to bed, alone, so I could sleep it off. His name was Jim Lassister and he saved my life that night. Jim and I became good friends, nothing sexual, just good friends. He came over the next morning, made me clean myself up and took me to my first AA meeting. At the meeting, I listened as Jim shared his story of being a recovering alcoholic."

"He sounds like a good friend Belinda."

"He had been living a life of sobriety for about a year. Unlike me, he had a loving and forgiving wife and family who stuck by him and continues to stick by him. He became my mentor Candace. I don't know what I would have done without him. I won't lie to you. I still want a drink. Sometimes I want a drink so bad I can taste it at the tip of my tongue. I can feel the vodka on my lips and imagine it sliding down the back of my throat while the ice clinks the inside of the glass. I want it Candace. I want it so bad, but I know I can't have it. I can't go back Candace. I can't hurt anyone else and I can't hurt me any more Candace. I just can't."

Candace looked at me like she was seeing me for the first time. She reached over and grabbed my hands in hers. We said nothing to each other. We sat there in silence, staring into each other's eyes and the tears streamed gently down both of our faces.

By the time we finished talking, two and a half hours had passed.

"Candace, let's talk again soon. You're welcome to come by my place anytime."

"Belinda, I would love that. I have to admit something to you Belinda."

I had no idea what she was about to say but I was concerned nonetheless. I wouldn't blame her if she didn't want to see me anymore. I didn't want her to think I expected her to forget totally about the past.

"When you gave me your number, I didn't plan on calling you at all. I talked to Elliott and told him I saw you. You see, Elliott knows all about my past and he loves me anyway. He was the one that told me I should call you and listen to what you had to say. He reminded me it is my duty and responsibility as a Christian to forgive. I hadn't forgiven you Belinda. When I ran into you, I realized I still harbored anger and bitterness towards you."

"I can understand Candace."

"When I got ready to call you, that's when my father-in-law passed and one thing led to another. One evening after dinner, Elliott asked me whether or not I had contacted you. I told him I hadn't. He said I had to do it. That's the day I called and invited you to church. Even after then I wanted it to be over. I wanted to believe that I had done my Christian duty, but today God has shown me that he wasn't finished with us yet Belinda. I'm glad he fixed it so I would run into you again. So, I said all of that to say I want you to forgive me too for being selfish Belinda."

"Candace, of course I forgive you." This time Candace reached out and gave me a piece of paper.

"Call me Belinda. I'd like to see you again soon, maybe this weekend."

I walked back home feeling a sense of exhilaration and relief. Another burden had been removed from my life, the biggest burden of all—the burden of un-forgiveness. Maybe there was something to this God thing after all. Maybe he really does love me I thought as I pushed the elevator button and headed back to my world of staying focused and getting it together.

Candace and I talked on the phone almost every day. I even invited her to attend some of the Three E classes whenever she was in Manhattan.

131

The class in the Bronx wasn't scheduled to start for another three to four months.

I thought I had finally escaped the horrid events of my past. I had re-established a relationship with Candace, become relatively active in church again and things were beginning to look up for me. Then it happened. The doorbell rang early and interrupted my morning period of solitude.

"Good morning. Miss Hamilton. I have a certified letter for you." The Postman said.

"Thank you. Where do I need to sign?" I asked while turning the long envelope over searching for a return address.

"Right here, Mam," the postman pointed to the signature line.

I hurriedly opened the envelope, curious about its contents. The contents of the envelope fell as if in slow motion onto the shellac hardwood floor. All I could see were the all too familiar words of the one who had haunted me for all of these past years. I couldn't contain the scream that rose from the pit of my stomach! Fear had taken over! I slammed the heavy oak door with all of the strength inside of me. I barely saw MochaJa running up the stairs for cover. My stomach tightened in knots as I held my hands up in the air and read the words I had come to know by heart:

I'm going to cut, slice and dice you up. You cannot get away, each day I watch you. Waiting, waiting for the right time to kill you Belinda! I'm going to do it slow, so you can feel the pain. I'm going to peel your skin off of you while you are still alive and replace it with a layer of hot tar, before I slice your throat.

"NOOOOOOOOOOOO!!!!" I heard the woman screaming...not fully realizing that it was me.

⁊Ɔ⁊

"One...two...three...four...and stretch. One...two..three...four and stretch. Okay ladies and gentleman, let's do two more sets of fours and then we'll call it a day," I said as perspiration poured onto my Nike sweatband.

I could barely teach my class as the thoughts of the letter saturated my mind. After working so hard to make my life worthwhile again only to be pummeled with this blast of terror from my past!

Lord, help me, I prayed within. I put on a brave front before the class, like I always managed to do around others. I couldn't let anyone know I was frightened. The person who was writing those letters could be anyone.

Maybe he or she was right here in my class. Maybe they had been following me wherever I moved. Paranoia had definitely set in. Who could help me now, but God?

"Belinda," Tamara called out to me just as we were finishing our stretches. I nodded to let her know I heard her.

"*Allright,* class, that's it for the evening. I'll see you again on Friday." I went over to Tamara's glassed in office on the other side of the workout area, hoping she wouldn't notice my uneasiness.

"Hey, what's up Tamara? You looked like something was bothering you?"

"Belinda, I don't know how to tell you this. . .but."

I knew it was bad news because she couldn't bring herself to look me in my eye. Had this terrible person approached Tamara about me? Did she know something I didn't?

"Belinda, it's about the Three E class."

I breathed a sigh of relief. What Tamara had to say couldn't be so bad after all.

"What about the Three E Class? The Bronx isn't going to do it? If that's the case, we'll just have to try next year Tamara. We still have four classes a week going on now and to be honest that's more than enough. You know that. So why are you worrying about that?"

"Belinda, the Three E Class has been cut from the budget-entirely. We just don't have the funds to carry it anymore. I've talked to the board of directors and there's nothing we can do. We can barely hold on to this meeting facility. I'm sorry, Belinda. You've done an outstanding job. The class wouldn't have survived this long anyway, if it hadn't been for your monthly monetary contributions. But it's over Belinda-we just don't have the funds."

"Over! You have the nerve to just call me in to your office and tell me the Three E Class is over, like it's nothing! Just like that you tell me—Belinda, the Three E Class had to be cut. I don't believe this. Do you know how hard I've worked to get this class to where it is? Do you! Do you know how much money I've invested in this group?" I couldn't contain myself. I knew I was shouting but I couldn't stop.

"All of my hard work and this is how I'm repaid. No one even so much as gave me any indication that this could happen. Maybe I could have gotten somebody to help us. How dare you do this to me Tamara!" I screamed and cried. People were beginning to gather around to see what was going on.

"Just tell me when Tamara. When is the last class?"

"Belinda, what's wrong with you? This isn't like you. Calm down." Tamera closed the door behind us. Her eyes were big as marbles. She knew I was behaving totally out of character.

"Talk to me, Belinda. Tell me what's really bugging you. I'll try to help you. You know I will." Tamera's voice was soothing and sympathetic.

"I...I can't talk about it Tamera. I just can't," I cried. "No one can help me, Tamera. No one can take away my past. All I can tell you is that I'm sorry for my outburst. I didn't mean to lash out at you. You're too good to me and I wouldn't want to do or say anything to jeopardize our friendship. Won't you please forgive me? I'm just going through something right now."

Tamera looked bewildered. She was so used to reaching out and helping others. But she couldn't help me with this. No one could.

"I...I have to go Tamera." I hurriedly turned and walked out of the door before she could see the tears beginning to form in my eyes.

I didn't know what else to say. I knew it wasn't her fault that the Three E Class was cut, but right now all I could feel was anger and hate. At that moment I felt nothing but contempt; not against Tamera but against myself. I was my own worst enemy. I was the reason good couldn't take up residence in my life for long.

Everything that was bad in my life was my fault and now there was someone out there who knew just how bad I really was-and they wanted to see me dead. I ran out of the building, not bothering to gather my things.

The rain coming down outside hid the tears streaming down my face. I ran until I saw the flashing lights. Darkness had pierced the sky and the lights stood out like a bright star. "The Vault Tavern and Grill," I stood there for a moment looking at the neon light flashing on...off...on...off. I took a step inside. I knew inside these walls there would be no one to turn me away or dash my dreams.

"Candaceaaaa!" I don't know how loud my voice sounded to her. All I know is that I had to talk to someone. I didn't care if the clock on the wall said 3:30 a.m. I had to talk to Candace!

"Belinda, what is it? What's wrong with you?" I knew she already knew without question what was wrong with me. How could she not know? I was the one who screwed her husband. I was the drunk. The pretty little drunk, I was nobody. I was worthless and useless.

"You mean you don't know who this is? Don't you recognize my voice Candace? I'm the great betrayer. I'm the one who used to be your friend. Instead I turned out to be your worse enemy didn't I Candace?"

"Belinda, stop it and tell me what's wrong with you?"

"Tell you what's wrong with ME? Don't you know Candace? Don't you know everything that's wrong with me? My life is what's wrong with me Candace. That's what's wrong. Everything about my life is what's wrong with me. Oh, don't worry little Miss perfect Candace. I haven't had a drink. Not yet at least. I did go by the bar and I did buy me a fifth of vodka but I haven't drunk it yet –but oh I'm about to. Why shouldn't I Candaceaaa!" I kept on screaming into the phone like a raving maniac. I was hurt. I was tired of being hurt and tired of being disappointed. I knew Candace was frightened now. She was afraid that I was *pissy* drunk. She thought I had fallen off the wagon.

"Listen to me Belinda. Please don't take that drink. Please just listen to me. You've come too far to turn around now, Belinda. You've done great things. You have a great job and a wonderful support group. You have the Three E Class. Don't you see Belinda. You have so much going for you?"

"No, don't you see Candace. I'm a failure. I always have been. I'm a drunk. I always have been. The Three E Class. I don't have the Three E Class. The Three E Class is no more Candace. It's ka-puff…gone…it's no more. Everything I do falls apart and I'm sick of it.

"Listen, to me Belinda. I want you to stop right now. Listen, please do this for me. Call your partner Belinda. Call whoever your partner is right now. I'm going to put on my clothes and be there as soon as I can. Please Belinda. Do what I say. I'm begging you."

I thought I heard the fear in Candace's voice but my mind was consumed with my own worries and problems. She wanted me to call my partner. Call Casey?

"You want me to call Casey? Is that who you want me to call Candace?" I began to hear what she was saying but I also heard the fifth of Vodka calling me too.

"Yes, call Casey, Belinda. I'll tell you what. Give me Casey's number. I'll call her right now. I'll call her for you Belinda. Belinda, give me Casey's number."

"I…I can't remember Casey's number right now."

"You have it somewhere Belinda, don't you? Is it on a message board or something? What about the refrigerator door? Find Casey's number and give it to me Belinda. You can do it."

Candace was frantic. Her husband Elliott had been awakened too. He whispered that he was going to start the car up so they could drive to my house as soon as they hung up.

"I'm going to stay on the phone Belinda until you go and get Casey's number. Okay?"

"Okay." I told her as if I was in a daze. I searched for my telephone message pad. I looked on the refrigerator door. I searched on the living room table. I couldn't find Casey's number anywhere. Just as I stumbled back into the living room I saw the number glued on the side of the telephone base.

"I…I found it," I mumbled to Candace.

"What is it Belinda? What is Casey's number?" Candace cried.

"It's 555-2129."

"Now, listen to me Belinda. I'm going to hang up and I'm going to call Casey right now. She's going to call you or come right over. Elliott and I are on our way too but it's going to take us some time to get there but we'll be there. Belinda, please, please don't take a drink."

I hung up the phone and curled up in a knot. I wanted to hide from the world. Hide from everybody.

I heard someone pounding on the door. I couldn't tell if I was dreaming or if someone was actually at the door. The ringing became louder.

"Belinda!" I heard someone screaming my name. "Belinda! Open up! It's me-Casey! Open up this door, Belinda!"

I pulled myself up from the sofa almost stepping on MochaJa.

"I…I'm coming." I opened the door and fell into Casey's arms.

"Belinda, tell me. Where's the alcohol? Where is it Belinda?"

"It's in the living room."

"Come on!" she demanded.

She led me by my hand, pulling me into the living room. She grabbed the fifth of vodka off the table.

"Take it Belinda. Take it and let's go and pour it out."

Casey forced the vodka into my hands almost knocking me to the floor. She led me into the kitchen.

"Now open it!" she screamed.

"I twisted the cap off slowly. I wanted to drink it so bad."

"Casey, please," I begged. "I just need one drink. Just one. That's all."

"No, Belinda. One drink, never. You can never have just one drink Belinda. You can never have just one drink," she repeated.

"Now pour it down the sink. Every last drop of it!"

I took the bottle of vodka and did as she said, crying hard, shivering at the thought of how close I had come to taking that drink. I collapsed into Casey's arms. So much fear and uncertainty was still inside of me.

I heard my name being screamed out once more. It was Candace.

"We're in here," Casey yelled out to her. Candace and her husband Elliott rushed in. MochaJa sat on the end of the recliner looking confused, lost and bewildered. If only MochaJa knew how close I was to death's door.

"Belinda, calm down. Everything is going to be just fine." Candace held me in her arms rocking me back and forth like a baby. I heard Elliott asking Casey if I had taken a drink.

"No, thank you for calling me," Casey said. "I made it just in time. She's going to be fine."

I awoke to the smell of bacon frying and coffee percolating. I rolled over and saw the time was 10:30 a.m. I was in a daze, still confused over what had happened. As I began to remember the previous night's events, I thanked God for my friends. I thanked him for bringing Candace back into my life. I thanked him for my AA partner Casey. I pulled myself up and sat on the side of the bed.

"Good morning, sleepy head," Candace said.

"Candace, what are you still doing here?"

"You didn't think I was going to leave you alone did you? I had to be in Manhattan today anyway. I have to check on my mother-in-law. And of course you know Casey had to get home to her family too. You gave us quite a scare last night or should I say this morning. I'm just thankful to God that He had your fingers to dial my number. You made it through a big crisis in your life Belinda and you did fine. You did all the right things. You called out for help. I'm proud of you."

"Thank you Candace. Thank you for being here." I was overjoyed and words escaped me. All I knew was I owed a lot to my friends. I owed a lot to God. Maybe I would just have to find out more about this man who Candace and Elliott loved and gave their lives to, after all last night He saved mine.

After my near devastating battle with me and alcohol, Candace and I began to spend more time with each other. I know she still didn't quite trust the fact that I no longer drank, but I knew in time she would see I was serious about never taking another drink. That night proved to be a big test for me and quite an eye-opener. I realized how vulnerable I was to alcohol. For the first time since I had stopped drinking, I saw how much alcohol had a control over me. I knew that I would forever be fighting a battle and having the strength not to take that first drink would always haunt me. I was determined to confide in Candace. I opened up to her completely.

"Candace, the morning the postman delivered me that threatening letter, I spun out of control. I wanted to escape my past but no matter how I tried, I just couldn't seem to shake it. I was tired of running. I was tired of being afraid and having to always look over my shoulder. I didn't know how to fight against this person who had such control over my life."

"Really Belinda?"

"When the Three E class was cut, I was thrown into another catapult of unleashed emotions. All of my energy, time and care, I had once placed in to my drinking, had been put into the Three E class. I couldn't take it when Tamara told me the class had to be discontinued. That meant I would have too much time on my hands to think about my past mistakes. I went into a self-induced state of depression. As for the letters, I couldn't tell you about them. I didn't want to pull you back into the whole nightmare with me. You've come too far Candace."

Candace listened to me and allowed me to talk and I did just that.

"Candace, I'm frightened. I almost wish this maniac would just go on and kill me since that's what he or she wants to do so badly."

"Belinda," Candace interrupted for the first time since I had been talking. "You have to pull yourself together girl, and get out of this depression you're in." Her voice rose to a high pitch. I could tell she was angry that I was talking like I was some powerless creature.

"You can't allow someone else to keep you in a state of fear, Belinda," she said. "You have to go to the police. Take the letter and the envelope. I'll go with you. Maybe they can match it up to some DNA or maybe there are fingerprints that can be matched. Something can be done Belinda-you have to fight back!" she screamed.

"I know but I'm afraid."

"That's the only way you're going to find your healing. And I don't want to hear you say that you wish this fool would kill you! I don't want to hear you talking like that ever again."

I hadn't seen Candace this adamant about her feelings in a long time. Listening to Candace lecturing me, I knew she still cared about me. Candace continued to speak.

"Belinda, there's something else. As far as the Three E Class goes; it's not worth it. I know you loved that Three E Class. I know it helped you to focus your energy on something positive but it's not the end of the world. You can start another class somewhere else. God knows you have the resources to do it. So just do it."

Candace spent countless hours talking to me and visiting me. She would often pop up unannounced just to make sure I hadn't answered the call of the mighty bottle. I decided to do like she said and the two of us took the envelope and letter to the police. They were going to contact the police back home and get them to fax the files of the other threatening letters I had received over the years. They were also going to run updated fingerprint checks and see if they could tie any DNA to the packages. I finally felt like I was taking control of my life.

After several weeks had passed, I felt myself returning to the land of the living. Candace' words were finally reaching me. They invigorated me to get up and move on with life and living.

"Candace, I think I'm going to start a business of my own," I told her one day over the phone.

"What kind of business, Belinda?" Candace's voice resonated a genuine curiosity and interest.

"I'm going to do like you suggested, open and operate my own Three E Spa. I have lots of connections with my financial background and I can cash in some of my stocks. All I have to do is find a location, do a little more research on the cost and go from there. What do you think, Candace?"

"Belinda! I think it's a great idea. Now this is exactly what I've been talking about. I knew you would wake up sooner or later. I've been praying for this day, Belinda. I've been afraid that you would take that drink but God answered my prayers."

"You're right, Candace. He did answer your prayer. It's been hard, but there's one thing I know, Candace."

"What's that Belinda?"

"I can't go back to the old Belinda, Candace. She's dead. She's gone and I will not resurrect her. I won't live in fear any more either. I owe you so much Candace. You know I want you to be a part of everything. Please say you will."

"Belinda, I'll do whatever I can to help you. That's a promise, because that's what friends are for."

A smile stretched across my face at the thought that life ain't all that bad after all. It was now or never-and I had decided that I wanted to live-Now.

"Candace, can you believe my dream is about to become a reality?" I chattered away nervously as I scurried around the 7,500 square foot building that was to house Three E Spa and Sauna Resort Center. True to her word, Candace had been at my side during the entire process. As a matter of fact, it was Candace who found the building and it turned out to be the perfect location at just the right price. The structure was in good, sound shape so there wasn't a great deal that needed to be done to the building itself. We put our heads together, networked with some existing members of the former Three E Spa and everything began to fall into place.

The center had an aquatics area for water aerobics, five Jacuzzis, three separate weight rooms, six separate exercise rooms and a store complete with Three E mugs, gear and exercise accessories. The reception area was decorated in cool colors of mint and salmon with lots of live plants spread throughout. Soft leather back and cloth chairs along with a plaid mint and salmon sofa complemented the décor. The receptionist area was state of the art and included a small exhibit of Three E products that members would be able to purchase from the store.

Over 250 invitations had been extended for the private open house black tie affair.

As the guests filtered in one after another, I felt like I was floating on a cloud! God has truly been working some good stuff in my life lately and I was thankful. As people helped themselves to champagne, wine and h'ordeurves, I made my rounds, being careful to stop and converse with as many people as I could. As I moved toward the area that had the array of food delights, I had catered; my eyes fell captive to the gentleman standing next to the table.

He held a sparkling crystal glass of white wine in one hand and with the other hand, he was gesturing as he talked to one of the directors of Harbor House, a rehabilitation facility for recovering addicts. I knew I had invited several big wheels to the event, but this was one person I didn't know. Perhaps he was the guest of someone there. I continued walking toward the banquet area. I was so close now that I could hear bits of their conversation.

"Chris, what do you think we can do about starting some other programs around this city like Harbor House?" I heard the obese director ask in a gruffly voice.

"Sir, I'm full of ideas. As a matter of fact, the person whose hosting this event tonight, I heard she's a recovering alcoholic. I'm sure this Three E Resort Center is going to take off. It's people like her who we need to tap into. I bet she has a closet full of ideas. If she came up with this brainchild, she most definitely has to have a good head on her shoulders.

"Why, thank you," I said, bowing my head slightly. "I couldn't help but over hear the two of you talking."

The stranger looked confused which made him even more handsome. His striking features made me tingle. His thick eyebrows and dark eyes seemed to be calling me toward him.

"Allow me to introduce myself," I continued. "I'm Belinda, the owner of Three E Spa and Resort Center. And you are?" I asked as flirtatiously as I could.

He reached out to meet my hand. "I'm Chris. And I must say, I am very pleased to meet your acquaintance Mrs. Belinda." His smile drew me in even more under his captivating spell.

"Miss, I'm not married," I told him. I hoped I didn't sound like some giddy schoolgirl. But I couldn't seem to help myself. "Thank you for the compliments. And if the two of you were serious about listening to some of my ideas to improve on programs such as this and Harbor House, then I'm interested."

Chris and I began to talk with ease. I could tell he was not like Carlton. He was articulate, intelligent and quite charming to say the least. When the band began to play one of my favorite tunes, Chris grabbed me gently by the arm and led me to the dance area. I breathed in the scent of his cologne and rested my head upon his chest as the soft music echoed throughout the Center. Nothing was said between us. We just enjoyed the music and each other. At the end of the dance, Chris told me he had to leave.

"Belinda, I'm sorry I can't stay any longer. I actually wasn't invited anyway. I came in place of one of the managers from Harbor House who wasn't able to come due to a family emergency. I haven't been in the city long but where I came from; I worked with organizations like Three E and Harbor House. What you are doing here is quite impressive Belinda. If you don't mind, I would love to get with you and get an in depth tour of the facility and learn a little more about what you'll be offering. Would that be okay?"

I tried to sound confident and calm. But it was hard. In just the short time I had met this man; I was already swept off my feet.

"Certainly, I think that would be a good idea. I'll walk you to the receptionist area and give you one of my cards."

We made our way through the myriad of people; finally we reached the secluded receptionist area.

"I'll just take me a minute. My cards should be behind the desk here." I moved around toward the back of the desk. I could feel his eyes on me. I sure hoped he liked what he saw.

"Here, you go Chris. Again, let me tell you. It was so nice meeting you. I hope we'll talk soon."

"Oh, you don't have to hope because we'll definitely be talking-real soon." Chris leaned his tall frame down and kissed me softly on the cheek.

"Goodnight, Belinda."

I don't know how long I stood there after Chris had left. All I remember thinking is that at last my love has come along.

Chapter Seven
The Reunion

I'd just stepped out of the shower when the telephone rang. Leaving a trail of soap behind me, I raced to pick it up. But it was too late; the person calling hung up. Thank God for voicemail. At least the caller left a message.

"Hello Belinda…. this is Candace. I was wondering if you would be home later. I'd like to stop by and chat with you about something. So let me know… Peace." Candace sounded nervous. Something must be wrong. Maybe nothing was wrong. I was getting remarried in a few months, and the anxiety of it all was apparently beginning to affect me. I was in a bad mood lately, and I wasn't a moody person by nature. Maybe it was those nagging flashbacks of my previous marriage to Carlton, what a disaster it was. In fact, the disaster ended with Carlton croaking, while rocking Ms. Bitch - Tina Suarez.

Rocking…that was funny; he was rocking all right-sex and cocaine. He was enjoying the best of both worlds. That is, until a third world took his sorry ass out-of-here. As far as I was concerned, the end justified the means; Carlton got what was coming to his dumb ass. I got what was coming to me too-a house and some matrimonial compensation, otherwise known as bread, dough, and El Dinero.

I didn't like to think about my marriage with Carlton, but how could I forget it? Like a reoccurring nightmare, it just wouldn't go away. Perhaps I deserved it. Perhaps God was punishing me… again. No, it wasn't God's fault. He didn't make me sleep with Eman. Perhaps it was the devil's fault. But, more than likely, it was my own horniness and loneliness, which led me to betray my best friend. Shaking off these bitter, negative thoughts, I telephoned Candace.

"Hi Candace, its Belinda," I said as Candace answered the telephone. Candace paused before speaking. "Candace, are you, are you there?" I asked.

"Oh, I'm sorry Belinda," Candace replied after breaking her silence. "I was on the other line with Elliott when you called. Are you free tonight?"

Candace didn't bother with the small talk. She didn't even ask me how I was doing. She obviously had something on her mind.

"Yes I'm free," I answered. "Come on over."

It was about 10:30 p.m. when the doorbell rang. It was Candace.

"Come on in girl," I urged Candace as we embraced. "You're looking good. Have you been on a diet or something?" I wasn't just flattering Candace; it was true. Candace looked radiant, and she seemed to be really happy.

"No Belinda, you know me and diets don't get along well," she said as we walked toward the sofas. "I'm just happy girl; maybe that's what you really see in me."

She was right. There was definitely something different and beautiful about her, and I was happy to see her smiling again. She deserved to smile again after all she had been through. Or perhaps more appropriately phrased, after all I had put her though.

Right after finishing that thought, it seemed as though I went into a deep trance. I could hear Candace talking to me, but my mind was busy racing back into time again. All of a sudden, I was back in bed with Eman, and he was rocking my boat. I remembered the passionate pleasure I felt and how he completely satisfied me that night. I remembered the look on Candace's face as she saw Eman kissing me goodbye. I...remember... the hurt. Damn Judaist, I mumbled under my breath.

"Belinda! Did you hear me?" Candace yelled at me, quickly bringing me back to the present. "Is anything wrong?" she asked.

"No" I said, shaken by my temporary detour into my notorious past. "I'm sorry, what were you saying?" I continued after collecting myself.

"I was saying that I have something really important to ask you." Candace looked me straight in the eyes. This must be serious, I thought. There was an awkward but brief silence as Candace paused between her thoughts.

"Wait Candace," I interrupted. "I want to ask you something first." My statement caught Candace off-guard. She said nothing; she just nodded in compliance. "You know that Chris and I are getting married in April, right?" Again, Candace just nodded yes. Speaking more nervously now, I continued. "I know I have no right to ask you, but I was wondering. I paused. I was having trouble finding the courage to ask Candace the question that was zooming around in my head. Candace, noticing my difficulties, took my hand, and gently squeezed it.

"What is it Belinda?" she asked softly. This sweet and humble gesture by Candace gave me the reassurance I needed to ask my question; I spoke up.

"Would you please be my matron of honor?" I finally asked. Again there was silence, as we looked into each other eyes. Then Candace smiled a little, and then a lot.

"I was going to ask you if I could be your bridesmaid!" she said as we both hugged each other, half-laughing, half-crying.

How ironic was this? I had ruined her marriage, now she was going to be my matron of honor. Had Candace finally forgiven me? She must have forgiven me. At last! Oh how I had waited years for this moment. It had been so long in coming, so very long.

We talked a few more minutes, and then Candace left. I went straight to bed. I was so happy. I felt like a little girl again on Christmas Eve.

I said a special prayer to the Lord and drifted off to sleep. Not long after I had fallen asleep, I heard noises outside my front door. It sounded like two people talking. Who in the world could that be? I asked myself. I tipped-toed to the front door and looked out the peak hole. There was a man and a woman engaged in a passionate kiss. What the hell is going on? I asked myself. What are they doing here? I looked out again.

This time the man had his hand underneath the woman's dress, and she had lifted her left leg up and around his waist. Wait a damn minute! That's not some man! That's my fiancé! And that's not some woman! That's Candace! I screamed! I tried my best to open the door, but I couldn't, so I just started to bang on it.

Just then I awakened. Someone was banging on my door. I sat up in my bed, still confused.

"Belinda, it's me. It's Chris. Let me in." Wow! What at nightmare, I thought. I had only been dreaming, but it seemed so real. I got myself together and finally answered the door. I grabbed Chris and kissed him so hard that I think I scared him.

"Is...everything Okay Belinda?" he asked, as confused as I had been just a few minutes earlier.

"Never better my love, never better."

"You haven't kissed me like that since I bought you your engagement ring," Chris teasingly said. "And speaking of rings" he continued, "how is the wedding plans going so far?"

"Candace is coming over this afternoon and we're going to get busy," I replied.

"Candace?" Chris asked, somewhat shocked.

"Yes Candace," I said. "Anything wrong with Candace?" I went on.

"I just find it kind-of strange, you know what I mean?" he asked.

"Yes honey, I know exactly what you mean. I was thinking the same thing, to be honest Chris. But despite everything that has happened between Candace and I, we are still best friends."

"That's the way true friends are," Chris uttered. "Men are different," Chris went on. "If the same thing had happened with two men, one of them would probably be dead. If they didn't kill each other; they would never speak to each other again."

For a moment, Chris sounded as if he was confessing to some previous romantic entanglement.

"Has that ever happened to you Chris?" I asked.

"Who me? No way!" Chris exclaimed. *But,* somehow I could tell that Chris had been the unwilling victim of "love-gone-bad" at some previous point in his life.

He never talked much about his past, but that didn't bother me. A lot of men are like that. I figured that once Chris and I were together for a while, he would open up to me. He had told me when we first met *'I don't have anything to hide from you; I want you to know that right now.'* So, I wasn't worried about any dark secrets or anything, but I was dying to know his small secrets. For now, I had to wait. Just then, a terrible thought popped in my head. What if the letter writer, Mr. *'I'm going to cut you in pieces,'* turned out to be Chris? Damn, that was a foolish thought, I said to myself. But there it was! No matter where I was or what I was doing, the Slicer man would always find a way to get back into my head. This son-of-a-bitch was ruining my life. I couldn't go one day without thinking about him! This man, this Slicer, was driving me crazy.

"Belinda!" Chris yelled at me. "You're day dreaming again sweetheart. You were thinking about him again weren't you?"

I couldn't lie; my face said it all, so I just started crying.

"It's going to be all right Belinda; I'm not going to let anyone harm you. I promise." Chris was holding me now, and rocking me like a parent rocks a child to sleep. And like a child, I felt so safe and so loved.

When I awakened, I was back in bed again, and Chris had left. Beside me, he had placed a note: *'To my beautiful bride-to-be. I love you more than I love me. Love-ya, Chris.'*

Chris was so different than Carlton. If I had to describe the difference between the two, I could sum it up in one sentence. Chris was everything that Carlton wasn't. I know this sounds cold, and I don't know why I was still so bitter about Carlton after all these years. Carlton was gone, and I should just let him rest in peace. But I couldn't, then and I still can't now. Everyone is always telling me to let it go. I did let it go, but it keeps coming back. Once Mama suggested that I see a shrink. Sarcastically, I replied that I didn't have time to see a shrink because I was too busy hiding from the Slicer/Dicer man and attending the Three E classes.

"See what I mean?" Mama said. "I rest my case," she concluded.

It was Saturday morning and Candace was coming over at noon. It was time to buckle down and make some firm plans for the wedding. Candace arrived at 12 o'clock sharp. I wanted to keep the wedding simple but special. Chris and I had already set the date for April the 25th.

"I'm curious," Candace said. "Is there any reason why you guys picked April the 25th?"

"Chris wanted to be married in March, but I convinced him otherwise," I stated.

"Why?" Candace questioned.

"You know the old sayings, don't you?"

"No I don't. Enlighten me sister," Candace said smiling.

"They say, if you wed when March winds blow, joy and sorrow both you'll know. Marry in April when you can, joy for the Maiden and for Man."

"Belinda, I didn't know you were so superstitious," Candace remarked.

"I'm not," I retorted. "But why take chances," I said grinning.

"You're a nut," Candace said. "What am I going to do with you?" she asked, shaking her head.

"Okay," I said, pretending not to hear her last comment. "Let's start sending out these invites."

"But I don't even know where the wedding is going to be yet Belinda," Candace said as she opened one of the invitations. She started to read: 'The honor of your presence is requested at the marriage of Miss Belinda Norris to Mr. Chris Stevenson on Saturday, the 25th of April at six o'clock in the evening at the Golden Gate Outreach Ministries, 22600 Dawson St., Bronx, New York.'

"Belinda!" Candace screamed. "This is our church."

"Surprise Candace! It was all Elliot's idea," I continued.

"I thought he was keeping something from me," Candace commented. "He's been acting strange all week."

"Okay girlfriend, lets get these invites out," I shouted. "Here's half of the invite list for you. I'll send out the other half."

We mailed out sixty-five invitations. Out of the sixty-five, I expected about 100 people to show up for the wedding. This estimate included kids and stray relatives.

We spent the rest of the day contacting and choosing the main wedding players: photographer, DJ, limousine service, etc...

Occasionally, I would call Chris to get his opinion concerning a certain matter. As usual, Chris had a definite opinion on whatever the issue was. Chris didn't have any trouble voicing his opinion either. I liked that about him. At the same time, he wasn't cocky or pushy, and he was a great listener. These qualities are rare in most men. But Chris was a different breed. After I had given up on love, Chris stepped in. He was my black knight in shinning armor. I had no doubts whatsoever that Chris and I would have a beautiful and lasting marriage.

The afternoon stretched into the evening and then into the night. We had accomplished a great deal and the day had been fun. Cadence had to leave; she was doing something at church a little later that evening. I thanked her for helping me, and I told her how much I enjoyed the day. She too had enjoyed the day, according to her.

As she stood in the doorway getting ready to leave, that awkward silence returned. It was if something needed to be said by one or both of us, but we didn't know what or how to say it. In the end, we simply hugged and said goodnight.

For the second time, I dreamed of Candace and Chris having sex. Why was I having these damn dreams? Was this a premonition or just my imagination running rampart? It was then I realized a sobering fact; Candace had forgiven me, but I would never fully be able to forgive myself. That's the price of betrayal, I thought, and I'd be paying my dues forever.

The big day inched closer and my nerves were unraveling. Even though I had obviously been through the wedding drill before, it didn't seem to be any easier planning my second wedding. But Mama had so wisely reminded me to keep my eyes on the big picture. 'The really big show,' as she called it.

The big show was on track all right, and it was rolling like a runaway train. At times I could almost feel it bumping me squarely in the ass. I just needed to hold on a little longer, just a little longer.

Unlike me, Chris didn't seem nervous at all. In fact and to the contrary, he seemed to be enjoying the whole wedding ritual. He was having his bachelor party tonight, and he was definitely feeling it. Everyone seemed to like Chris, and tonight his male friends were hooking him up for one last bachelor bonding bang.

"Don't have too much fun tonight," I kidded him.

"Baby, you know I can't even look at another woman without thinking of you," he said grinning from ear to ear. When he smiled like that, I could see the devilish little kid that still lived within him.

"Good," I said grinning back. "Keep it that way."

"Baby when was the last time I told you how much you mean to me?" Chris asked.

"Tell me again," I demanded.

"Okay," Chris agreed.

"Go ahead baby, I'm all ears, I urged."

"Without you I would still be me, but I wouldn't be myself. You have redefined me in ways I never thought possible. Your soul has mingled with mine, and created a new me. Without you there *is* no me."

Chris knew how to get to my heart, and how to get to my panties too. What could a sister do after hearing that from her man but to get naked and get busy? We did both, and we "did it" for about two long hours. I must admit; I had some ulterior motives for this impromptu booty-call. I was making sure that Chris arrived at his bachelor party with as little testosterone as possible. Yeah, sisters are like that.

Chris didn't come back to my house that night, but he called me at least three times. I knew after the second call that the sexual *Mojo* I served on him was working. Chris was also drunk the third time he called me, and he was obviously having a good time. He told me that he wished I were there with him. I told him to enjoy himself and not to worry about me because we had our whole life to be together. That seemed to please him. He said goodbye and went back to his party. I smiled and went back to sleep.

Time seemed to fly by, and the wedding train had a full head of steam now. It was rolling like a bat out of hell. The wedding was less than two weeks, and it was time to make one final check of all the preparation. I called Candace.

"Hi Candace.... Belinda."

"Hi Belinda, what's up? How-you-been?" she added.

"Fine girl," I replied. "Look, I want to go over the wedding plans again. Can you stop over?"

I had gone over the plans earlier with Chris, but I needed my trusted confidant to look at the plans from a woman's point of view. And, it was another excuse to be with my best friend. We were closer than ever, and I cringed at the thought of almost loosing her in my life. I shook off those negative thoughts and got out my planner worksheet. I started going down the checklist: church reserved, photographer, video technician, etc. The list was looking good. So far, there were no major issues that I was aware of.

Judging from the RSVPs replies we received, we were expecting about 115 people to attend the wedding. That's just about what I had predicted. Damn I was good, I thought.

My mother had purchased the wedding dress that I had chosen. I thought of how beautiful it was as I checked it off on the list. I had chosen a rum-pink chiffon dress with no beadwork. The soft bustles would hang just below my kneecaps. The bustles looked very Victorian.

I decided not to wear a veil, but I did choose a simple headpiece. Naturally I didn't try all of the wedding attire on at one time. People say its bad luck to wear the complete wedding outfit before the wedding. Ah, the bridal shower; I checked it off. That was happening tomorrow. Sisters love to be pampered, and I was no exception. Besides that, I could get caught up on the latest gossip.

Candace arrived and we meticulously went over all of the details: from the ceremony to the reception. While I wanted to keep things really simple, I wanted everything to flow smoothly. I had an advantage though; it was my second time around and I had twice the experience at planning these things.

"Yeah," Candace agreed. "Everything seems to be right on track." When Candace mentioned the word "track", I thought about that runaway locomotive again. I could hear the warning whistle in my mind. But what was it warning of?

Occasionally I would mention my wedding anxieties to Chris. He would tell me: "Chicken Little, the sky is not falling; that's just a little matrimonial acorn falling on your head." Maybe he was right. He would say: That's not a runaway locomotive at all; it's a love-train.

Interrupting my thoughts, Candace asked, "By the way Belinda, how did Chris propose to you?"

Recalling that particular day, I responded.

"We were at the "Jazz House" on Brighton Blvd. We had just finished eating our dinner and we were listening to one of the local jazz bands. They started playing a jazzed-up version of Stevie Wonder's "Ribbon in the

Sky." Halfway through the song the keyboardist started talking between the melodies. Chris also went to the restroom. Then, all of a sudden Curt, the keyboardist, said:

'Belinda, will you be my ribbon in the sky for the rest of my life?'

Girl, I was totally shocked! I was looking around and everyone was looking at me. At that moment Chris reappeared. He tapped me on my shoulder and when I looked around, he was on his knees with a small jewelry box in his hands. The box contained the engagement ring."

"No kidding girl."

"Chris opened the box and asked, 'Belinda, with all my heart I ask; will you be my ribbon in the sky for the rest of my life?' I knew Chris loved me but honestly; I had no idea he was going to propose to me that night."

"So what you said girl?"

"I said, yes baby! I will always be your ribbon in the sky. Then I cried. The joint erupted with cheers and applause, and Chris slid the engagement ring onto my finger. We danced through the rest of the song. I will never forget that night."

"Damn girl," Candace said. "Now that was good."

"Chris is good," I said staring at Candace. "I mean he's really a good man, and I was so fortunate to find him."

"You deserve him Belinda," Candace said smiling again. At that moment, I remember being so happy. Candace was happy. The whole damn world seemed to be happy, as far as I was concerned.

Candace and I finished looking over the wedding plans. Everything was a *"GO."* The green light was on, and now it was just a matter of time.

My bridal shower was planned for the next day, and Candace was the hostess. I arrived early to help Candace set up. She had told me earlier that she already had help, and that she didn't want me helping with anything. But I arrived early anyway. Perhaps I just wanted a few private moments alone with her before the other guests arrived. Candace and I grew closer and closer to each other everyday. She was more than a friend now; she was family.

There was a guest book set up at the entrance of the front door, and a stack of blank "Thank you" cards beside the register. The idea was to have the guest register, and then put their names and addresses on the blank cards. At the end of the shower the cards would be placed in a basket and shook up. One card would be drawn from the basket, and the winner would be given a prize. Candace had decorated the hell out of her house. I really felt honored as I entered.

"Damn girl," I said in amazement. "You didn't have to do all this for me."

"The hell I didn't," she retorted. "We're going to do this thing right! Right?"

"Right," I said, still looking around at the decorations.

We sat and talked for a while before the guest began to arrive. There were about fifty people, as near as I could tell, in attendance. Candace had a table set up with all kinds of food goodies on it: Buffalo wings, meatballs, and all manners of vegetables and dips. She had also arranged a few games for the shower. Although I inquired about the games, she wouldn't tell me. She told me to wait and see.

The theme for my shower was "lingerie." Each guest was asked to bring a gift of lingerie to the shower. I had enough kitchen crap, so I decided I didn't need a kitchen shower. Besides that I reasoned; what woman would choose a blender over a strapless corset?

Once the majority of the guests had arrived, Candace walked to the entrance of the door and asked them for their attention.

"My name is Candace, for those of you who don't know me; I'm your hostess for this special event tonight. We are here to celebrate the wedding of my best friend Belinda and her fiancé Chris. First things first, did everyone register and fill out a blank thank-you card? If you didn't, please do so as soon as you have a chance. The door prize will be drawn from the cards."

The real reason for having people fill out the blank thank-you cards was to make it easier to send back the thank you notes. The last bridal shower I had, before I married Carlton, I had trouble figuring out who gave me some of the gifts because some people didn't put their names on them. I also had trouble finding the addresses of some people. I learned a few tricks from my first wedding.

"Secondly," Candace continued. "Each of you was given a gold safety pin to pin on your dress. No one is allowed to cross their legs at any time during the shower tonight. If you see someone with her legs crossed, you may take her pin and pin it on your dress. The person with the most gold pins at the end of the shower will win a prize. Thirdly, I want each of you to take out a pin or pencil and a small piece of scrap paper. When you're finish, we're going to play our first game."

Everyone looked around at each other, puzzled but excited about the upcoming game. There was laughter initially, but later silence, as everyone zoomed back in on Candace. "Ready?" Candace barked. Everyone nodded their head in agreement.

"Okay, the name is this game is 'two of a kind.' Go ahead and put your name at the top of the paper. You have two minutes to make as many separate words as possible out of two names: Belinda and Chris. You can only use each letter once per word. Ready-set-go!"

Pencils and pens started flying as though the sisters were competing for the Pulitzer Prize.

"Okay! Stop!" Candace yelled. Candace quickly collected all of the responses and announced the winner. "And the winner is Marie Williams!" I will now read you the winning names: "Linda, in, is, be, his, sin, ran, band, sand, can, clean, rise, led, sled, bed, head, red, dice, rice, end, bend, siren, hen, ice, nice, land, able, and scare."

Marie was a coworker of mine, and everyone was amazed at the number of words she was able to make in two minutes- everyone except me. It didn't surprise me at all. Marie smoked 'coke' like it was legal. I had no doubts whatsoever that she smoked it up before coming to my shower. Marie was one of my cool white friends.

She was smart as hell, but she had been smoking cocaine for at least a year now, and she was headed for trouble, big trouble. She told me her husband had introduced her to cocaine. She also told me how she "did" three men one night while "lighting it up." I told her she would have liked Carlton because they had so much in common, and if she wasn't careful, they would have one more thing in common: croaking while smoking and stroking. She just laughed at me, and told me not to knock it before I tried it.

After the first game, the liquor started to flow and the sisters began to loosen up. In a few minutes, I would be fully caught up on the latest gossip. Laughter would erupt every few minutes or so, usually as a resort of someone loosing her pin. Not crossing your legs is almost impossible for most women, unless your name was Betty Chambers.

Betty was not only the biggest whore at my shower; she was unarguably the biggest whore in the Bronx. In high school, she was affectionately named: "Ready Betty," by the varsity football squad. They called her that because she dropped her drawers so much she finally stopped wearing them at all. She was even caught "serving it up to" the Driver's Education teacher in the back seat of the driver's Ed car. It only took Betty about fifteen seconds to loose her gold pin. Someone jokingly remarked:

"Damn Betty," I bet that's the longest you ever kept your legs closed." The living room exploded with laughter, including Betty. She didn't give a damn, and didn't seem to be bothered at all by the jokes. In fact, she seemed to enjoy them more than anyone.

The evening progressed with more games and more liquor. Soon it was time to wrap things up. Everyone commented on how great the shower had been. A few called their insignificant others to come and get them, while others doubled up and left. Candace offered accommodations for the night for anyone who had indulged too much. Three sisters took her up on her offer. I stood at the door and thanked everyone again for coming, and reminded each of my upcoming wedding date.

Candace and I loaded up my car with all of the lingerie goodies the ladies had given me. My car was stuffed with panties and bras everywhere. It looked as though I had just returned from an orgy convention. No such luck, jokingly I thought to myself.

By the time I arrived home, I was wonderfully exhausted. The bridal shower was a lot of fun. I substituted the liquor for diet sprite instead, and no one except Candace and a couple of other friends knew the difference. Once I didn't think it was possible to have fun without drinking, but I guess I was wrong. I had always associated the one with the other. I was sober now and I loved being sober.

As any "surviving" alcoholic victim will tell you, you can never be completely cured of this dreaded disease. It doesn't matter if you haven't had a drink in fifteen years; you're always just one sip away from a liquid hell. I was doing okay though, thanks to the help from people like Candace. You can't cure yourself; I tried to. I almost killed myself in the process. I have a long way to go but I think, *'I'm going to make it after all...'*

The big day had finally arrived, and I was as nervous as a new bride. Hell, I was a new bride; sort of. It was time for the really big show, and I suppose I was as ready as any bride could be. The wedding was scheduled for 6 o'clock p.m. I woke up at 4 a.m. and could not go back to sleep. I sat in bed and rattled the wedding checklist off in my head, as though it were a song. Everything still seemed to be on track. There were no obvious showstoppers. It was time to get up and at-*em.*

Since I couldn't sleep any longer, I may as well take a nice long bubble bath. The bubble bath relaxed me, and I was able to think a little clearer. I slid back in the tub and felt my wedding anxieties slowly fade away. "Just what the doctor order," I thought. The bath was so relaxing that; I almost fell asleep.

"Knock! Knock! Knock!"

"Belinda sweetie, are you up?" I heard my mother calling. It took me a second or so to come out of the blissful slumber I was in.

"Hey Mama," I said. "Is that you?"

"Yes darling, it's me. How are you feeling this morning?" Mama asked, entering my room.

"Oh I'm fine Mama, just fine." I stepped out of the tub and dried myself off. I could hear Mama humming a church song in the other room.

"Pass me not oh gentle savior. Hear my humble cry. While on others thou are calling. Do not pass me by." I joined in…

"I'm singing Savior oh, oh, oh Savior, hear my humble cry. While on others thou are calling. Do not pass me by."

I could hear Mama chuckling outside. Church had meant so much to both of us in our lives. When I was a child, every Sunday, Mama would drag me off to church, me kicking and screaming. I tried every trick in the book to keep from going. Mama was much to smart for my tricks though. She had an answer for everything and every trick. When I hid my shoes and told her I couldn't find them, she would say:

"The Lord says come as you are. So if you can't find your shoes, you just have to go barefoot." When I pretended to be sick, she would say: "If Jesus brought Lazarus from the dead, surely he could cure your stomach ache, so come on." Once I even tried to use a little psychology on Mama.

"Mama," I slyly asked," how do you know there's really a God?"

"Because the Bible says so," Mama replied.

"Who wrote the Bible?" I quickly shot back.

"Prophets wrote the Bible Belinda."

"What if the prophets made God up?" I asked. "Have you ever seen God Mama? Has anyone ever seen God Mama?" Seeing where I was headed with this particular line of interrogation, Mama quickly cut me off.

"Hold your breath Belinda," Mama calmly ordered me.

"What?" I responded—shocked.

"Just hold your breath until I tell you to stop, " Mama said.

I didn't know where she was going with this one, but I liked playing games so I eagerly complied with her demands. It was fun for about thirty seconds. As I stood there with my cheeks and eyes bulging out, Mama didn't say a word. Finally I couldn't hold my breath any longer. My mouth flew open and I let all of the used air out. When I had gotten my breath back I looked at Mama, waiting for an explanation.

"Are you trying to kill me?" I asked.

"What makes you think you were dying?" Mama replied.

"I didn't have any air, and you can't live without air," I yelled, now somewhat angry.

"Are you sure you can't live without air?" Mama persisted.

"Mama, everybody knows you can't live without air."

"How do you know that you have air?" Mama asked. "Can you see it?" she added. "Checkmate!"

Mama had beaten me at my own game again. From then on, I stopped playing those games with Mama. She was too clever for a ten-year-old kid. In hind site, dragging me to church was the best thing Mama ever did for me. This thought made me think of something else Mama used to say. She would jokingly sing, *'I got a Christian soul and I'm super bad.'*

Noon rolled around. LaKrisa, a friend of mine, came by to give me a pedicure and a manicure. While LaKrisa was taking care of my nails, one of my hairdressers stopped by to give me a perm. All of my friends were collaborating to make it a special day for me, and I loved every bit of it. Chris called me at 1:30.

"Hi Baby, it's the man of your life," Chris jested.

"Hi Denzel," I jokingly answered.

"Ha ha," Chris continued. "What has Mr. Washington got that I haven't?" he asked.

"Nothing baby, absolutely nothing," I replied.

"I was just checking to see if everything was all right with you baby. Are you feeling it?"

"I'm feeling it," I said. "And it feels just fine. The green light is on and soon I'll be yours forever."

"Mine forever, that's sounds so good to me. I can't wait," Chris said in a soft, sincere voice. Chris had decided not to see me before the wedding. He said he wanted the full impact of seeing me for the first time in my wedding dress. The limousine would pick me up first and bring me to the church and then return to pick up Chris.

At 3 o'clock Candace arrived. We hugged and discussed the ceremony one last time. She was my Matron of Honor. Candace telephoned all of the wedding players to tie up any loose ends. Surprisingly, there were none. We made one final check of the checklist. Everything was looking good.

The limousine driver picked me up at 4:45. It only took us about fifteen minutes to reach the church. I went inside and started to get dressed. There were already about thirty-five people sitting in the church. They stood up an applauded as I entered.

I carried my wedding dress in a traveling bag. It was the one item I insisted on carrying myself. Mama and a few other friends brought the rest of my wedding accessories inside. Before I started dressing, I walked around the room and acknowledged everyone in attendance so far. Then I briefly spoke with Elliott about the ceremony.

After speaking with Elliott, I returned to my dressing room. Just before I closed the door, I looked out. The next time I come out of this door, I thought, would be to marry Chris. I slowly closed the door. I was closing the door to one life and opening it into another. For this reason, I deliberately although self-consciously, closed the door very slowly.

At 5:20, Mama informed me of Chris's arrival. According to Mama, Chris didn't seem nervous at all. He briefly said hello to everyone and then proceeded to his dressing room. The big show was finally about to begin. By 5:45 both Chris and I were ready. All the main wedding players were present. Everything was going so smoothly. I kept waiting for something to go wrong, but it never did. It was 6 o'clock and time to get married.

The organist started playing. Chris entered through the front doors with his immediate family. The family sat down, and Chris proceeded to the altar. Next, Elliott and Mac entered the front door. Mac was a close friend of Chris and Chris's best man. Then Mama and Mrs. Stevenson, Chris's mother entered. Behind Mama and Mrs. Stevenson, Tina, my flower girl followed. She was Elliott's niece and extremely smart for a four year old.

I was next, and as I strolled up the aisle with Daddy, I saw Chris looking and smiling at me. It was as if he was seeing me for the first time. And judging by the look on his face, he loved what he was seeing. I stopped a couple of steps back from Chris. Finally, the wedding processional was done. Elliott addressed the church:

"We are gathered here today in the sight of God and angels, and the presence of friends and loved ones, to celebrate one of life's greatest moments, to give recognition to the worth and beauty of love, and to add our best wishes and blessings to the words which shall united Belinda Norris and Chris Stevenson in holy matrimony."

As Elliott proceeded, I could feel my heart beating rapidly. Chris was still cool, calm and collective. He appeared to be focused on every word Elliott was saying. He was enjoying the actual ceremony itself. Elliott continued:

"Marriage is a most honorable estate, created and instituted by God, signifying unto us the mystical union, which also exists between Chris and the Church; so too, may this marriage be adorned by true and abiding love. Should there be anyone who has cause why this couple should not be united in marriage, they must speak now or forever hold their peace."

The only person I could think of who had any possible reason for us not being married was the Slicer, whoever he or she was. I wondered if the Slicer was in attendance. I was almost tempted to look around.

"Who is it that brings this woman to this man," Elliott continued.

"I do," answered Daddy. Daddy stepped forward, placed my hand with Chris's and then stepped back.

"Chris and Belinda, life is given to each of us as individuals, and yet we must learn to live together. We receive love from our family and friends. We learn to love by being loved. Learning to love and living together is one of life's greatest challenges and is the shared goal of a married life.

But a husband and wife should not confuse love of worldly measures for even if worldly success is found; only love will maintain a marriage. Mankind did not create love; God created love. The measure of true love is a love that is both freely given and freely accepted, just as God's love for us is unconditional and free.

Today is a glorious day the Lord hath made-as today both of you are blessed with God's greatest of all gifts-the gift of abiding love and devotion between a man and a woman. All present here today-and those here in heart-wish both of you all the joy, happiness and success that the world has to offer.

As you travel through life together, I caution you to remember the true measure of success, the true avenue to joy and peace, is to be found within the love you hold in your hearts. I would ask you hold the key to your heart tightly.

Within the Bible, nothing is of more importance than love. We are told the crystalline and beautiful truth: "God is Love." We are assured that "Love conquers all." It is love, which brings you here today, the union of two hearts and two spirits. As your lives continue to interweave as one pattern, remember it was love that brought you here today; it is love that will make this a glorious union; and it is love which will cause this union to endure."

When Elliott reached this portion of the ceremony, I was trying my best not to cry, but I was unable to hold the tears in. Chris could sense the emotional state I was in. He looked at me, smiled, and gently squeezed my hand for encouragement. This simple gesture by Chris was all I needed to calm down. Elliott continued:

"Would you please face each other and join hands?" Chris took my hand again.

"Chris, do you take Belinda to be your wife? Do you promise to love, honor, cherish and protect her, forsaking all others and holding only to her forevermore?"

"I do," Chris replied.

"Belinda, do you take Chris to be your husband? Do you promise to love, honor, cherish and protect him, forsaking all others and holding only to him forevermore?"

"I do," I answered in turn. Elliott resumed his speech.

"A marriage ceremony represents one of life's greatest commitments, but also is a declaration of love. I wish to read to you what Paul wrote of love in a letter to the Corinthians a long time ago. I believe this is a true model of love, and it's a model of love I would hope you both would pursue in your marriage.

'Though I speak with the tongues of men and angels-but do not have love, I am only sounding brass or tinkling cymbals. Though I have the gift of prophecy and understanding all mysteries and all knowledge, though I have all faith so that I could remove mountains-but do not have love, I am nothing. Though I bestow all my goods to feed the poor, and though I give my body to be burned but do not have love, it profits nothing.

A love endures and is kind. Love is not envious or jealous. Love wants not itself, is not puffed up, does not behave itself unseemly, seeks not its own; it is not easily provoked, and thinks no evil. Love does not rejoice in unrighteousness but the truth.

Love bears all things, believes all things, hopes all things, and endures all things. Love never fails. Where there are prophecies, they shall fail where there be tongues, they shall cease, where there is knowledge, and it shall vanish away. For we know in part and we prophesy in part, but when that which is perfect is come, that which is part shall be done away with.

When I was a child I used to talk as a child, think as a child, reason as a child. When I became an adult, I put aside childish things. At present we see indistinctly, as in a mirror; but then we shall see face to face. At present I know partially, and then I shall know fully, as I am fully known. So faith, hope, love remain, these three; but the greatest of these is love. You may exchange vows at this time."

"I Chris, take you, Belinda to be my lawfully wedded wife, knowing in my heart that you will be my constant friend, my faithful partner in life, and my one true love. On this special and holy day, I give to you in the presence of God and all these witnesses my sacred promise to stay by your side as your faithful husband in sickness and in health, in joy and in sorrow, as well as through the good times and the bad. I further promise to love you without reservation, honor and respect you, provide for your needs as best I can, protect you from harm, comfort you in distress, grow with you in mind and spirit, always be open and honest with you, and cherish you for as long as we both shall live."

Though the words Chris spoke were somewhat standard for a wedding, they were special to me because I knew he meant every single word. Next it was time for me to present my vows to Chris.

"I, Belinda, take you Chris to be my lawfully wedded husband, knowing in my heart that you will be my constant friend, my faithful partner in life, and my one true love. On this special and holy day, I give to you in the presence of God and all these witnesses my sacred promise to stay by your side as your faithful wife in sickness and in health, in joy and in sorrow, as well as through the good times and the bad. I further promise to love you without reservation, comfort you in distress, encourage you to achieve all of your goals, laugh with you and cry with you, grow with you in mind and spirit, always be open and honest with you, and cherish you for as long as we both shall live."

To my amazement, I didn't stumble or stutter once. Chris's reassuring soft stare eased all of my previous anxieties. Now it was time to exchange rings. Elliott spoke again.

"Wedding rings are an outward and visible sign of an inward spiritual grace, signifying to all the uniting of this man and his woman in marriage."

Mac handed Chris his ring. Chris placed the ring on my finger.

"With this ring, I thee wed. In the name of the Father, and the Son, and the Holy Spirit. Amen."

I placed the ring on Chris's hand and said the same. Elliott then read a passage from Ephesians.

"Submit yourselves one to another as the fear of God. Wives, show reverence for your own husbands, as unto the Lord. For the husband is the head of the wife, even as Christ is the head of the church and He is the

savior of the body. Therefore, as the church is subject unto Christ, so let the wives be to their own Husbands in everything. Husbands, love your wives, even as Christ also loved the church, and gave Himself for it; that He might sanctify and cleanse it with the washing of water by the word; that He might present it to Himself a glorious church, not having spot, or wrinkles or any such thing; but that it should be holy and without blemish. So ought men to love their wives as their own body. He that loves his wife loves himself. For no man ever yet hateth his own flesh; but nourishes and cherishes it, even as the Lord cherishes the church. For we are members of the body, of His flesh, and of His bones. For this cause shall a man leave his father and mother, and shall he be joined unto his wife, and the two shall become one flesh. This mystery is profound and I am saying this as it refers to Christ and to the Church: however, let the husband love his wife as himself, and let wife love her husband."

The ceremony was drawing to a close, but I wasn't in any hurry now. In my mine I heard the train conductor shouting, *'Next stop Newly Wed City!'* This love train had almost reached its final destination.

Elliott then read us our wedding charge:

"Chris and Belinda, as the two of you come into this marriage uniting you as husband and wife, and as you this day affirm your faith and love for one another, I would ask that you always remember to cherish each other as special and unique individuals, that you respect the thoughts, ideas and suggestions of one another. Be able to forgive, do not hold grudges, and live each day that you may share it together-as from this day forward you shall be each other's home, comfort and refuge, your marriage strengthened by your love and respect."

Next, Elliott offered a prayer.

"Dear heavenly Father, our hearts are filled with great happiness on Chris's and Belinda's wedding day, as they come before You pledging their hearts and lives to one another. Grant that they may be ever true and loving, living together in such a way as to never bring shame or heartbreak into their marriage. Temper their hearts with kindness and understanding, rid them of all pretense or jealousy. Help them to remember to be each other's sweetheart, helpmate, friend and guide, so that together they may meet the cares and problems of life more bravely. And with the passage of time, may the home they are creating today, truly be a place of love and harmony, where your spirit is ever present. Bless this union we pray, and

walk beside Chris and Belinda throughout all their lives together. We ask these things in Jesus name. Amen."

The Unity Candles ceremony was next.

"Chris and Belinda, light the candles that symbolize your separate lives, your separate families and your separate sets of friends. I ask that you each take one candle and that you light the center candle. The individual candles represent your individual lives before today. Lighting the center candle represents that your two lives are now joined to one light, and represents the joining together of your two families and sets of friends to one."

I could see Mama beaming in the background. She was obviously enjoying the ceremony as much as, if not more than, I was. It was now time for my favorite part of the ceremony, except for the pronouncement as Husband and Wife, of course. Chris and I had a red rose attached to our lapels. The roses were for the Rose Ceremony, which was next.

"Your gift to each other for your wedding today has been your wedding rings-which shall always be an outward demonstration of your vows of love and respect and public showing of your commitment to each other. You now have what remain the most honorable title, which may exist between a man and a woman - the title of "husband" and "wife." For your gift as husband and wife, that gift will be a single rose. In the past, the rose meant only one thing-it meant the words "I love you." So it is appropriate that for your first gift as husband and wife, that gift would be a single rose. Please exchange your first gift as husband and wife."

Chris and I exchanged roses. As Chris pinned the rose to my dress, he whispered, "I love you Belinda."

I tried to tell him the same, but I was too choked up. His loving words caught me by surprise. He simply nodded, acknowledging my sentimental predicament. At this point and unbeknown to me, Chris had arranged for someone to play the song "Wildflower by New Birth." It was one of Chris's favorite oldies. The song moved me and brought tears to my eyes again. After the song ended, Elliott resumed the Rose Ceremony.

"In some ways it seems like you have not done anything at all. Just a moment ago you were holding one small rose, and now you are holding one small rose. In some ways, a marriage ceremony is like this. In some ways tomorrow is going to seem no different than yesterday. But in fact today, just now, you have given and received one of the most valuable and precious gifts of life - one I hope you always remember-the gift of true and abiding love within the devotion of marriage.

Chris and Belinda, I would ask that wherever you make your home in the future, whether it is a large and elegant home or a small and graceful one- that you both pick one very special location for roses. On each anniversary of this truly wonderful occasion, you may both take a rose to that spot both as a recommitment to your marriage, and a recommitment that this will be a marriage based upon love.

In every marriage there are times where it is difficult to find the right words. It is easiest to be hurt by whom we most love. It might be difficult sometimes to find the words to say 'I am sorry or 'I forgive you; 'I need you' or 'I'm hurting.' If this should happen, if you simply cannot find these words, leave a rose at the spot which both of you have selected. For that rose then says what matters most of all and should overpower all other things and all other words. That rose says the words; 'I still love you.'

The other should accept this rose for the words, which cannot be found, and remember the love and hope that you both share today. Chris and Belinda, if there is anything you should remember of this marriage, it should be that it was love that brought you here today. It is only love which can make it a glorious union, and it is by love which your marriage shall endure."

I loved the Rose Ceremony. But now it was time to hear the words that I had been waiting to hear for so long.

"Chris and Belinda, in so much as the two of you have agreed to live together in Matrimony, have promised your love for each other by these vows, the giving of these rings and the joining of your hands, I now declare you to be husband and wife. What God has joined, let no man put asunder. Congratulations, you may kiss your bride."

As Chris held me gently and gave me a long passionate kiss, I felt the love train coming to a slow and gentle halt. At last! We were now husband and wife.

After we were married, we took what seemed like to me, a hundred or more photographs. Flashes went off as often as my previous wedding memories were going off in my head. I knew Carlton would find some way to *bogard* his way into my wedding.

We finished the photography session and allowed the guest plenty of time to get to the reception before we left the church. Next, we proceeded to the hotel where our reception was being held. The hotel contained a beautiful ballroom. Candace, with the help of a few friends had arrived and supervised the preparation of the reception room.

"Ladies and gentlemen, Mr. And Mrs. Chris Stevenson." Elliott, announcing us, also started the applause. The crowd stood, clapped and cheered.

As Chris and I walked in, we were impressed. Everything looked completely professional and beautiful. Candace had worked her magic once more. We had divided the reception into three events: cocktail hour, dinner and dancing.

The doors to our reception were kept closed until we had freshened up and checked everything out one last time. Candace arrived shortly after we did.

"Girl, you have outdone yourself again," I commented when she came in. "Everything is just right," I told her.

"What did you expect?" Grinning wildly, Candace responded.

Shortly after that, more guests started to arrive. As soon as everyone arrived, I sat in a chair near the guest of honor table and prepared myself to throw the corsage. I sat with my back toward the crowd. The single women gathered behind me, anxiously waiting for my toss. I could hear the talk and laughter in the background.

"Okay Belinda, are you ready sweetheart?" Chris asked me.

"Yes I am."

"Okay, on the count of three…One…two…three…!"

I flung the corsage behind me, high into the air. I could hear footsteps racing for the corsage. It sounded like a stampede. Damn, I thought, there must be some lonely, horny ladies in here. All of a sudden, the once boisterous crowd fell deadly silent. The sudden stillness scared the hell out of me. I looked up at Chris, but he was not looking at me. Instead, he was fixated on the crowd.

"What the hell was going on?" I thought. I turned quickly, almost falling out of my chair. Then I saw what the commotion was all about.

There standing in the middle of the aisle with the corsage in her hands, was none other than my old friend Sheila. She was silent but smiling wildly. At first I didn't know what to make of it. My heart raced through a gamut of emotions-first, extreme happiness.

I hadn't seen her in a while, but not a day had went by in which I didn't think about her. I heard from a mutual friend that Sheila was taking an experimental new drug. This drug had shown promising results with people like Sheila. I didn't think much of this news when I heard it. I didn't think anything could bring her out of comatose personality. But there she was, standing there with a smile and my corsage. I slowly approached her, not knowing what to expect. When I reached her, I stopped briefly and just stared at her.

"What's wrong with you, you crazy or something?" Sheila suddenly shouted.

The room burst out in laughter, and I burst out in tears. Apparently the medicine had worked and Sheila seemed to be her old self again. What a beautiful day this had turned out to be. But that wasn't the only beautiful surprise. As I was hugging Sheila, I just about dropped dead when I noticed another member of the old crew.

It was Celeste, and she was standing in the back of the room with presumably her man. She didn't attempt to move toward me at the time; she just stood there smiling. I could almost read her mind. She was saying 'hello old friend. It's good to see you again.'

She must have been reading my mine also because after a few seconds of staring at each other, she gave me a wink, as if to say, 'It's okay, everything is all right now.' I winked back and blew her a kiss. We would talk later. After that, I grabbed Sheila and would not let her out of my sight for the rest of the reception. I wanted to make sure I wasn't dreaming.

We had so much to get caught up on, and there was no time like the presence, as far as I was concerned. Chris was great; he didn't get jealous of Sheila, like most men would have. He understood perfectly.

The cocktail hour started and the liquor began to flow. The liquor smelled good to me. A shot or two would really go down real good right now, I thought. I was tempted on a couple of occasions to smuggle a snort. But Chris and Candace never let me out of their site. I think they had formed a plan to keep me under some type of "sobriety surveillance" for the evening. Candace had thought of everything.

The cocktail hour quickly came to an end, and dinner was served.

The food was quite delicious and plenty. The wedding photographer and the wedding video technician buzzed around the reception hall all night, taking photos and video recording the entire event. From my seat at the head table, I could see a couple of women eying Chris. Why not, I reasoned? He was a handsome man. If I were in their shoes, I'd be eying him too.

Mama was still having a good time. By the way she was acting; you would have thought it was her wedding. She circulated the room like a Diplomat. But now it was time for the main event-the reception party.

"Ladies and gentle, may I have your attention?" Elliott announced. "Chris and Belinda will have the honor of the first dance, and then the dance floor will be opened to all. Please rise as a sign of respect for these newly weds. The intoxicated crowd stood up and started clapping. Chris and I took the floor. The D.J. put on the first cut; "Always and Forever," by *Heatwave*. Chris held me softly.

"Is everything all right baby? Are you having a good time?" he whispered in my ears as we were dancing.

"Yes sweetheart, I'm having the best time of my life and I want to thank you. I love you so very much Chris." I was crying again as I struggled to tell Chris how much I loved him.

The evening continued swiftly, and as soon as it had all begun, it was over. The party was almost over, but I didn't want it to end. I could have danced all night, but I could tell Chris had other things on his mind. Finally, it was time to leave. We thanked everyone once more and then jumped into our Limo. We headed to a five-star hotel in N.Y. for our honeymoon night. We decided to take a second honeymoon in the summertime to Belize, a country in Central America after the political situation subsided. I wanted to go there because Belize had some of the most beautiful beaches in the world. A friend of mine took a vacation there, and she said the beaches were so blue and so clear; you could see two hundred feet down. And the tropical fish were a marvel. For a few American dollars, a person could really have a great time there.

At least I thought we were headed to the hotel. The driver didn't seem to be heading to the hotel though, but Chris didn't seem too concerned.

"Where is he going?" I whispered to Chris.

"Oh, I asked him to make a quick stop before going to the hotel," he answered.

Suddenly, the driver came to a stop in front of a large, nice-looking house. "Friends of yours?" I asked.

"No," Chris said, smiling like the cat that ate the mouse. Chris exited the Limo and opened my door. By now I was wondering what was going on? Then Chris *swooped* me off my feet and carried me to the door.

"Welcome home baby," Chris said kissing me on the way to the door.

Chris had bought a house for us, and it was a beautiful house. Juggling me in his arms, he pulled out a set of keys and opened the door. There were all kinds of welcome signs in the house. The presents were arranged in two columns, leading all the way up the staircase. There were cards, gifts and flowers everywhere.

On the table was a giant card from Mama. The card read: *'Congratulations baby, enjoy your new life, Mama.'*

It was almost the perfect end to a perfect day-almost. By now I was ready to get Chris in the bed. I was going to make it a night for him to remember forever. Chris was ready too. I couldn't help but notice while he was carrying me, his manhood had awakened.

I walked around looking at all of the beautiful presents. One of the presents read, 'Read me first!'

The gift was wrapped in a beautiful rainbow colored box. There was no name on the card. I had to open it. I carefully untied the pink bow wrapped around the box. I slid my fingers underneath the wrapping paper and removed the tape. I felt the child inside of me taking over again. I slowly opened the box top.

"Chris! Chris! Chris!" I screamed. Chris came running from another room, only to find me completely freaking out.

"What's wrong Belinda? What is it baby?" I was only able to point to the box. There, in the box was a butcher knife, embedded into what look like someone or something's heart. Next to it was a note that read: *'Beautiful wedding, hope your funeral will be as nice!'*

"Oh my God Chris! He was there! He was at our wedding, I moaned in a low self-defeating voice. "He's going to kill me; he's going to kill me," I said in disgust.

"No one is going to kill you Belinda. I won't let them," Chris said holding me in one arm and putting the lid back on the box with his other hand.

"Do you think we should call the police?" I asked Chris.

"No," Chris said.

Candace and I had wondered if the Slicer might attend the wedding. We had the photographer take pictures of everyone who attended the wedding and the reception. *Whomever it is, is somewhere in the pictures.*

"Wait a minute," I said suddenly. "There was a guy in a black tux that kept looking at me all night at the reception, now that I think about it."

"That was Willy," Chris said half-smiling.

"Willy? Who the hell is Willy?" I asked confused.

"Willy is a good friend of mine, who happens to be a cop, and who was your personal bodyguard for the night," Chris explained.

Chris had thought of everything, and I never had a clue.

"Let's go to bed and forget about this for now, okay baby?"

Chris's voice was soothing and reassuring. Although the Slicer had ruined the best day of my life, he had shown his hand, and perhaps he had finally made a mistake.

That night we made love over and over, until we drifted off to sleep. The next morning when I awakened, I quickly went down stairs to see if the box was still there. Maybe I had only dreamed the incident. No such luck, the box was still there. I unwrapped some dishware gifts and made breakfast. As I scrambled the eggs, I subconsciously attempted to recall every single face at my wedding and my reception. Everyone was a suspect in my mind.

"Hey you," a voice called from behind me. Startled, I almost dropped the bowl of half-beaten eggs.

"Oh Chris…you scared me."

"I see," Chris said, hugging me. "How did you sleep last night?" He asked.

"Very well, and you?"

"Like a king," Chris answered, displaying his boyhood smile.

"Listen baby," Chris said, grabbing a piece of toast. "I've got some friends who have volunteered to help us move our things in this weekend, if that's all right with you. We can move you on Saturday and me on Sunday. Meanwhile, that will give you and I time to pack. I'll get the fellows to help me and you can get the ladies to help you. Then, we'll move everything on the weekend. What do you think?"

"Sounds good," I told Chris. After breakfast, Chris had to meet with the closing attorney, to complete some paperwork. I couldn't wait for him to leave. I had something on my mind. As soon as he left, I called Candace.

"Candace, can you come over right now?" Candace must have sensed the urgency in my voice.

"Sure Belinda, but is there something wrong?"

"Yes, something is wrong…the Slicer has sent me something."

Upon hearing this, Candace slammed the phone down and raced over to my place to get the rest of the details. In the meantime, I called the wedding photographer and the wedding video technician and begged him to bring the finished photographs and videos to my house by noon. It took some doing, but I managed to persuade him. Fortunately, money still does talk.

It was around 10:30 a.m. when Candace arrived. I showed her the box, which was still in the house.

"Maybe you should call the cops so they can take fingerprints or something," Candace suggested, looking at the knife. "I wonder where that organ came from," she continued.

"Probably a cat or something," I said. "I know I should call the police

Candace, but somehow I know the police won't find any prints. The Slicer is too smart for that."

At 11:20 the photographer arrived, and shortly after he arrived, the video technician brought the videos over. The Slicer was somewhere in the pictures or on the video. One by one, we looked at every picture; there were 127 pictures in all.

We laid every picture on the floor, forming a giant square of assorted photographs. If any picture contained someone Candace or I didn't recognize, we placed it in a different stack. After about two hours of looking and re-looking over the snapshots, we were able to account for all but seven people.

Next, we looked at the video. We had so much fun watching it; we almost forgot why we were watching it.

"Woooo!" Candace shouted.

"What is it Candace?" I asked.

"Rewind the video," she insisted. I rewound the video a few seconds and then hit the play button.

"Stop, right there!" Candace shouted.

"What!"

There it was the box. Now all we needed was the—'who, when, where, how and why.' But there was doubt about it being the same box as the one the Slicer had sent me. I couldn't stand to look at the box any longer so I threw it in the trash. Maybe one of the seven unidentified people in the photographs was the Slicer.

It took us about a week, but we were finally able to identify the other seven people. They were either relatives or friends of friends. None, as far as we could tell, had any reason to stalk me. Who was this person making content on making my life a living hell, and why was he or she haunting me? What had I done? These questions kept playing over and over in my mind. I was pretty sure the Slicer was someone I knew, perhaps someone I knew damn well. From time to time, I had an uncontrollable, absurd thought; *what if Candace was behind all of this? What if she hadn't forgiven me at all?*

I felt guilty for even thinking these thoughts, but I couldn't help it sometimes. Your mind starts to play tricks on you after awhile. I was beginning to distrust everyone. If I didn't discover who this madman or madwoman was soon, I'd probably go crazy.

Chris and Willie came up with a plan to find out who brought the box to the reception. Over the next few weeks, I was supposed to personally deliver *thank you cards* to everyone who had given me gifts. Of course I would always have someone along with me, like Candace. During the conversation, I was to suppose to say how much I appreciated their gift. Next, I would tell them about the gift with no name on it. I would ask them if they saw anyone bring the gift in. It was a long shot, but it was worth trying.

We visited a dozen or houses, and it seemed as if we were wasting our time. We stopped at Doris Gray's house. When we rang her doorbell, Kathy her six year old daughter opened the door. Doris was standing behind her.

"Hi Belinda, how are you?" Doris said motioning for us to come inside. "Candace, it's nice to see you again."

"How are you Doris?" Candace said, exchanging pleasantries.

"Just fine," Doris replied.

"Look Doris, I just wanted to thank you for the Cappuccino machine. I really love it," I said as Doris closed the door.

"You're welcome, but you didn't have to come all the way over here just to tell me that," she said smiling.

"The wedding and reception was so perfect, I just had to stop by everyone's house and thank them personally," I coolly replied.

Candace seemed impressed with my quick wittiness. She gave me a *'damn you're real good'* glance.

"I got a lot of good presents, but yours was my personal favorite," I continued. "By the way, someone gave me a box full of x-rated videos girl."

"Who gave you that?" Doris asked.

"I don't know. They didn't leave a card, but the box had a rainbow cover. You didn't happen to see who left it did you?"

"No, I don't think so," Doris responded.

"What's x-rated?" Kathy asked her Mom.

"Honey, it's kind of hard to explain."

"I saw the x-rated box at the party," Kathy blurted out. Doris laughed, but I was about to die upon hearing this.

"Kathy honey, did you happen to see who brought the x-rated box to the party?" I asked.

"A man," she said bluntly. I couldn't believe it; Kathy had seen the Slicer!

"Do you remember what the man looked like sweetheart?" I asked Kathy.

"He had money in his shoes," Kathy immediately responded.

What did she mean by *'money in his shoes,'* I thought? I looked around at Candace and Doris, both of whom were smiling. Doris had no clue I was interrogating little Kathy. If she had, I'm sure she would have thrown me out of her house. For all she knew, I was just amusing Kathy. But Candace knew, and I could see the anxiety in her eyes too.

"What kind of money did the man have in his shoes?" I asked, smiling at Kathy.

"Pennies," she barked out.

Pennies...That was it! The Slicer was someone wearing penny loafer shoes.

"Oh," I suddenly said, pretending to have just remembered something. "I've got to run. Thanks again for the gift Doris. I'll see you later." I grabbed Candace and ran out of the house.

"Don't tell me..." Candace said. "We're going to go back and look at shoes now, right?"

"Right," I said jumping into the car.

We went back to my house and spent another hour looking at shoes in the pictures and videos. Unfortunately, we didn't see any penny loafers, but we were sure someone had to notice the shoes. It was only a matter of time before we would find out, or so we thought.

I think the Slicer knew he had finally made a mistake. He or she disappeared for a few weeks. I was sure now this person was someone I knew well; probably someone I had spoken to when I went door-to-door, thanking people for their gift. But which one of them was the Slicer? *Was it Candace, Sheila or maybe one of the girls from our childhood group?* I felt as if the Slicer was somehow connected to my childhood.

I couldn't quantify my feelings, but I was sure all of this madness had something to do with the games we once played with the boys; getting them turned on, testing and teasing them, and then stopping short of going all the way. For that matter, where was Richard now? What had he been doing since getting out of jail for raping Sheila? No, I thought... it couldn't be him.

Weeks passed. I was married and happy again, and I knew Chris would never make me unhappy. I had gotten a handle on my drinking and Candace and I were best friends again. The world was finally *right by me*, and I was really enjoying life. I was no longer dead. I was alive, and it felt good to be alive!

Sitting on my sofa and thinking these thoughts, the theme from *The Mary Tyler Moore Show*, returned to my mind, playing itself again, 'You're *gonna* make it after all...'

Chapter Eight
Time for Change

Rodney

Muggy wet heat entered my bedroom on a Friday morning in the middle of July. I've always wanted satin sheets, but since my air condition was on the blink, the sweaty sheets sticking to my body was unbearable. Thank God it's Friday, it's been such a long week. I've only been in Charlotte for four months, and it seems so different compared to the Bay Area. My job was placing tremendous stress on me.

As a chemical engineer with three process engineers as my subordinates, my job was continuously on the line. I was the one who had to evaluate their decision making process, and if things went wrong, I was certainly the one to be blamed. Ensuring those young fresh out of college process engineers didn't blow up the plant was indeed becoming overwhelming.

On the social scene, a local magazine company interviewed me and named me one of the ten most eligible bachelors in Charlotte. Never, did I want to be spotlighted or placed in a competitive position—but it happened and my privacy was invaded.

After the interview, women constantly made themselves available to me. The men to women ratio in Charlotte must've been ten to two. Never in my life had I seen so many women. Once, for a week, I monitored how many women in comparison to men entered the grocery store. The results were astounding!

After work, some of my new friends would take me to some of the happy hour spots. They were cool places to visit, but never could they compare to the places in Oakland or San Francisco—like Sweet Jimmies or Geoffrey's. The women of Charlotte were different. They asked the same questions like, where you work, what you do and what you drive, placing me into a category of some type. I knew it was just a placement game. In the clubs they only wanted to find out who was making the most money; then they would move on, if I didn't say what they wanted to hear.

I knew the game and sometimes when I felt like it, I would play along with them. I would tell them sometimes I was a farmer, and I raised road kill, like armadillos or squirrels for a living, anything to get them away from me and off my back. But, some of the women had this uniqueness about themselves. It was always easy to discern the wanna bee's from the hood rats, and the *I'm too much for you,* and someone else I know with a lot of money has to introduce you to me; I just ignored them.

After about two months, my co-worker Derrick took me out after work just to unwind. I'd already told him I wasn't in the mood for collecting telephone numbers or even rapping to a female. It wasn't difficult at all for me to be filled with the presence of a lady, but I just wasn't in the mood that day. We went to the Hilton off of North Tryon Street. The bar area had a settled crowd. Most of the people were there just to unwind, the same as us. When we walked into the place, I immediately noticed the stare the bartender delivered while he tried to read our demeanor.

With his white apron tied sloppily around his protruding beer belly, he stood tall and erected, wiping the insides of a glass with what looked like a dish towel. He stared and wiped continuously until we made our way to the bar.

Derrick was medium built, standing about five foot ten. He wore his hair in a neat, short Afro. He didn't hesitate letting it be known that Afros were back in style. Like most single men on the prowl, Derrick kept his hair and clothes in tact. I knew after a drink or two he would be in the mood to talk about someone's clothes, especially if they were wearing loud colors.

The last time we went out he spotted a man in a purple suit, with matching shoes and hat. I practically had to put my hands over his mouth to stop him from laughing. He said that was the way some of the men in the south dressed; he thought it was ridiculous.

Although I didn't agree with the way some of them dressed with the loud colors of pink, lime, yellow and orange; I knew there had to be a reason. I came to the conclusion that when African-Americans were brought over as slaves, we left a homeland that encouraged us to wear flamboyant colors. During festivals and celebrations we'd walked the streets of the motherland with brilliant bright colors; and nothing was said. The men wore Koo Fee hats with long Dashikis—bright colors were vivid to the eyes. I thought perhaps through centuries our chromosomes sustained characteristics of loud colors used in Africa, and this was the reason our southern brothers still had it in them to dress with the bright colors some men wouldn't be seen in at their own funeral. Nevertheless, my justification in the defense to the southern brothers didn't make any difference to Derrick. He dismissed my comments, waved his hand in a downward motion and said, "Yeah, right. Man you're crazy as hell. That fool is just country!"

Derrick didn't notice how the bartender was staring at us—but I did. I walked behind Derrick, listening to him talk about the other co-workers we had just left.

"Rodney, did you see that new girl that works in the front office?"

"Yeah I saw her man." I responded calmly but still keeping my eyes on the bartender, but unable to figure out the look he had on his face as we approach the bar area.

After sitting down and receiving our drinks from the bartender, I felt something was wrong with him. I began to savior the sweet taste of the Crown Royal down my throat. The burning sensation reached my stomach as my eyes caught a glimpse of two of the prettiest beauties I'd yet to see in Charlotte. They approach the bar area with the stride of owning the place. Gracefully they strolled up to the bar directly across from Derrick and me. We turned our heads simultaneously saying, "Damn!"

Like most men would *zoom in on* one particular female in a crowd, the one with the tight pants was my choice. She was elegant. My eyes followed her until her rear end met the leather covered bar stool. If only I could have been that stool was the thoughts running through my mind. She had on tight black pants that displayed every curve of her succulent body. Her firm round hips slowly sat down while her friend chattered away.

They sat directly across from us; my eyes were trying desperately to peruse her entire body before the bar would cover my view. Before she sat down I could see her small waist line and my eyes continued to roll up to the upper portion of her body. She had small full breast, the kind that would make a person assume they were filled with silicone, but they weren't! She was real and well put together. I'd been cool thus far with the females in Charlotte. I'd only talk to women and would leave it at that. But this woman was bringing out some sparks inside of me I'd wanted to lay at rest.

After a previous breakup with my girl friend in Oakland, I knew how susceptible a person could be. I was in the rebound stage of my life. Women knew this was the most vulnerable position any man could be in, to satisfy their needs.

Constantly, I avoided jumping into bed with strange women. My co-worker Derrick thought it was kind of strange; me just talking to women whenever we went out and not trying to sleep with them. I reassured him I was not gay; I just wanted to take my time with women in a new environment. Neither did I use the old sympathy trick on women, by blurting out the fact of just losing my girl friend. That trick for sure would have won me a trip to bed with numerous females in Charlotte.

During my Player's days, all I needed to hear after informing women of a recent break up was, 'awe, you poor baby,' and the next thing I knew we were at their place or mine sharing a wonderful time.

My past was not one of the shy types. I'd gone through so many women it was pathetic, before I managed to settle down with one. I would have given Wilt Chamberlain a run for his money. Nevertheless, I just wasn't into it anymore.

When I was younger I was somewhat shy towards women, for some reason I didn't have the player instinct that existed in me later on in life.

All of my friends had the gift to talk to the school yard girls, but I didn't. When they would talk about the girls they had, I didn't have anything to contribute to the conversation. Until one day a young lady told me I was cute and had some pretty eyes. When girls say a guy is cute it merely means he's not ugly; but neither is he fine. This was easy to relate to, but the pretty eyes thing left me confused. Constantly, I'd wondered what they meant by that.

In the mirror I'd stare trying to figure out what they were trying to say. Was it the shape of my eyes, I'd asked myself. Then, it dawned on me that it would always be during the day light hours when I would be told this. I began to look deeper into the mirror.

Shockingly, I discovered what they were seeing. My eyes that were brown had this bluish gray line around the pupil. When the sunlight reflected off of them, they gave off this grayish brown look. It was as if they were blue, gray and brown altogether. Now I knew why they always said I have some pretty eyes. It went to my head, especially, since I knew and so did the girls that they weren't contacts.

After realizing my eyes would get the attention of girls, that's what I would use most of the time. When I met potential dates I would stretch my eyes open so hard, and place my face directly up to theirs. I wanted my dates to see my beautiful grayish, blue and brown pupil. I had to stop that; my eyelids began to hurt at night. I was stretching them so much that the ball of my eyes almost began to protrude out of its socket.

One young lady had the nerve to ask me what was wrong with my eyes after I stretched so hard to get her attention. I became a womanizer until I grew older and realized, that's not what manhood was all about. I guess I had to live and learn.

Crown Royal on the rocks relaxed me after a hectic day. While having the glass to my lips, my eyes took another look at the young lady across the bar. Surprisingly, she was looking in my direction also and our eyes locked in on one another. I knew the game and I knew what her next move was.

After being in the singles life for such a long time, history had taught me I should say hello from a distance, if her eyes is still *locked* on mines. After I say hello she will return the jester then she will talk to her girl friend about me, if she thought I was cute. *But*, she is going to tell her girl friend not to look in my direction.

Most of the time that's when I would put my hand on my chin resting my elbow in my other hand; like having my arms cross but one in a vertical position. Staring at them both, until they would just give in or ask what the hell I'm looking at! When I was lucky, they'd start laughing and asked me to come over.

In Oakland I learned a long time ago how to play the night club game. Women wanted the men they choose, the most I'd ask for was a dance. When I would have a drink with a woman, I'd play the waiting game when both of our drinks ran out. Although, I had money and could have bought many drinks, I wanted to be with the women that thought buying drinks was a minuet issue. Those were the ones I thought had it going on. I didn't want a woman that came to a club and didn't have at least a hundred dollars in her pockets. That should be standard issue, I thought.

During one incident of the waiting game I remember I had three hundred dollars in my pockets, but at the bar I watched as the ice cubes melt in my glass and I continued to sip, suck and drink what was once a shot of Crown Royal.

The lessons I had learned in California had spoiled me. Some of the women should have known I just wanted them to offer me a drink. I've always been a gentleman, but in California in a night club environment— when a man meets a lady and the first thing out of his mouth is, *'let me buy you a drink.'* He's a damn fool, and is ready to be milked! He might as well wore a red jacket to the club and the women knew it.

Even if a woman was broke, but she saved up her money and came out to the club with a hundred or more; I had more respect for her. We'd sit at the table drinking all night long. Money was placed on the table, waitress coming back and forth, but of course she had to buy my drink first. We'd talk about why I didn't offer to buy her a drink.

One occasion at Geoffrey's in Oakland the drinks were fifteen dollars *a pop*. Candy a friend and a waitress there shared a booth with me. We laughed as we watched this brother making a spectacle. After buying about four or five women drinks and they all leaving him for someone else, he made it to a table with four women. Of course they all were riding together. Between them and the other women he had bought drinks earlier, they must have *milked* that brother out of at least five hundred dollars that night. Maybe, he had it like that; but it was so obvious he didn't—he was only given the opportunity to walk them to the car and waved good bye. He stood with the stupid grin on his face and a wrong number in his hand.

Candy and I laughed endlessly that night. There were so many times we would see the same scenario, but still couldn't figure out what it would take for the brothers to understand—or to figure out the mind set and mentality of some of the young ladies in the night club scene.

Candy was my friend; she was an artist and an actress. In between jobs she would work at Geoffrey's to help make ends meet. We rolled around in the sheets a couple of times, but we remained friends. It was one of the hardest things I'd ever had to do in my life. She was a baby doll—extremely close to impeccable.

The young lady that sat across the bar reminded me of her. When I sat my glass on the bar—I notice her staring, but now she turned her head away. Unexpectedly, she stepped away from the bar stool and started walking my way; without saying a word to her counter part. Why I became so nervous watching her foot touch down on the shinny floor, I don't know. Each step rhythmically moved in a left over right pattern.

Being frighten at this point would have been an understatement, but this was the type of woman I had wanted. The bold/blunt type—the kind that will ask me, 'can I buy you a drink.'

Her hair was straight and tied in a bun. Her girl friend watched her walk over to where I was sitting, wondering what she was doing. The strap from her purse was hanging off of her shoulders, so she slid it back to her collar bone; still walking gracefully. A short walk but it seems as if it took forever. Finally the elegant woman stood in front of me.

"Hi, I'm Celeste Lewis. What's your name?" she extended her hand.

I was in a state of shock; I knew I wasn't in California. Never would I expect a woman from the Carolina's to act like this. All of the southern women would think, 'That's so un-lady like.' How wrong they would be, 'cause Celeste presented herself more than in a womanly like manner. Everything about her was classy. I waited for a woman of such caliber since I've been in the Carolina's. I was tired of looking for it, so I decided to relax for a while.

"My name is Rodney Anderson. It's a pleasure to meet you Celeste." We shook hands and for a moment we stared at each other. I dared to give her a glimpse of my pupils. I was afraid they would've locked up on me.

The warmness of her hands sent a sensual feeling throughout my body. Derrick stood with his mouth wide open, wondering what I did to have such a beautiful creature standing in front of me. Celeste's eyes were like the sweet tone of a whisper. Her melodious style was so unusual than any other woman I'd met.

Immediately after I told her my name she glanced at Derrick. His bushy eye brows shot upward into his forehead. His hand extended outward to shake hers—practically before I could spurt a word out of my mouth.

"Celeste, this is Derrick." Their hands joining momentary, then she looked back towards me; not hearing a word Derrick was saying to her.

"It's a pleasure to meet you Celeste."

Recognizing the greeting from Derrick, Celeste turned her head to him once again and paid due respect.

"Nice to meet you too Derrick."

"Won't you have a seat Celeste, can we talk?" I pointed towards the stool next to me. I asked in hope to get to know who the fabulous creature that stood in front of me was.

She leaned her hand on the bar counter. From the corner of my eyes I could see the bartender glancing while still wiping, what could have been the same glass when we first arrived? Still, in my mind I knew there was something wrong about him.

"I'd like that Rodney, but I left my friend over on the other side of the bar."

We all turned to look and see if her friend was taking in the new situation with ease, apparently she was; at that moment she looked at us from the top of her small framed—what appeared to be reading glasses. She held a flyer of some sort in her hands; carefully nursing a lime colored Margarita.

"Derrick, why don't you go keep my girlfriend company while Rodney and I talk?"

"Okay." Derrick said wondering if she was going to be as friendly as Celeste. "Will she bite?"

"No, just tell her I sent you over, and I'll be right back. Her name is Diane."

Diane was nice looking too. The glasses didn't hide her beauty. Unlike Celeste she seems to be more laid back. I could hardly wait for Derrick to get up off of the bar stool so I could hear what this woman had to say. My patient was fading so I gave him a stare as to say, 'you're not up yet?' Derrick understood my look and he expeditiously walked to where Diane was sitting.

The stringy hair bartender was staring at our moves, finally he put the glass and dish towel down. Celeste sat down on the bar stool while I sipped down the remainder of my watered down Crown Royal. I wanted to suck one of the ice cubes to gain some sort of composure. But I couldn't, I had to talk to her and make her feel comfortable. I was more than scared of this woman. She was more than any man could ever ask for in a woman—just from sight; it was easy to see she was a *full package*.

My glass landed on the bar and the ice cube swirled around the glass in a circular motion. Moisture from the cold glass surrounded my finger tips. Our eyes met while she repositioned her purse that was hanging off of her shoulders.

"What're you drinking Rodney?" She asked with a smile that would make a man get on his knees and beg to be with her for life.

"Crown on the rocks." I replied. Not knowing she would be the type to just go ahead and order it for me.

"Okay, I think I'll have the same." She motioned to the bartender for service, and then she began to reach into her small square shaped leather purse.

The bartender approached us and smile. She pulled out a wade of money thick enough to wrap around a cat's neck for a choker. I wondered what in the world she was doing with such a large roll of money, I held my reaction back. She could have easily taken one of the crisp twenty dollar bills out. I knew this was a test. I was being confronted differently. I believed she wanted to see my reaction.

"May I help you?" The stringy hair bartender asked. He looked at her with a smile, for a quick second we made eye contact. His mannerism was of an uncomfortable one, I didn't know if he was nervous because of Celeste or me. Celeste continued to display poise, I just sat and stare; wondering who should I be analyzing her or the bartender.

"Two Crown Royal on the rocks." Celeste said. Then she placed two twenty dollar bills on the counter while the bartender walked away.

Celeste turned herself around once again facing me. I was nervous not knowing what would come next from this flawless beautiful lady. She was dark skinned with small dimples in her cheeks. Straight shiny black hair complimented all of her features. It was easy to observe she knew how to work the bar scene.

"So Rodney, tell me who you are in one sentence." Celeste said with a curious grin, as she tilted her head to the side.

"That's kind of hard to do in just one sentence Celeste, but I'll try."

"It shouldn't be that hard, just tell me the good qualities."

"Okay then, I would have to say, I'm gentle, kind, and an easy going person—unless provoked in the wrong way."

"Oh that's good, I like how you handled that question."

"And you Celeste, who are you?"

"I don't need an entire sentence to describe myself."

"Really and why not?"

"I just need three words."

"What would they be?"

"Mysterious, hot and precise!"

"Why those choice of words Celeste?" I asked waiting for more to come from the precious jewel of a woman. I also noticed Derrick had developed a conversation with Diane and seemed to be having a good time. Then the bartender returned with our drinks. He placed them in front of us and stepped back, wiping his hands with a dish towel.

"That'll be seven fifty each. Is this together?" He looked at me, although he could clearly see the forty dollars Celeste had set on the bar in front of her.

"It's together. Here keep the change." Celeste passed him a twenty. Good ethics should have told him she wasn't going to tip him the next round. Celeste gave me her attention again after she sipped the Crown over ice.

"Hum, that's good, haven't had that in a long time." She put the drink down on the bar gently, while glancing around the bar area as if she was scanning the place. "I used those words for a reason. But a person really would have to get to know me to understand why."

All the while I thought she forgot about the question, but she didn't.

"Oh really? I wonder if it would be to their advantage getting to know you."

"What do you think, sweetie?"

"They say never judge a book by its cover, you know."

"If I have to say so, the pages inside this book are a good read," Celeste said, smiling while she lifted her glass up for a toss. Her dimples seemed to be larger, or perhaps it was the Crown Royal making me see things.

"Prose," she said. I knew the word was German from one of my classes in college. Some sort of style this woman had; to be using a European word on me as we tossed.

"So Celeste, how long have you been in town?"

"I never said that I was from out of town, Rodney."

"You didn't have to." I took a sip of the Crown, while she waited for me to finish. "I can easily tell."

"Oh really, and how can you tell?"

"Besides the absence of a southern draw, the way you carry yourself. I watched you from the moment you stepped in the bar."

"Oh really, why didn't you come and try to talk to me then?"

"It's not my style baby girl." My confidence level was building up while my drink was slowly disappearing from the glass.

"And what is your style Mr. Rodney? How did you know I was going to come over to you?"

"I didn't, I was just hoping you would and at the same time admiring your beauty. I know you probably heard it a million times. But Celeste, you're real pretty and you have the most beautiful eyes I've ever seen." I knew the eye thing would get her buttered up. Her response was the next thing I wanted to see.

"Oh, that's so sweet of you Rodney. You really know how to pour it on a lady, huh? Yeah, I hear that a lot, but it's never too much. Coming from you I can sense the sincerity though."

"I'm definitely sincere about it Ms. Celeste or is it Mrs. I didn't see a ring."

"It's Miss. and you're right, I'm not from here."

"Oh okay, if you don't mind me asking. Where are you from?"

"Chi town, baby boy, originally from Boston though."

"Yeah, I can tell how you strolled your pretty self over here. Most southern girls walk like they're carrying a load on their backs, and I said most, not all!"

"Is that right?"

"Oh yeah, and another thing most southern girls are not going to offer to buy a man a drink, they're not ready for that."

"You sure do know a lot about southern girls. Sounds like you've been psychoanalyzing them."

"No, I just been around."

"Been around or been through them?" We both laughed gingerly and I could see how comfortable she was getting with me.

"Let me get the next round," I asked.

"Sure go ahead."

I waved the bartender, indicating for two more rounds. With my eyes on Celeste I could see her beauty even more. She knew I was staring at her excessively, I couldn't help myself. Celeste was bringing feelings out of me I had tried to put away for a long time. I was warm on the inside and the thoughts of holding her raced through my mind. I watched as she fidgeted on the bar stool. Occasionally she would turn to see if her girl friend was okay. Derrick was making sure of that. Never had he been given the opportunity to be with a pretty woman like Diane so easily.

The bartender handed the drinks to us. I paid and tipped the same as she did. Although, I should have thought about the tip she had already given him, my mind was someplace else—on her and getting to know more.

It was strange when we talked, the conversation of what type of work we did never came up. I did wonder, but continued to keep the conversation on the level she wanted it to be. She only wanted us to talk about each other and not what we did or who we were attached to.

When the bartender sat our drinks down, Celeste picked up her twenty off of the counter and wrapped it around the wad of money she had. It was as if she was letting the thin haired bartender be aware she had money. Something was happening, what I had not a clue. But it was obvious something was going on. I started to wonder if there was a possible connection between the two. I wasn't a detective but I knew there was something wrong with the stringy haired bartender. Now, I knew Celeste was on some sort of mission. She was *too* fine to be working the bar on a professional level, and she had too much class to be a lady of the night. Those types of women were easy to pick out.

As the night began to settle, Celeste suggested the four of us get together in one of the booths and share drinks while we talked. It sounded like a good idea. The beady eyed, stringy haired bartender followed us to where Derrick and Diane were seated.

"Diane this is Rodney Anderson. Rodney, Diane."

"The pleasure is mine Diane. Are you enjoying yourself with my friend Derrick?"

"Oh yes he's such a nice guy."

"Hey guys, there's a nice booth over there we can use." Celeste said.

I nodded my head agreeing to the new location, and then I turned in the other direction only to notice the bartender still staring down my throat. We left the bar and sat in the half moon shaped booth. Derrick and I allowed the ladies to go in first. After sitting down I felt kind of awkward not knowing where to put my arms. Finally I put one arm on the back of the seat behind Celeste; not hugging her, just letting it rest. When the waitress came, I pulled out some money just to let Celeste know I wasn't some dead beat.

"Diane, I already know what Celeste and I are drinking. What can I get you and Derrick?"

"I'll have a Margarita, thanks Rodney."

"And I'll have a Crown on the rocks," Derrick said, as if he was anxious to get back to his conversation with Diane."

"Hey guys I was just starting to tell Diane about my visits to my grandparents' farm in Ohio."

Derrick must have been tripping. I knew he never spent a day on a farm, and his grandparents lived in the city. But I didn't want to burst his bubble, so I listened.

"I remember one time I went to visit my grandparents and it was time to eat."

We all stood anxious to hear what Derrick had to say. He was truly an entertainer after a few drinks.

"I reached into the cabinet to get a dish, then I held the antique china in my hands for a minute only to notice how clean the dish was."

The drinks arrived to the table; it was just a moment's interruption. *But,* Derrick had the girls' total attention. He continued to tell us about his visit to the farm, while I paid and tipped the waitress.

"I was so amazed at how clean and shiny the dishes were. I asked my Grandpa, 'Grandpa how do you get this dish so clean?' He replied, 'Oh it's just as clean as cold water will get it.' Then I went and fixed me some of that good ole beef stew he had on the stove."

We were all listening to Derrick. But since he had Celeste's attention also, I thought I'd take a quick glance at the suspicious looking bartender. He was on the phone, talking to someone while staring at Celeste and Diane. Quickly I turned away and continued to listen to Derrick.

"That was some good stew. Afterwards I asked Grandpa what to do with my plate. As he was getting out of his chair he said, 'Oh just leave it there. Cold water will take care of it.' When Grandpa went into the next room, I could hear him yelling as he kicked his lazy, sleepy old dog. He said, 'Cold

Water, get your lazy, good for nothing ass up.' The dog came walking by me and began licking my plate."

"Awe, ha, ha. Man that's some funny stuff. Cold Water," Celeste responded in laughter.

"I don't get it. Was the dog named Cold Water?" Diane asked.

"Yeah girl," Celeste interjected. "You slow or something?"

"No, I guess I just missed the punch line."

I continued to sip my drink. We must have ordered at least three more rounds. Celeste and Diane were staying at the Hilton in separate rooms. Celeste was feeling pretty comfortable with me and after so many questions and answers; she told me she never *gave it up* on the first date in so many words. Another good quality in a woman I admired. If only some of them could stick to it after a few drinks, I thought to myself.

While turning around to look at Celeste, she moved closer to me. She was now about an inch away from my face.

"Am I too close to you Rodney?"

"No, as a matter of fact, I think you're just right!"

It seemed as if music was being played. I was an inch away from the prettiest moist lips I'd ever seen. Her legs were crossed and clinching.

It was clear to me her precious jewels were not to be violated. What wasn't clear was—could this be a game of enticement? Why bother, I thought. If there wasn't going to be after play—forget about foreplay.

I started wondering if Celeste could just be teasing me. Here I was staring at those sweet juicy luscious lips and I wanted to kiss her badly, but I knew she would just pull away. Embarrassing me, no, I wasn't going to fall for that. Being only inches away from her I had to prove myself. I noticed Derrick and Diane had stopped what they were doing to enjoy the entertainment.

Thinking quickly, I reached for my glass of Crown and took an ice cube out of the glass and gently rubbed the cube around her lips. She gasped; Derrick and Diane had a surprised look on their faces. Celeste's eyes closed. Then she opened them.

"Awe, that was so nice. You sure do know how to cool a woman off, don't you?"

"I really don't know if I wanted to cool you off, but from what you've said, perhaps it's best," I said to her in a calm voice, while Derrick sat with his mouth opened wide enough for a fly to enter.

"Tell you what Rodney." Celeste squirmed in her seat. "I don't normally do this, but let me run upstairs and change. Then I want you to take me to the liquor store and get my own bottle of Crown, okay?"

"Okay baby girl, I'll be here when you get back."

"Come on Diane." Celeste practically dragged her out of the seat. Derrick and I looked at each other. We knew the girls wanted to have a conference. As soon as they were out of view Derrick nudged me on the shoulders.

"Man that was a slick move. Damn! She seems like she's on fire and digging you man."

"No man it's all just play. But when she gets back we're going to the liquor store. I think she's going to invite me up."

"Really, I know you're glad we drove separate cars and met here."

"Yeah, but I know we are not going to do nothing. She just wants some company. And she knows I wouldn't respect her if she did."

"Man that's crazy! What are you looking for a girl friend or some fun?"

"Awe, we just getting acquainted, how is it looking with Diane?"

"Man she got a boy friend here in Charlotte. I think that's the reason they're here. You lucked up. She says Celeste doesn't have anyone."

"Yeah, I kind of figured that from how she's trying to play me."

"I know man; she can drink and still be in control. And that dude of Diane's sure is a lucky cat."

"Hey man, have you been noticing how the bartender's been looking at us with the girls since we've been here?" I nudged my head towards the bartender and Derrick turned to look, then he leaned across the table.

"Maybe he's just jealous, Rodney."

"No, I think something else is up with this guy."

₧₧

Celeste changed her clothes, and was now wearing a pair of jean shorts with a tight fitting T-shirt.

"Okay, you changed your clothes." I said with a surprise—but wasn't.

"Yeah, I wanted to relax a little, you know." She paused for a second before turning to Derrick. "It was nice meeting you Derrick, you're so funny. Are you ready to ride Rodney?"

"Yeah baby, I'll see you Diane, nice meeting you. Hang in *there* Derrick, peace out."

Softly, we walked out of the hotel. I knew the bartender's eyes were following us. There wasn't a guy in the place that wasn't watching Celeste when she came down in those shorts that were cut so short they were close to being a G-String. But the girl gave class to wearing clothes a hooker would probably wear.

Finally we made it to my black Lexus SC with its peanut butter seats. I opened the door for Celeste. When I stuck the key in the ignition the steering wheel adjusted to my height and the surround sound stereo system came on with some sweet jazz from the CD player. The DVD rolled out and Denzel was on the screen. I gazed at her as I reached for the button to let the sun roof roll back. My Lex and a queen; what more could I have asked for? I thought.

I pressed the handle on the steering column to a pre-programmed destination. I had frequented the ABC store off of Village Lake quite a bit. I could have gone to a store that was closer, but I just wanted Celeste to hear the sweet voice of the computer as it said, 'Destination, ABC store, Village Lake Rd. estimated time of travel twenty minutes. Estimated distance is eighteen miles.'

I had no plans to use the vehicle's instructions; I guess I was just showing off—just a little. Celeste angled herself displaying more of what was under those jean shorts. I could see her nice firm legs while she crossed them in the passenger's seat. She smelled like sweet jasmine. Everything about this woman was erotic.

"You said you haven't been here long, huh Rodney?"

"No, not long at all."

"You're going to be a good catch for someone. I know they're after you like white on rice, huh?"

"Not really, I'm just checking out everything now. I'm not trying to get attached to anyone. You know what I mean?"

"Yeah I know what you mean. I like that in a man. You know how to take your time. They say when a man takes his time he can do everything right."

"Oh okay, well I guess that does have some logic to it. It gives you more time to concentrate on what you're doing when you take it slow."

"Oh, I was thinking the same thing. Was that computer right when it said it'll take twenty minutes to get to the store?"

"Why, are you getting impatient?"

"No, I just want to get back and take a bath. That's all."

Instantly I started wondering why this woman was telling me enticing information. I really didn't need to know she wanted to take a bath. I thought this was another one of her mind games, so I just dismissed it.

Purposely I passed several liquor stores to give her a tour of the city. While riding on I-277, the loop around the skyline of Charlotte, I noticed the warm breath taking feeling Celeste was embracing from the scenery. The sun had begun to set. Its golden rays were reflecting off of her and it just intensified her beauty. I could hardly keep my eyes on the road.

I've always been impressed with the wonderful skyline of Charlotte. It was difficult at first for me to believe how a small country town could look so nice. It was growing and many others were migrating to the wonderful town. I loved it!

We cruised around the city and I took the off ramp to downtown. We drove downtown then back onto the freeway to Independence Blvd. I stopped my vehicle to get the Crown Royal at the ABC store as originally planned. Like a gentlemen I came to the door to let Celeste out, but I noticed her extending her hand; as if she wanted me to help her out of the car. Knowing she wasn't at all handicapped, but I couldn't help but to obliged to her offering.

She really didn't need me, it was just the point of having a gentlemen's touch. I think it was significant to her.

All eyes were on her. People stopped in their tracks to stare at the beautiful creature that was walking beside me. I felt as if we were walking down the red carpet to the Hollywood Awards show.

Celeste grabbed my hand as we walked into the liquor store. She made sure everyone knew she was with me, even if it was just a *front*. While we were in line she took it to another level by holding my hand with both of hers. She came closer to my side and leaned her head on my shoulder, while standing in line.

It was breath taking how this young lady was cuddling me in public. While we were in line she noticed an expensive bottle of Hennessey. The top shelf liquor was in a display box, surrounded by a silk gold material. The bottle was fancy shaped with an elegant top on it. Everything about it was saying it was too much for my pockets. The price tag on it said $1,895. Celeste lifted her head off my shoulder when her eyes spotted the bottle of Hennessy.

"Oh that's how much she paid for it?"

I had no idea what she was talking about, so I questioned her.

"Who Celeste, who are you talking about?"

"Oh, my girlfriend back home, Carla. She told me she paid $2,500 for it. It must be cheaper here in the South.

A lump came to my throat but I played it cool, knowing it would just be by luck, if my taste buds were to ever savior the expensive drink that sat behind the counter—guarded by the teller.

"If you ever want to get me something, that would make a nice, present."

I just stood and looked at Celeste as if she was out of her damn mind. Instantly, I controlled the jester that had engulfed my facial expression. I just responded kindly.

"I sure will."

"*Yeah right!* I bet you will. Rodney I don't care how much money I may have, I would never spend that much on a bottle liquor."

"I hear you Celeste. But from the way that wad of yours looked at the Hilton, it doesn't seem like you're hurting for nothing."

"I was wondering when you were going to get around to talking about that."

"Oh really, and what made you think I would be talking about it."

"For one thing, you should ask yourself if a lady pulls out a roll like that, is she buying something or selling something."

Her comment left me kind of confused. I paid the clerk for the bottle of Crown Royal. But still wondering where this conversation was going.

"Okay, now you've got me curious." Puzzled, yet I continued while my mind began to shift gears. "If you were selling something, there were discreet buyers. Perhaps that stringy haired bar tender."

"Hey, Rodney you're pretty observant huh. Let's talk about it later, I'll fill you in."

We made it back to the Hilton, as expected all eyes were on Celeste in the parking lot. While strolling to the elevator she clung to me just like she did in the liquor store. Celeste was beautiful. Her dark skin was evenly toned all over. After pressing the button for the third floor she laid her head on my shoulders and looked me in my eyes.

"I was wondering why you haven't asked me why I'm nestled so close to you."

"I figured you would tell me sooner or later," my broken voice responded.

I was nervous, but, couldn't let her smell the fear inside of me. The elevator stopped on the third floor. We stepped out and Celeste led the way.

"I wanted you to feel how it would be to have me as yours."

Celeste began to search her small purse for the card key to the room. She looked at me while sticking the card key into its slot.

"Not that I'm loose or anything like that—'cause I'm not!"

"Okay, I understand. Then tell me why you were *all up on* a brother like that. What was I supposed to think?"

"Just think how things would be if we were together. How did you feel? 'Cause to tell you the truth Rodney, I think *you are all that and some.*"

"Hey, without a doubt the feeling is mutual. And thanks Celeste, I didn't know you felt that way."

"I don't believe in holding back Rodney, I say what's on my mind."

"In that case say Rodney then, 'cause I want to be all over your mind."

"*Alrighty then!* You getting kind of bold aren't you. I bet after a little of that fire water I will see a little more of the true Rodney huh?"

"I don't think so, I have to drive. Most of the times I like to drink water in between my drinks. It sort of dilutes it."

"Okay, I have some bottled water in the fridge," Celeste said as we made our way into her nice smelling room.

She went directly into the bathroom while I placed the bottle of Crown on the dresser. Music was needed, so I turned on the TV to the video station. A slow ballad was being played. Celeste knew the lyrics. Her voice traveled from the bathroom while I easily assumed she was just fixing herself up.

With fresh lipstick on and obviously feeling more at ease, she stepped to me, standing in front of me looking as sweet as candy.

In fact her name should have been Candy, instead of Celeste.

"Rodney do you mind taking the bucket and getting us some ice?" The ice machine is right down the hall."

"Sure Babe," I responded.

"Here take the key; I'm going to start getting ready to take my bath."

Celeste passed the key to me while my mind was blank with the thoughts of her in the bath tub. This girl was moving too fast for me. Although I knew the speed; I just wanted something a little slower. Or did I? I questioned my thoughts, only to come to the conclusion that at this point anything might go.

During the entire walk to the ice machine I wondered why things were going so easy. She didn't strike me as being an easy woman. Still, we were getting along remarkably well. How could she feel me out and know I wasn't a rapist or something? I suppose after she saw the type of vehicle I drove she was more comfortable with me. Somehow I believed she would have invited me no matter what I drove.

The cubes of ice fell into the bucket and some spilled to the floor. Anxious I walked back to the room and opened the door—the bucket in one hand, card in the other and high hopes of an intriguing evening resting on my mind.

Celeste danced around the room to the song *"Kiss Of Life,"* by Sade with her cup in her hand. It already had some Crown Royal in it and she couldn't wait to get some ice. She had changed her clothes again. With only a silk robe on, it was easy to notice the curves and grooves of her voluptuous body. If she would've stood still I could easily have used her rear as a coffee table and sat a drink on it.

Her dimension was as if her family of the past served many laboring days in the hot fields of the south picking cotton, cropping tobacco or whatever it took to survive. Unaware their body structure would form a shape that would be passed down from one generation to the next.

A smile dressed my face as I thought, *'I'm so glad her great grandmother was a hard worker out in the fields.'*

"What are you smiling about?" Celeste asked.

She caught me in my thoughts.

"Nothing, just thinking to myself, and admiring your beauty."

"Thanks, I had to get out of that tight stuff. Come sit down on the bed."

Celeste sat her drink down on the night stand and bounced her happy self on the bed. Cheerful she was; almost like a kid in a candy store.

After putting the ice in my cup I poured about a two inch shot and sat beside her on the round bed. Her thin robe was tied tight. It had moved quite a ways up her smooth, firm thighs.

"So, how are you feeling Celeste?" I questioned, trying to start a conversation.

"Oh, I feel warm, and bubbly. This is some good stuff."

"Yeah, but I better take it easy; I've got to drive you know."

"Okay, so you have a little self-control."

"When it comes to me, I'd like to say I'm in control."

"Really!" she turned her head in amazement.

Celeste stood up and pulled at her silk robe that I knew was filled with bareness. I had begun to feel warm, aroused from her beauty.

I was continuously trying to hold back my desires and stick to my dating rules. But, she was pushing me to a breaking point. Not knowing what would be next—I knew this woman was full of surprises.

She walked over to the wall by the door and flicked off the lights. The movement of her silhouette from the street lights shone in through the window gracefully. She walked to the lamp looking bare, and flicked on the lamp.

"I'm feeling kind of tense do you know how to massage Rodney?"

She wanted me to touch her flesh. My fingers tingled from the thought. It was happening—if I touched her I didn't know what it would lead to, I thought.

Celeste clicked off the lamp and disrobed down to her waist. She tied the straps of her robe around her. From the side in the dimmed lights I could see the perfect shape of two teardrops that stood erected like torpedoes or missiles about to fire.

"Could you rub me between my shoulder blades, Rodney?"

"Yes Celeste, with pleasure."

It was more than pleasure for me, it was an honor. Just to touch her I knew would be the highlight of my evening. Quickly, I stepped behind her about an inch away from pressing my nervous body onto hers. My hands glided themselves to her leveled shoulder blades. My fingers massaged her tight muscles in a circular motion. She awed at the motion of my fingers. I could feel her sensation tingling through my hands.

"Awe, that feels so good Rodney."

"Yeah, baby you're kind of tense."

"I know, I'm not stressing or anything. I guess my muscles just tighten up sometimes."

My movement and technique began to amaze me. I was sending Celeste into a trance with my gentle touch. She was in another world I could easily tell. Celeste' moans grew louder while she was enjoying the massage. The intense sounds were as if we were engaging in romance—but we weren't. My body wasn't even touching hers, only my hands were on her shoulders. I wondered what was going on but continued to participate in a level of foreplay I had never encountered.

"Awe, yes. It feels so good." She cried.

Celeste was now at a higher level. She discarded the robe and it fell to the floor, exposing her pure secrets. I was astounded from her nakedness and she turned around and pulled me to her.

Our bodies met, with my swollenness being the only barrier between us. Her soft lips connected to mine and we kissed passionately. *A nice dry kiss—not sloppy and wet.* Her movements on me were intense while we kissed.

Suddenly, she became louder with her moaning, her grip on me tightened and she began to shake. Shivering recklessly she began kissing me all over my face. She *grinded* me as if she was trying to put her body inside of mine—while making the sounds of pure ecstasy.

Her nails in my back felt as if they had broken through my silk shirt. I felt her gripping me tightly, breaking right through my epidermis. She shook and squirmed, almost squeezing the breath of life out of me. Then it happened! She exploded right there before me, standing next to me. Two bodies connected as one without me ever entering her tunnel of love or breaking the seal.

The awe feeling capsulated her aurora, she was pleased. I could easily tell from her soft whispers of outward breaths. Calmness had no control of Celeste and she wasn't finished. She started again, but this time I interrupted the mood. I slid away from her before she could start again; realizing I wanted something a little bit more than flesh or mere pleasure.

"I can't do this, Celeste!"

"Why, isn't *this what* you want!" She questioned as she picked up her robe and covered herself up.

"Oh yes, it's what I want. There's nothing gay about me. But, I'm just looking for a little bit more."

"Oh really? And what is it that little bit more you're looking for? I'm feeling like I'm throwing myself on you, and you have the nerve to resist. Don't you know how many men would be dying to be in your shoes?"

"Hey, I know that you're fine and all that, and believe me it's tempting than a mother...., but not like this. When you told me you don't roll like that on the first date. I was cool with it, 'cause I was trying to be like that. I want to find that special someone like you were in the bar. *The girl who does things differently, to make me feel good, like you did by offering me a drink first.* I thought that was unique. And I like that." I tuned my head away from her, hoping not to have offended her.

Celeste walked over to the lamp and turned it on. The bulb wasn't that bright and she seemed to have not been upset because of my actions.

"You're a strange brother, I like that!" she said as she twisted her flawless body towards the window. "Tell you what, I'm gonna share something with you."

"What are you talking about, Celeste? I think you tried to do that already."

"Don't flatter yourself too much my brother. Like I said before, I do think *you're all that*, but you know they come a dime a dozen. Remember when me and Diane came up to the room to change?"

"Yeah, I remember. What are you hinting around to?"

"Look under the pillow, baby boy. I think you'll find an explanation."

I was curious at this point. Wondering what Celeste was talking about. At first I thought she was the type of woman I was looking for, but when she came across as the average I knew she wasn't in my league. Despite how she turned me on and made me aroused; that came a dime a dozen also—to me! Now she wanted me to look under the pillow. For what—I wondered, but I went to the bed to see what it was she wanted me to see.

While walking to the bed my mind was reminiscing on her behavior when we held each other. Never had I seen a lady reach her peak from the connecting of two bodies in such a short period of time. Damn! She turned me on and didn't realize it.

The bed was still made with the hotel blanket wrapped around the pillow. I pulled the blanket back and tossed the pillow aside. Underneath the pillow were an envelope and a shiny nickel-plated nine millimeter. The site of the gun was a complete surprise. But being from California I was use to it. Most of the females stayed *packed* for their own protection.

"Leave the piece, I want you to open up the envelope," Celeste said while she went towards the door to turn on the other light.

"I'm going to turn on this light so you can see."

I picked up the envelope, opened it and began to read the letter.

If you've gotten this far you may be the one for me. My life has been difficult and I've been through so many trifling relationships. Feel fortunate that I've asked you to read this, 'cause if you were a thuggish brother and tried to take what you wanted, I would've blown you away with the piece that's lying next to this letter. Believe that!

I figure you wouldn't have believed me when I told you that I had no intention of giving you some of this body. So, I wrote this way ahead of time and I put the time down, so you wouldn't think that I use this letter on all of the men I meet. As you can see the time is the same time I left you at the bar and came up to my room;5:45.

I felt you Rodney, and despite what you may have told me, I just wanted to see with my own two eyes if you were the type that would screw the first bimbo that would drop her drawers for you. I don't need a man like that! Even if he is drinking, I like to know if my man can handle his own. You would never have gotten any of this, and if you didn't understand no and tried to man handle me, your ass would have been shot!

But thanks for being the potential man that I'm looking for. Now, we can relate and I will be open to you, telling you who I am, and we can get to know each other a little better. If you're scared I understand, but you're not. You're the one. That's why you're reading this letter.

Now grab me and kiss me, I'm yours if you like. It will take some time to have all of me. Just be patient, okay? I've seen what I like. I just go after it in a different way. Celeste.

A picture of a rose was at the bottom of the letter. I held the letter in my hands and Celeste looked at me innocently and sweetly. She waited; I came over and hugged her gently—passionately kissing her. A moment of breath we shared with our eyes inches apart. I could feel her, she was mysterious and exciting. No longer did I feel the boring relationship of the past that always turned out to be never as good as it was the first time. The thought of the gun never entered my mind as I gazed into her soft brown pupils. She was more than a dream as we stared at each other and I held her tight once again—in my arms.

"Rodney." She smiled innocently.

"Yes Celeste."

"I didn't fake that orgasm."

I boiled inside wondering how many more surprises she had in store for me.

The next couple of days Celeste and I had lunch and dinner together. We made it a point not to get close to each other. We both knew it would only lead to intimacy. After about a week of dating, two days passed without a call from her. I knew she was in town with her friend Diane; therefore, I didn't want to smother her with phone calls. I gave her space to socialize.

While walking to the bathroom the telephone rang. It was her.

"Hey Rodney."

"What's up baby girl? How you been?"

"Oh fine, been going through some things with Diane."

"Really? What kind of things?"

"You wouldn't believe it if I told you Rodney."

"Try me!" I could hardly wait to hear what was going on. My bladder was about to burst and I knew she heard the stream of my waste products as it dived into the bowl.

"Okay *peep* this Rodney. You remember that stringy haired bartender right?"

"Yeah, I remember him.'

"He's not a bartender anymore. Don't know what happened to him, but apparently he was a supplier."

"A supplier of what?"

"Drugs, silly."

"What does that have to do with you?"

"Diane's boyfriend has been missing for weeks. That's why we came here. That stringy haired bartender knew who we were because Diane's boyfriend used to flaunt a picture of her in a bathing suit to the other druggies. Instantly, he knew who she was and why we were there."

"So what happened?"

"After asking around about his whereabouts, we were directed right back to the bartender. So, Diane and I followed him."

"This is beginning to sound like some James Bond stuff, baby girl."

"Yeah I know. Anyway he led us to a drug house. Crazy Diane had the nerve to knock on the door. I had her back though. I wasn't about to let nothing happen to my girl."

I continued to listen to my new friend's story. It was exciting. This girl was full of surprises, with unpredictable moves.

"So, what happened then."

"The person that answered the door called for him and he came to the door. Rodney, he was a sight for sore eyes. His teeth were rotten and he must've weighed a buck five."

"Dang!"

"Not only that, his new crack head lady followed him to the door. She had the nerve to ask him, 'what's going on baby?' I almost fell out. Diane said a few words and I pulled her out of there. They weren't worth the bullet. He had been in that crack house for over two weeks. The bartender knew it all along."

"Sounds like you had some excitement Celeste."

"Yeah, but things have cooled down here, but I have to go somewhere else."

"What do you mean?"

"Diane will be cool here. Her parents moved here and bought an antique shop and a bookstore. They're retired, so she'll be all right until I get back."

"Get back from where?"

"New York. I've got a friend that's getting married again."

"Really?"

196

"Yeah, I haven't seen her in a while so it'll be good to see her and a couple of my old friends from Boston."

"I heard that. *Ain't* nothing like seeing old friends."

"Yeah, my girl Veronica says she's been trying to track me down. The wonders of email and cell phones, you know."

"Yeah, I can relate."

"Hey Rodney, why don't you come with me? I'd like to introduce you to the crew."

"I don't know, that's a long trip. I'd like to put my Lex on the road, but I heard ain't nobody up there with a car that doesn't have a dent in it."

"Awe, we'll be alright, you can handle it. Besides, we can talk all the way up there. And I'd love to show you off. Plus, I don't want to be by myself. Everyone else is going to have a man with them. Please, I don't think I can take so many men hawking me like at her last wedding."

"I could use the trip. I tell you what; give me a couple of days to work it out with my job. Things have been hectic there anyway."

"Cool, let me know in a couple of days."

"Alright, but let's have dinner, I've been missing you."

"Have you? Boy I've been missing you too. The more I think about you, the more I know it's getting close to that time. You know what I'm talking about!"

"Yeah girl, but it's cool that we're putting in the mileage and getting to know one another. I respect you more."

"Same here, let's make it seven. I'll meet you at Stevie's, exit ninety off of 77 south, turn left and go about a mile. *Me* and Diane went there one night."

"Okay *see* you then. Peace, cupcake."

Celeste and I managed to stay together but away from getting too close. Each moment with her was exciting. That night at Stevie's it was difficult to finish eating my fish without thinking about her. I was challenging myself; but it was a challenge for something good. Her company was all I needed and the thought of me spending my money and not *hitting* it was of the least.

She had her own money and later I learned the girl was loaded. Her dad had passed away and left her with enough to do whatever she wanted. At dinner she told me in his Will he stated he wanted her to travel and not be confined. He wanted her to see the world and it would all be on him. She found favor in Chi-town.

We asked for a doggy bag and went back to my place for a movie and fell asleep in each other's arms on the sofa.

197

The south has a way of waking a person up. Either it's the noisy sound of the roosters crowing or the enjoyable hot, morning rays of sunrise. Anxiously, I was in a hurry to get to work that morning. I wanted to put my vacation time in and be with her. I knew it was time, and I wanted it to be right. New York would be as good as any other place. I began to picture it as being romantic.

Our sexual acts could not occur on the road going there. A full night's rest to have performance level at its peek was necessary. Planning the event of intimacy was rolling through my mind while driving to work. I had to stop thinking that way, but for sure spontaneous romance was not needed. We needed to plan everything to the last detail. After all we both deserved it for waiting.

My job approved my vacation leave. All the while I wondered if it was a set up. Most of the times when they agree to what I wanted it seem as though it would come back to haunt me. There was always someone standing in line waiting for my position. If it wasn't on the job, it was with the women I were involved with. Either, really didn't matter now—they both came a dime a dozen.

I had left Celeste at the crib when I went to work that a day. At the job Derrick thought we had sex after I told him I left her there. A little male bonding went on at work. All of the high fives and him seeming to be happier than I was while thinking I *had hit it*. I just pretended, and then erased the thoughts from his itty-bitty mind of any difference.

When I returned to my place things were like I had left them, but a true player always knows a woman goes through his things. No surprise there.

Women always want to check out their competition or see how many bills a man may have before they make their claims. Nosy as hell they are, but Celeste could get away with it.

୫୦ ଓ୨

I couldn't see it, but it was there; the moist smell of the Atlantic Ocean was near. Celeste sat comfortably cozy in the passenger seat. We were heading to the Big Apple traveling at top speed on Interstate 95. That time of the morning the birds were singing, while folks were embracing the sticky atmosphere. The air conditioner was at its maximum level and the radar was on. Cruise control was set at a hundred, 'cause she said she wanted to get there in a hurry.

Celeste had fallen asleep while we *cruised* the Interstate. She had missed my narrow escape from the Virginia police officers at the border. Luckily, I had been paying attention to the radar or they would have caught me for sure. When she woke up we talked before she dozed back off again. I could easily tell she was exhausted; but while she was up she managed to fill me in on her girl friends.

Celeste told me about the *games* they played when they were young. I was astounded; the game sounded viciously cruel. Nevertheless, she had turned into a baby doll and I liked her.

Her friend Belinda was getting married, Celeste had sort of familiarized me with the others also. There was Veronica; according to Celeste she was the most *hoodlum* of them all.

Celeste said Veronica had the don't care attitude and she was the first in their group to sport a piece—after the incident that went down between one of her friends named Sheila and a guy, I believe his name was Richard.

Apparently the girl was injured severely. She also mentioned a new girl had been added to their bunch, but she didn't know her name. I noticed Celeste became a little upset when she was telling me the new girl was the matron of honor. Somehow it seemed to me as though, she felt one of the girls from the crew should have held that position. Her friend Belinda had fallen out with the girl about something a long time ago, but they had managed to sort out their differences.

Celeste woke up when we approached one of the tollbooths in D.C. She had slept right through the previous two refueling. Her hair was a little messed up when she woke up, She instantly began to get herself together with the mirror on the passenger's sun visor.

"Man, I look a mess."

"Awe baby, you look fine."

"Yeah right! Where are we?"

"D.C. You slept though the last couple of stops."

"Oh, really. How are you holding up?"

"Cool, I got me some sunflower seeds and some water. There's a bottle in the back for you in the cooler."

"Good, I could use some."

"Hey Celeste."

"Yeah."

"Tell me some more about your friend, the one that's getting married."

"What is it you want to know? She looks good. All of us do."

"Not that baby. How long has it been since you last saw her? How long has she known her husband-to-be?"

"Now that I don't know! But it must've been about five or seven years ago when I went to her first wedding."

"Oh she got divorced?"

"Nope, he croaked. I wasn't about to go to his funeral. I don't do funerals. But I told my girl I couldn't come, and she understood. So you see why I'm trying to make it up to the wedding."

"Okay, I hope this one stays alive for her. If he doesn't, your girl may be working something vicious."

"Oh Rodney stop it, she ain't even like that."

"How do you know."

"Cause I know my girl."

"Yeah right!"

"No, for real. She's a little bit on the uppity side—but she's cool."

"Someone you'll give your right arm to?" I asked while staying focused on the road.

"No, I wouldn't give my right arm to her—I'd give her both of my arms."

"Oh, it's like that!"

"Yeah, that's my girl. We can stay away from each other for a decade and still be down like that."

"Women can be tight like that, huh?"

"*Fore sho*, aren't you and Derrick like that?"

"No, we're just associates. I travel alone."

"Sometimes that's best, especially for a guy. But all I got is my girls."

"I understand."

"Is that sign right? It said New York 12 miles?"

"Yeah, we're almost there."

"Okay, I've been here once before. Spent the weekend with my girl Veronica."

"How'd you like it?"

"It was cool, we had a good time."

"Yeah, I know what you girls call a good time."

"Whatever, Rodney." She smiled and I returned the look. It was amazing how this girl made me feel, and I was still able to keep my hands off of her. It was beginning to be hard, but I knew I had to.

The metropolis of New York greeted us with a different atmosphere. A sort of hard to explain environment, it was busy. I'd never encountered scenery like New York displayed before in my entire life. It was completely overwhelmingly. Exciting were the thoughts rushing through my mind. Celeste dialed the number to one of her girls to let them know we were in New York from her cell phone. After someone answered, she retrieved a pen and pad for directions.

"Veronica, *girl tell* me what exit number," Celeste said to her.

She seemed as though she was happy talking to her friend. I had to pay attention to the road. Just from glancing down at the other cars on the road, I noticed there wasn't a car on the road that didn't have a dent in it, just like I had told Celeste earlier. The car's rears were covered with bumper stickers. I knew this place was wild so I said a quick prayer not to be carjacked or have an accident.

Celeste and I checked into a hotel in Manhattan. We had double beds and she was becoming more desirable. Holding back my desires for her became unbearable in the hotel room, but I had to.

We had dinner and afterwards she received all the details and the directions to the wedding. I knew she wanted to go be with them, but Celeste was the thoughtful type. She knew we just had a long drive, and I was tired, so she wanted to stay and keep me company. Although I insisted she go visit her friends she said she'd rather stay and pamper me. In a way I was glad to be exhausted, after her smooth hands massaged my shoulders I fell into a deep sleep.

The next morning Celeste woke me up with a gentle kiss on my cheek. She had ordered room service. The smell of bacon and eggs were the inspiration I needed to get my day started. After showering, I asked Celeste to call her friends to ask what the colors for the wedding were. With only two tuxes and a dinner jacket I knew one had to fit the occasion. Both my white and black tux was double breasted. Some would say they were a bit outdated, but it didn't matter to me. My banded collar formal shirt would make me feel in fashion.

Celeste had the directions. We arrived at the huge church a littlelate, it didn't seem to bother her though. As long as she was able to see her friends she was content with the reunion. Her friend Belinda was shocked to see her, quickly all of her girl friends escorted her away to the area I assumed where the woman needed to be. One of the groom's friends instructed me what I needed to do. Black Tux was appropriate, I was glad we all didn't have to match.

After the ceremony crowds of people stood around joyfully. Everyone gathered around Celeste, I stood in the back. There were so many pretty ladies there, but it was obvious which ones were from the crew. The girls shared a similar look along with idle laughter. Celeste introduced me to everyone and then the girls went off into their own little worlds. The groom was taking everything in with ease after the first dance was completed. I could only assume he knew he would have his bride for a lifetime, so he was willing to share her with her friends.

The girls were overwhelmed with each other. Belinda and Celeste hadn't seen each other in a while. I became acquainted with Chris and the other gentlemen that were there. We ate, drank and had casual conversation about the type of work we all did.

After the reception was over we all went to Belinda's house. Chris and Belinda's honeymoon was set for the summer. While at Belinda's place partying they invited us to church and then to brunch afterwards the next day. We accepted the invitation.

Belinda and Chris appeared to be a happy couple; I couldn't wait to be in their company again. Celeste had a gleam in her eyes indicating she couldn't wait to get married—unfortunately that was the last thing on my mind.

At the hotel I was no longer tired. In fact I could have gone a couple of rounds of good sex with her, but it wasn't the right time. We had separate beds, but this girl was taking me to my limits—I swear to God! We both had enough Crown Royal under our belts and I still don't know why nothing ever happened. She teased me by stripping and taking a bubble bath. Celeste called for me to come and rub her shoulders.

The suds were beginning to dissipate. With the large sponge in my hands I rubbed her back gently. It was easy to see her flesh in the water at that point, the bubbles were now gone. The girl was beautiful!

I went to bed that night with dreams and the thought of what possibly could have happened if I tried something with Celeste. Would she had given in, or perhaps embarrass me by saying no. Waiting would be the key. Time would answer a lot of my questions.

The next morning the sunlight almost blinded me. I felt good, but instantly I noticed Celeste was not in her bed. In the bathroom doorway she stood with the telephone in her hand. Shapely, and distinguished looking in every way yet she looked a bit upset. I could hear her talking louder and asking questions. Something was wrong. The name Belinda was constantly being repeated. It was time for me to get out of the bed and find out what was really going on.

Celeste gazed into my eyes while I stood at the doorway of the bathroom waiting. Anger had surrounded her dwellings. Patiently, I waited to be told what was going on. She hung up the telephone, and I could hardly wait. She walked to the bed and sat down, with her hands in a cross fashion. The smooth chocolate colored girl looked at me with her hypnotizing eyes filled with tear duct glands of water. I knew something was wrong.

"Belinda, Belinda is missing!" Celeste said. She was frantic as she sat at the side of the bed.

Tears poured freely down her soft cheeks and dribbled onto the floor of the hotel room. I came to her aid, gently putting my arm around her. My arms gently embraced her for comfort while she placed her head into my chest. It was easy to assume she needed me now. Strange how a woman that displays herself to be so strong can be broken down emotionally, I thought.

Just as I was thinking about her emotions being a sign of sensitivity, Celeste jumped off of the bed and headed for her luggage. Now I knew why we didn't fly, she knew she may need to bring a piece. From her suitcase Celeste retrieved a shoulder holster. She strapped the holster around her neck and tied off the bottom straps around her waistline area. The nickel-plated nine-millimeter was next. She locked and loaded a magazine— pulling the charging handle back. She slid the gun into its carrying holster as if she was back in the Wild West. Celeste slid her jacket on to camouflage the piece and quickly stuffed a box of ammo into her jacket pocket.

"Lets go Rodney!"

"Where? Where are we going?"

"We're going to find my girl. Belinda is missing!"

"Did someone call the police?" I questioned her, but I could see the expression on Celeste's face was saying she didn't have time for the small talk. She was displaying a different side of her. In some sort of way, it reminded me of that question she asked when we first met. Her answer was mysterious and precise. Could it be the precise part of her that yielded the weapon? I was puzzled but quickly grabbed my coat and we were out the door.

When we made it to Belinda's place, the police were already there. Several other cars were parked along the street. The neighborhood was quiet; that morning had a mist that seemed to have kept everyone inside—especially the folks that had partied the night before. Candace met us at the door with tears in her eyes as she and Celeste embraced. Everyone sat in the living room; some were stirring about from the kitchen to the bathroom.

The police had their surveillance equipment all around the house. The phone was tapped, and anxiously they waited for it to ring. Her new husband, Chris, paced the floor, when the police were not asking him questions. Our hands clinched when we greeted. I expressed my sympathy while covering his hand with both of mine.

Chris knew we were all there to help, but what he probably didn't know was the type of friends Belinda had. Although he owned a security agency filled with ex-policemen; the girls were conspiring how to find Belinda without the help of the policemen.

The police were reviewing the tape from the wedding and the reception. Candace interjected, she recognized someone in the taping. She wasn't positive, but she was sure she had seen the man in the video. Then it came to her he could have been the man that was behind her in line the day she ran into Belinda at the coffee shop. She wasn't sure though, but she told them anyway where she thought she could've seen him.

Celeste was taking in all of the information. She tugged Candace by the arm and signaled for Veronica to meet them in the kitchen.

The women were in the kitchen. I thought they were just doing girly talk. When Veronica left the kitchen I noticed her slipping by the coffee table and scooping up the picture of the suspect the police had printed off their computer. Quickly she rolled it up, while everyone was talking about going to Starbucks and asks questions. From the way Celeste was directing things in the kitchen, I knew she was up to something. I also knew Candace was a preacher's wife. Whatever Celeste was planning I knew she wouldn't let the preacher's wife know she had a gun.

While I was talking to Chris, Elliot and police officers, a few of Chris's buddy's arrived. It was feeling like we were on some sort of fugitive hunt. The police told everyone to remain cool. I think they became a little upset when Elliot's friends arrived with their weapons in view attached to their bodies. They were licensed to carry them, but the policemen's eyes were all over them.

Celeste pulled me to the side and told me, 'lets go.' Veronica and Candace joined us and we rode in my car. We went to the newsstand that was around the corner from the Starbucks. Celeste must have known the police were on their way to the Starbucks, so she wanted to take a chance at someone seeing the gentleman at the newsstand that was next to Starbucks.

The girls stepped out of the vehicle hastily; Celeste leading the way. Immediately they started questioning the guy at the stand.

"Excuse me sir, have you seen this guy around?" Veronica asked the gentleman. He looked her up and down, before responding.

"Girl, you sure is pretty."

"Look sir, I just wanted to know if you've seen this guy around here."

"What will you give me if I tell you where to find him. You think we can hook up."

Celeste was getting a little antsy. She heard the guy trying to come on to Veronica and she must have felt that it was the wrong time. She dashed over to the man and grabbed him in the collar and took out her nine millimeter and slammed it into his neck. The man was shocked and so was I.

"Look mister, we're trying to find this guy, now do you know him or have you ever seen him before, huh?"

Fear surrounded the newsstand owner. He couldn't believe that these beautiful women could have him at gunpoint. I was seeing an entirely different side of Celeste. She was beautiful, but from that point on I dared not to get on her bad side—she was dangerous. The guy looked down at the picture carefully while Celeste clinched his collar with the muzzle almost into his esophagus.

"Yeah, I've seen him before. He comes by almost everyday."

"Where does he live?" Celeste continued to question him.

"I don't know but he wanted to know where he could shoot some pool one day. So, I told him to go down to 130th and Lenox."

"Okay, what's the name of the pool hall?"

"Shakies!"

Celeste released him, but remained pointing the gun on him until we all were in the vehicle. I was feeling like I was in the Wild West or something with this girl.

Celeste and Veronica were in a zone I'd never seen before, it seemed as if they were in tune; but Candace had not a clue what she was getting into. We drove down to Shakies. It was a low life pool hall filled with smoke.

While in the vehicle I tried to convince Celeste to stop waving her gun at folks, especially when we got into the pool hall. She said she would be cool this time.

There were about six tables in the joint, paintings dressed the walls and the lighting was dim—except for the low hanging lamps over the table. The men stopped shooting to look at the women that accompanied me.

This time I thought it would be proper for me to ask the questions. I told Celeste and Veronica to let me find out about the guy this time.

The owner sat behind a counter, reading the newspaper with a cigarette hanging out of the corner of his mouth.

"May I help you, son?"

"Yeah, I'm looking for this guy. I was told he comes here from time to time."

He looked at the picture, and then he looked up at me with a snarl written all over his face.

"You ain't no cop! You look like one of those Ivy League boys. What you want to know about that *fella* for? He doesn't seem to be your type. Especially with all those pretty girls you have with you."

"So you've seen him before?"

"Maybe I have and maybe I haven't!"

I knew the game. He wanted money. I slipped him a twenty while the girls were checking my moves.

"Yeah, he comes through here. Couple of the boys followed him one day. They say he lives in an abandoned building on 128th a couple of blocks over."

"What's the building number?"

"Maybe I can remember the number, maybe I can't."

Here we go again; I had to slip him another twenty.

"265, whatever y'all do, you ain't heard it from me," he said.

"Alright and thanks."

We left the pool hall anxious to find Belinda. The girls were hyped. Celeste was busy in the front loading up another magazine with more bullets. What in the world she was thinking of I don't know. She became quiet, and constantly looked around to see if we were being followed. We arrived at the abandoned building. It was trashed and steps were missing on the walkway. When we stepped out of the vehicle, Celeste began to give orders—Veronica and Celeste were going to enter through the front, while Candace and myself were instructed to enter from the back.

I was a little worried not having a weapon or anything; but the adrenaline from everything that was happening gave me a rush. In the back area of the building it was trashy. Mattresses and garbage were all over the area. The fire escape ladder was hanging down to the ground, which made it easy for me to climb up to the first floor. I told Candace to stay in the back and wait for me, but she said no; she wanted to come too. I think she was frightened and I really couldn't blame her.

By the time we made it to the first floor Celeste and Veronica were in view. Celeste placed her index finger to her lips indicating for me to be quiet. With the other hand she had the shiny nickel-plated nine-millimeter. She entered each door on the floor as if she were a police officer.

Candace was on the telephone whispering. I could only assume she was talking to Elliot. Like a fool and without a weapon, I started going through some of the rooms on the floor looking for the guy that was in the photo. The entire floor was empty, so we all went up the stairs to the second floor, stepping quietly as we could. At the top of the stairs we heard a noise and muffled voices coming from one of the rooms. We fell back against the wall, trying to listen, but were unable to distinguish what was being said.

Celeste directed me to move closer to where the voices were coming from. I complied and stuck my ear to the door to hear what was going on. A loud scream rippled through the door. I knew someone was getting hurt inside. I nodded to Celeste. She gave me a nod back indicating to me to bust down the door.

Celeste had made me feel like a gangster, although I should have felt stupid for not having a weapon. With all of my might I tore the door down. The door fell and so did I. Celeste quickly stepped over me with the weapon pointed in the air. Off to the side of the room sat Belinda, tied to a chair. Blood ran from her mouth, her legs had open wounds and a puddle of blood surrounded her.

Belinda's head hung down. She looked like she was almost dead. Her hair was all over her head, and most of her clothes had been torn off. A woman stood over her. Suddenly her eyes and Celeste's eyes met—stillness over came them both. I could tell they knew each other, in fact I think she was at the wedding.

The lady stood up with a sweater cap on her head, it was then I saw the knife she had clutched in her hands. Celeste didn't hesitate firing the gun at her and she fell to the ground. Just as the lady hit the ground, I saw another female behind her. Again, with the precise expertise of a marksman, Celeste landed a bullet that hit the woman square in the chest.

Suddenly and without warning a loud pop rang in the air. It was a bullet that practically breezed by us! We dashed quickly for cover underneath a table. Celeste fired back.

Candace never entered the room, but when Veronica and I backed out of the room, I could see she was shaking like a leaf. Celeste was still inside hiding behind whatever furniture she could find and firing back.

I glanced inside while sitting on the floor trying to see what was going on. It was the same stringy haired guy in the photo. Who the two girls were I don't know.

The sound of sirens began to whistle. Thank God, help was on its way. Celeste didn't care. She emptied the first magazine and reloaded another. This girl was treacherous. I thought she was having a good time.

The police raced up the stairs. Celeste and the guy had a shoot out. Finally he must have made his way to the fire escape. The police barged in while the guy was making a getaway. The back up unit hadn't made it to the rear of the building yet. The guy was able to climb down the ladder to make a getaway. He fired at the police, and they returned fire; but they were unable to hit their target. He was almost at the street making a clear getaway. Thank God that the back up unit was arriving.

Chris and his men met the guy at the corner and yelled for him to stop, but he fired at them and they returned fire and shot him down.

Inside the room stood Celeste, one of the ladies lying on the floor raised her head to Celeste total surprise. She turned her head towards Celeste. Celeste glared deeper at her and recognized the woman who was now standing in the pool of Belinda's blood.

"Sheila!" Celeste yelled. "Girl is that you?"

"Yeah it's me Celeste."

"What in the world is going on girl? What are you doing?"

"Girl stop tripping, I was about to cut Belinda loose when y'all walked in."
"Oh really?"

"Yeah girl, it's a long story and believe me it's a long story."

"I've got the time." Celeste said, then I watched as she raised the weapon on one of her old friends.

"Girl put that thing down and come over here. You know we have an oath."

"Yeah, that's cool and all, but you have to prove that to me. 'Cause all I seen was you standing over Belinda with a knife."

"Come here girl so I can stop you from tripping." Sheila said while pointing at the body that was on the floor. "Celeste you remember her?"

"Dang Sheila, you know who she looks like."

"Yep, that's her. Remember. That's right, that's her."

"Oh no, what in the world is she doing here."

"That's what I wanted to tell you."

"What!" Celeste yelled while lowering the gun.

"Celeste, you remember when we were kids we dropped her off in the room with that guy, when we were playing Choo, Choo."

"Yeah, that's her."

"Well, I don't know how I ran into her here with Belinda. I was after that stringy haired fella."

"Say what?"

"Yeah Celeste, that guy at first was like a Sugar Daddy to me during High School. But later on he started taking it from me I was afraid to tell anyone."

"Dang girl, not only did you get a serious beat down from Richard, but someone was taking it too!"

"I've followed him for a long time now, and then I found out that he was trying to get in contact with Belinda; so I stood back and watched." Sheila paused for a second to catch her breath. "I knew the day he was going to get her, he kept getting closer to her. I waited and when he snatched her up, it was time for me to try to help."

"Go ahead, I want to hear this."

"I followed him with Belinda. It seemed like she was on some kind of drug. He carried her up the stairs. The moment they get inside the other woman appeared. They started to argue in the other room and that's when you shot at me."

"Girl I wasn't shooting at you, I hit what I shot at! She was coming up from behind you 'bout to stab you!"

"Thanks then."

"Hey Sheila who is she? I remember the face." Celeste asked while her and Sheila looked down on the body sprawled on the floor.

"Girl that's Rosalyn. You know that new girl from that game of Choo, Choo we used to play."

"What?"

"Yeah, that's her."

"Now what in the world does she have to do with all of this?"

"I don't know, but when I was about to get out of the hospital, someone told me that a friend of mine had the AIDS Virus. They said she got it from playing a game and she was a virgin too."

"Come on Sheila, how do you know all of this?"

"Girl I'm telling you what was told to me. She's had it for ten years they say."

"Look, she's still breathing!" Celeste said, and then the police barged in and surrounded everyone.

"She needs help, she's still breathing," Veronica yelled to the police. Clearly they assumed who was innocent or perhaps the victim.

One of the officers quickly communicated on his radio to the dispatcher for an ambulance. The girls started untying Belinda. She was weak and weary. Celeste was rubbing her all over, trying to help her regain consciousness. Belinda and Rosalyn were taken to the hospital.

The police rounded us up to question us, but I could see in Celeste eyes she just wanted to get to the hospital to be with her friend, Belinda. Veronica was frantic to say the least. We didn't know what Belinda's disposition was. Her husband Chris left with the ambulance. We all told the police we had to go. Quickly, I jumped behind my wheel. The girls were nervous, but they jumped into the vehicle too like it was a chariot.

At the hospital, we were told Belinda's condition was stable. What a relief that was. The doctor also told us about Rosalyn. The bullet hadn't pierced any vital organs; she would be okay. The police listened to Sheila's story. Celeste relayed it to me on the way to the hotel. To put it all in a nut shell; Rosalyn played the childhood game when she was a virgin and contracted HIV that day, and swore to get vengeance on the crew, starting with Belinda.

Her life was destroyed and she never slept with a man. She must've heard about the letters coming to Belinda so she wanted a piece of the action of destroying Belinda.

The stringy head dude that had been molesting Sheila since childhood, lost his mind when Richard abused Sheila. He seek vengeance on everyone in the crew, starting with Belinda, he wanted to kill them all.

Sheila said she had seen him in the hospital a couple of times visiting her when she couldn't talk. She told Celeste hatred boiled inside of her at the sight of him, but at the time she couldn't remember why. Then he stopped coming to see her. That's probably when he started coming after Belinda.

Sheila said they were arguing in the other room over who was going to kill her, when she came to Belinda's aid.

I remember seeing the girls embrace one another, but didn't know what was going on until we were riding. I didn't know what to think. I didn't even know who this woman was in my car. All I knew was that she was too exciting for me. The girl left me scared.

All of them were different. On one hand there was the preacher that married someone that had been the best friend of his wife. But she slept with his wife ex-husband. But he tells her to forgive her, whoa! Then they become the best of friends again—never seen that with Black folks.

Then the girl Veronica is straight up fine and with hoodlum and yet has Wall Street poise.

Celeste was fine like the others, but with an itchy trigger finger and I'd have to say, she was crazy as hell.

The girl Sheila from the hospital was filled with drama. They were all good looking girls. For sure I am not leaving out the groom. He had a security team that I thought were always two steps behind everyone else— maybe it's just me, but I wondered if everyone around me had social issues.

I left Celeste in New York with all of her things and didn't even *hit it*. I thought about it, but all of the drama had just made me loose the desire for her. But like Derrick said, we all have issues—it was justified when I experienced the life styles of these notorious women way of life.

℘ ℺

Back in Charlotte I continued with my slow life. I kept in contact with the girls, they became my friends. Celeste call a few months later and told me they were having a Christmas party and they all wanted me to come. She said Belinda was well. Sheila moved in with Veronica and everyone was doing well. She told me Veronica and Terrance was together. Perhaps she came to terms with the fact *money doesn't make a man, the man makes the money.*

I look forward to seeing them again at the party, but somehow I know their way of life and the *Games* they play will always escalate. But who wouldn't want to be at their party—gorgeous women that will always have the men in their lives catering to their needs.

As for now, I haven't touch a bottle of Crown Royal, my drink is Hennessey. Nor do I ever want a lady to buy me a drink; it will only remind me of my new distant friends.

The End

Book Club Discussion Guide

∞ Do you know of similar 'games' such as the one played in *Show A Little Love 1?* What was the nature of the game (s) you played and the outcome for all involved?

∞ How does 'the game' contribute overall to the story line of *Show A Little Love 1?*

∞ Belinda Norris is an attractive woman, and she knows it, and often flaunts it. How do you feel about Belinda's self assuredness and the way in which she handles herself?

∞ Who is your favorite character (s) Why ?

∞ In today's society, cheating on one's spouse or significant other is at an all time high. Belinda blames her deed of cheating on alcohol. Does Belinda have a legitimate excuse? What blame, if any lies with Emanuel? What blame, if any lies with Candace?

∞ What do you, the reader, glean from the story about the power of forgiveness? Is forgiveness always necessary when mistreated by another?

∞ How does the title, *Show A Little Love*, fit the story line?

∞ What theories if any do you, the reader have about the Slicer and his/her identity and motive for the threatening letters to Belinda?

∞ Veronica, Celeste and Sheila played significant roles in Belinda's life. How do you feel about each of their characters and the way their lives turned out?

∞ Who is your least favorite character (s)? Why?

About the Authors

Clayton F. Brown is the author of the novel *"Under the Green Tree,"* 2002. He was the president of the Charlotte African-American Writers Group. His debut novel received the first-time Writer's Achievement Award from the North Carolina Art Society, 2003. He was also given the Golden Pen Award at the Charlotte African-American Literary Art Review One, 2002, for his contributions as president of the writers group. Presently, he conducts fiction and ghostwriting workshops as a volunteer for the Charlotte Libraries. Professionally, he writes procedures and policies as a technical writer within the chemical industry. Clayton is also a freelance Ghostwriter and a mentor. He's originally from the South Bronx; he later lived in Orangeburg, South Carolina. You may contact the author at claytonfbrown@gmail.com.

Tony L. Bellamy is the author of the book *Down in the Grove, Shattered Hearts and Wounded Spirits*, which is a nonfiction compilation of human-interest stories. He resides in Charlotte, North Carolina suburbs area. Tony has been invited to speak at several state universities and schools throughout North Carolina, where he facilitates domestic violence workshops as a result of the content of his book. You may reach the author at tbellamy2002@yahoo.com.

Ulysses McDowell Jr. was born and still resides in Charlotte, North Carolina. He is a graduate of Myers Park, High School and Pfeiffer University, where he received a bachelor's degree in criminal justice. Ulysses is a retired Master Sergeant from the United States Marine Corps. He's also retired from the Federal Reserve Bank where he was the senior supervisor and Federal Reserve Law Enforcement Officer. He can be reached at urarity@aol.com

Shelia E. Bell is a multi-award winning author, literary consultant, and editor. She is a graduate of Belhaven College in Jackson, Mississippi. Shelia was the founding president of Memphis African-American Writers group and is also the founder of BWABC (Black Writers and Book Clubs Literacy Association). You can reach her at sheliawritesbooks.com. Instagram: @ sheliaebell Twitter: sheliaebell

Printed in the United States
By Bookmasters